THE WITCH

mary ann mitchell

Previous praise for SIREN'S CALL:

"SIREN'S CALL is horror of the human kind. There are no supernatural beings in this serial killer thriller but Serena is the personification of pure evil. She repels readers just as Stephen King's monsters do because they can't believe she is capable of such atrocities. The denizens of Silky Femmes are all criminals to one degree or another which is one of the reasons this book is so chilling and mesmerizing."

— *Futures Mystery Anthology Magazine*

★★★★ 4 out of 5 stars!

"This is truly an edge of your seat read. I highly recommend Ms. Mitchell's read."

— *K. Ahlers, Independent Reviewer*

★★★★ 4 out of 5 stars!

"I urge my fellow readers this is a book you will find hard to put down as I read it in only 1 day. I look forward to reading more of Ms. Mitchell's books in the future."

— *TP, Independent Reviewer*

"Mary Ann Mitchell's book is a story about fallible people making the best decisions they can in a dark and dreary world that's only a short drive away from anywhere we live. It is the dark journey into this reality that makes this book truly worth reading, and heeding. For the demons and drives that plague the protagonists in SIREN'S CALL remind us of their very real presence whenever we flip open a newspaper or turn on the TV."

— *Thor the Barbarian*

"Mitchell's fine prose and characters should keep your interest until the good ending."

— *The Horror Fiction Review*

THE witch

mary ann mitchell

Gold Imprint
Medallion Press, Inc.
Printed in USA

Published 2007 by Medallion Press, Inc.

The MEDALLION PRESS LOGO
is a registered tradmark of Medallion Press, Inc.

Cover Illustration by Adam Mock

Printed in the United States of America
Typeset in Caslon 540

10 9 8 7 6 5 4 3 2 1
First Edition

DEDICATION:

Thank you, John, for all your support.

chapter 1

Down a long wooded dirt road there lives a witch in a secluded cottage. No, the cottage is not made of gingerbread. It is made from the bones of animals and humans. Notches are cut into the bones so that each bone fits snugly into the bone next to it. The bones have been carefully prepared and lacquered to give the house a gloss in the afternoon sun. The doors and windows have tiny bones meshed decoratively into each other. Flourishes rise up the sides of the cottage, leading to a widow's walk of ex-husbands. Some of the husbands were gentle and loving, and those bones she put to the front so she can always be reminded of them. The cruel, uncaring husbands' bones are used as connective material, out of sight, covered by a putty-like substance that is of her own making. Please do not ask what it is made from.

For a witch, she is a pleasant-looking woman with small, brittle bones surrounded by several layers of fat that give her a grandmotherly look. Her hair is coarse and cut bluntly to her shoulders. The color is a reddish, blondish grey, with dark greasy spots marking where she had laid her head the night before. Her facial features are delicate, with a small pug nose, huge almond eyes, and full lips, the bottom one making her look pouty.

Her clothes are simple and second-hand. No clothes-horse, this witch. She uses the clothes she collects from her visitors who never leave. She can always find room for another set of bones. Currently she is thinking about building an extension to the cottage, although she does worry about losing the well-planned flow of the house.

A garden is situated to the right of the house. Here she grows herbs for her brews and vegetables for her stews. Long stalks of corn have about ripened. Soon she will take her scythe to the plants.

The day we arrive, the stone path that leads to the front door is slick. She has just finished watering the lawn and cleaning off the path. Her home is very tidy. As we walk the path, please look out for the squiggly snakes that like to bask in the sun. Most of the snakes are harmless. One or two are poisonous and quite large, but they are also lazy, and I'm sure you'll be able to outrun them.

THE WITCH

When you climb the steps to the front door, you'll see a brass knocker. It is the shape of a twisted braid of garlic. A memento from when she was trying to get rid of her third husband. No, you'll not find his bones here. Actually, you'll probably not find him within a million miles of this house. The break-up was not amicable.

Carefully lift the bottom bulb of the knocker and gently rap it against the door. She has sensitive hearing, and you don't want to irritate her before you even get to meet her. And, by the way, IT will be in view as soon as she opens the door. Very proud she is of IT.

Yes, yes, she's at home. I can hear her oversized shoes shuffling across the floor. This is the time of day when she usually cleans. She'll be shaking out her bed covers and dusting the few pieces of furniture. The mirror on the hall wall she always keeps covered. A fine silk scarf dangles from the top edges of the mirror's frame. Note the frame when you go in. Bone and teeth speckle the frame. She has painted them delightful colors that shine in the dark.

Don't dawdle! I must insist you rap now before I rush off to hide myself.

"Rap, rap, rap."

The shuffling feet are coming nearer. I must now depart.

The doorknob turns, and the door slowly opens.

The visitor is wondering what the hell he was thinking when he agreed to come here.

"Hello." The witch's voice is charming. There is a

hint of a tinkle, making the visitor feel at ease.

"Hi," the visitor says.

The witch carefully looks the visitor's figure over and must like what she sees, because she invites the stranger into her home.

In walks the visitor, eyes darting all around the hall searching for IT.

"Would you like to come into the parlor and sit?"

The witch leads the visitor into the next room, but the visitor hesitates, taking several backward glances.

"Come, sit in this chair."

The visitor thinks the chair looks curiously like a skeleton waiting to be padded. Looking around the room, the visitor sees something much more comfortable. A pile of plush pillows are strewn across the center of the floor. Immediately the visitor heads for the downy softness.

"Fine, fine. I will sit here myself. You are selling something?" The witch waits patiently; a smile barely lifts the edges of her mouth.

"No, not at all."

"Fine, fine." She earnestly stares at the visitor, waiting for conversation to begin.

"I'm here looking for something."

"And do you see IT?"

The visitor glances around the room and notices only a table with several lit candles upon it.

"No, but then I was told I should see IT immediately upon entering your cottage."

"Mmmm. Something I would keep on display." The witch thinks deeply about this. "You must mean the egg. The Russian egg. The bright golden-colored one I used to have."

"Used to have?"

"So what is your name?"

"Brandy."

"You mean like the liquor?"

"Yes, Mom was in her cups when I was born. After birthing me, she called out for another brandy, but the doctor mistook it to be my name."

"Tsk, tsk. I so do feel for you. To be named after an alcoholic beverage cannot be pleasant," the witch consoles.

"Being born to an abusive parent was much worse than being called Brandy."

"Such a shame. Would you like something to eat or drink?"

"No, I won't be staying long."

"Please, please don't go. I am very much enjoying your company." She shows her teeth, and not a single one is straight.

"Besides, I wasn't looking for the egg."

"No!" She taps her fingers on an arm bone that looks as if it has come from a giant.

"It would have been nice to see the egg, of course, but that was not my main purpose in coming here." Brandy crosses his right leg over his left.

"Ah, a puzzle you are giving me." The witch snuggles

her rear deeper into the bones of the chair. "I love puzzles. Sure you wouldn't like something to eat or drink? It may take me a very long time to solve this puzzle."

"Nonsense. I will tell you what I am looking for. You won't have to guess."

"No! No! Much disappointment if you don't let me play the game. And you wouldn't want to disappoint a frail, old woman, would you?"

"I don't really have the time to waste."

"Waste time? One never wastes time when one is engaged in deep thought. Clues. Perhaps you could give me some clues. That might speed up the time it takes me." The witch sits forward in her seat and leans her head to one side.

"Okay, if this is important to you."

"Important? Much is important, but certainly servicing your visit with the appropriate object is most important at this moment." She claps her hands. "Quick! Quick! Give me a clue, but don't make it too easy for me to guess what you are looking for."

"I've been sent by a troll."

"Is that your clue?"

The visitor nods.

"What kind of troll?"

"An ugly one."

"But they are all ugly. How am I to guess if you won't play the game seriously?" Frustrated, the witch rubs her nose so hard the visitor believes it will fall off.

"He was a talkative troll."

"How do you know the troll was a he?"

The visitor shrugs.

"I really don't know how to determine their sex, madam. And I wouldn't be interested even if I could." The visitor thinks all this talk a waste. Why couldn't the troll have told him exactly where to look?

"Ah, but the sex is important. You see, female trolls always tell the truth, and male trolls never do."

"He could have lied to me about the—"

"No, no, please don't give the answer away. We must play this game through. Now, your first clue is that you were sent by a troll of indeterminate sex. This truly gives me pause. You see, I know many trolls both alive and dead."

"This one is alive, I assure you, for I was just speaking with . . . er . . . the troll." The visitor wonders whether IT could be buried under the pile of pillows on which he sits. Attempting to be inconspicuous, he begins to peel away layer after layer of pillows.

"If you are uncomfortable there, I will change seats with you," the witch eagerly offers.

The visitor, thinking the skeletal chair looks not only uncomfortable but morbid, stops engaging in his pillow toss.

"No, madam. The chair certainly looks well-made, but I have a bad back, and I don't think having bones sticking in my back would help."

"You do have bones sticking in your back. Nice bones, I'd say from the look of your physique. Your little

vertebrae are probably a pretty sight."

"Shall we return to our guessing game, madam?"

"A live troll of indeterminate sex sent you here. And where is this troll now?"

"I presume he is waiting outside for me."

"And why do you presume that? Did he tell you he would wait?"

"No, but . . . Why wouldn't he?"

The witch yawns and stretches her club-like arms.

"Because he would get terribly bored waiting for you."

"I don't intend to be long," answers the visitor.

The witch claps her hands.

"It is time for another clue. Please try to give me a better clue."

"Better than what I have given you?"

"You've hardly gone out of your way to assist me. But that is fine, for we don't want me to guess too soon and spoil your visit."

"Arachnid."

The witch jumps up from her chair screaming. "Where? Where?"

"That was meant to be a clue, madam."

"Naughty, naughty." The witch giggles and reseats herself on the skeleton chair. "I have some in the basement, if that's what you're after."

"I am looking for a particular one."

"Oh, and does this spider sing or dance? Perhaps he calculates quickly inside his head. Or better still, he may

be able to lift weights one hundred times his size."

"Madam, I am looking for a giant mummified spider."

"I don't have him anymore. Used him for a spell, you see. Can I get you some bat wing or toad legs instead?"

"But he or she swore you still had IT in your entrance hall."

"He lied."

"Why would he do that?"

"I still have a mummified leg or two, if you'd like to see them." The witch stands. Suddenly she seems to tower over the visitor.

"But the spider was important to me."

"Why? Are you related?"

"Hardly, madam. I was going to write my thesis on the spider."

"Well, I still have a leg or two. You could go ahead and write a thesis about them. The legs are very long and dark, and I'm sure they have all kinds of secrets embedded in them. Come and I'll show them to you." The witch reaches out her right hand toward the visitor.

"Where are they?" he asks.

"In the basement."

"Can you not bring them here?"

"Oh, they are so long and thick. Much thickness for a spider's leg."

"How did you get them down to the basement in the first place?"

"A troll helped me."

"An ugly troll?"

"One of the ugliest," she says.

"And did he promise to send me to you?"

"Not you per se."

"Just a live human body?"

"He always does. You see, I need a wart from a human hand."

"Well, I have none," Brandy says, raising his hands into the air so the witch can view them.

"Wait! Wait!" The witch prevents him from lowering his hands. "Must see! Yes, must see." Holding his hands tightly in hers, she scans the flesh. "There, there," she screams, jumping up and down. "An immature one. It needs time to grow."

"I don't see anything."

"Very tiny, the wart. Teensy-tiny wart."

"Well, the wart probably isn't big enough for you to use."

"Mmmmmm. Big enough."

"If the wart is barely visible to you, how would you remove it?"

"The hand will do."

Brandy jumps to his feet.

"Madam, I have no intention of losing a hand. Since you do not have the entire spider, then I must go. I'm sorry; this has been a waste of time for both of us."

"Daddy, how come the witch can see the wart and Brandy can't?"

"Ah, Stephen, that is the question. Can she really see a wart on his hand, or does she have some evil plan to use all of Brandy?"

Dad leaned back against the head of Stephen's bed, the oak solid on his back, a support he could use right now.

"So, let's see now."

"Madam, I must insist you stand out of my way so that I may leave."

"Leave? Why leave? Some cake or biscuits? A spot of tea? No? A taste of my home-brewed sherry? Aren't you having a good time? I will be ever so lonesome if you leave." The witch's face melted into a sulk.

"Dad, do witches really steal human bones, and if they do, how do those humans walk around?"

"They don't walk around after their bones are stolen."

"Is that why Robin is in a wheelchair? Did a witch steal her bones?" Stephen's round eyes became wider and rounder.

"No. Robin has nerve damage."

"A witch stole her nerves. Is that what the witch makes her putty out of?"

"Yeah! Yeah, as a matter of fact, that is what building putty is made from."

"Even the kind that holds our house together?" Stephen began pulling his covers up over his chest.

"Oh, no, we have special putty. We have animal-free putty."

"Good," stated Stephen.

"So anyway, the witch is dragging Brandy down the cellar steps when a loud crash is heard at the front door."

"I thought she was offering Brandy something to eat."

"But he turned the offer down, and in her frustration she grabbed hold of Brandy and pulled him over to the open basement door."

"Why was the door open? We never keep the door open. Mom used to say that it got too damp in the basement."

"Mom wasn't living with this witch."

"So none of Mom's bones are holding up the witch's house?"

"Mom's bones are ashes, Stephen. You were with us when we sprinkled the ashes at sea."

Stephen nodded his head seriously.

"So in rushes the troll. You see, he had a conscience and began to regret sending the young man, Brandy, into the witch's cottage."

"The troll's not going to save Brandy, is he?" Stephen looked disappointed.

"Not if you don't want him to. Which will it be?" Dad gave a thumb's up followed by a thumb's down.

With an evil glint in his eyes, Stephen raised his right fist high into the air.

chapter 2

Mother watched her little boy giggle when his father tousled his hair. Her son's small feet and chubby legs reached high into the air to push away Daddy's tickling fingers. The boy's hiccups stopped the play, and Daddy reached for the carafe on the night table. The glass was in Stephen's outstretched hands. His father poured a half glass of water and put the carafe back on the table. Slowly the boy drank, bubbling the water occasionally with soft giggles.

By the time the hiccups stopped Daddy had turned on the nightlight and turned off the bedside lamp. He pulled the covers up over his son's body, tucking the material under the boy's chin.

They wished each other good-night and muttered their stale warnings about bedbugs biting. Daddy closed the door behind him, and the room fell into peaceful silence.

Love swept across the room to every corner. Mother and son love. Stephen closed his eyes, turned to his side, and scrunched up into a fetal position.

Mommy sat on the bed's plaid blanket and stared down at the little boy she had planned to teach so much. Father now had that responsibility.

A low throaty snore issued from the boy's little mouth. She smiled. Even as a baby he had snored. Perhaps it was not her grumbling stomach that made so much noise when she was pregnant with him.

She touched his fisted hand but felt nothing under the weight of her fingers. Her hand appeared to make contact with the boy's flesh, but it was just a visual deception. Mommy couldn't savor the feel of his silky flesh or smell the little-boy smell of candy, rich desserts, dirt, fresh wounds, and antiseptics. Only her eyes could remind her of the little boy she birthed. She brushed her hand across his cheek and felt only the vacuum in which she existed. Tears flooded down her cheeks. Why had she left him? she wondered. He needed her so much, and she hungered for his love.

Her hand traveled up to her neck. She felt the raw, deep band on her throat. She remembered looping the noose, sliding the thick rope over her head, and that was all. Had she kicked the chair away? She must have done so while in a trance. She scraped at the indentation in her flesh. She wanted to wipe it away. A nightmare. *Let it all be a nightmare.*

Maybe she could kiss Stephen's forehead and awaken him. How many times had she tried to tiptoe into the room just to watch her little boy? He was such a light sleeper he always caught her. Not anymore.

If only Stephen could understand how Daddy, his lover, and Grandma had made her mind ill with their deplorable behavior. None of them would ever have her forgiveness. It sickened her to think they could still touch and play with her little boy and she couldn't. They had robbed her of her right to him. And now they would warp his little mind against her. Not with meaty lies but with subtle shakes of the head and pity in their voices.

"Poor Mommy ran away from the fight and abandoned the child that had come from her uterus."

They would make her sound pathetic, uncaring, even crazy. Over the years Stephen would assimilate their inaccuracies, and as a man he wouldn't recall the days spent in his mother's love. He would feel relieved she hadn't done something terrible to him while she had been taken over by insanity.

"I will never allow that to happen," she said.

The boy didn't twitch, his lids didn't flutter, and the sound of his breath remained steady.

"Bring me back, Stephen. Wish me into your world again. The forces in this house can help you. Use them. Go down into the basement and guide the malevolent powers that are now in disarray."

chapter 3

"Stephen worries me sometimes. He seems to have a twisted sense of justice. The other night he voted to kill off the innocent character in the fairy tale I was telling him."

"Jacob, are you still telling him those scary stories?"

Jacob managed to steer around a big rig that had been blocking his Toyota Tercel.

"They're only stories, Mabel. Besides, neither Stephen nor I care for sweet tales right now."

"But stories about witches and trolls and leprechauns that steal babies . . ."

"Some of those tales my mom told me when I was little."

"Does Stephen ever talk about his mother?"

"Rarely. Sometimes we go down by the shore and throw some wild flowers into the water. He's very particular about the flowers he chooses. They all have to be in blossom and brightly colored."

"He still includes her in his nightly prayers, doesn't he?"

Jacob sighed.

"Would it hurt, Jacob, to kneel down at night with your son and say a prayer? My daughter had him saying prayers every night, and now that she's been dead two months you've ruined all her work."

"I'm an agnostic, Mabel. I don't pray."

"Not even for your son's sake? I bet he never gets to church anymore." Mabel waited for Jacob to say something. "From now on, I'll come down each Sunday morning and—"

"Mabel, you don't drive."

"You can pick me up, and the three of us can attend services." She glanced sideways at Jacob.

"Stephen doesn't miss church. Hell, we usually go fishing every Sunday."

"You teach him to kill fish and eat them on the Lord's day?"

"The apostles were fishermen." Jacob stepped down harder on the gas pedal. Normally Jacob got along with his mother-in-law, but the topic of religion was a sore point.

"Not on the Lord's day," she said.

"Mabel, the apostles worshiped on Saturday. I usually have to head into the office for a few hours on Saturday, so we never fish on the Jewish Sabbath."

"You're not Jewish. You and Stephen are Christians."

"Agnostics," he corrected. "Actually, there's a touch of pagan in us. I can feel the need to fly. The need to communicate with the gods and goddesses. The full moon has me out baying." He looked at Mabel and smiled.

"Why did my daughter have to marry a Loony Tune?" But she smiled back.

"I was irresistible. You know that. Why else would you have shown me all those dishy youthful photos of yourself when Cathy brought me home to meet you?"

He made his mother-in-law blush. He loved to do that, because she was actually prettier when she blushed. Mabel had just had her fifty-eighth birthday, but her skin was still pale and soft, almost wrinkle-free except for the puppet lines reaching down to the corners of her mouth. Her hair was pale blond fading into white, and her well-shaped physique only hinted at a mature plumpness.

Jacob pulled up in front of the elementary school

in which she had taught for the past thirty years.

"I'm not kidding about church, Jacob. Children should be raised in a Christian manner."

"Even Moslem children?"

"My grandson should be." Her eyebrows arched, but Jacob refused to give her any promises. "I don't have time to argue now. This evening expect a call from me."

"Stephen will be happy to hear from you."

Mabel shook her head and got out of the car.

chapter 4

A piercing screech greeted Jacob when he walked into his kitchen. Stephen jumped out from under the kitchen table wearing a handmade mask of a wolf.

"Hey, Molly, you didn't warn me about the monster in the kitchen."

"Did I scare you, Dad? This is just a mask," Stephen said as he pulled the mask off with his paint-stained hands. "Molly helped me to make it for Halloween. She's going to make a fuzzy suit to go with it."

Seventeen-year-old Molly stood at the kitchen threshold. Her baggy pants and sweatshirt covered what Jacob knew to be a tight firm body. He wondered why she always chose to keep herself so covered up.

"I hope you thanked her," said Jacob.

"Sure I did. Thanks, Molly."

"Hey, I'm going to expect something in return," she said.

"Like what?" Stephen's eyes opened wide.

"A good little boy trundling off to bed when he's told."

"Dad," Stephen whined.

"Stephen," whined back his dad.

"I should have had you tucked in already before your father got home. I only allowed you to stay up to show your father the mask."

Stephen grimaced.

"It's okay, Molly. Why don't you take off for home, and I'll see to this ferocious beast."

"It's a wolf, Dad. See!" Stephen modeled the mask again.

"Okay. Will you be needing me at all this weekend?" Molly asked.

"No, I'm taking the entire weekend off to be with my son."

"Will we pick flowers and go to the shore?" Stephen asked.

"If that's what you want to do, but shouldn't we also plan on doing something else?"

Stephen shrugged.

The telephone rang.

"I'm feeling psychic tonight, Stephen. I'll bet that's Grandma."

Enthusiastically, the boy ran to answer the telephone.

"I could stay over if you need help getting Stephen to bed," said Molly.

"Who was that big lumberjack I saw with you the other day?"

"Randall. He's on the school football team."

"Why don't you go home and give him a call? By the way he was looking at you, I'd say he'd like to hear from you."

Molly stopped starring into Jacob's eyes and looked down at her white and black running shoes. Her body tensed.

"We're not serious," she mumbled.

"Sorry to hear that. You should really find yourself a steady boyfriend." Jacob opened the refrigerator door and pulled out a can of beer.

Molly looked up at him and said, "I'm sorry about your wife." Her eyes pleaded with him.

Jacob popped the can and took a slug of beer.

"I mean, I don't think we did anything that would have caused her to-"

"Molly, go home and do your homework. You've got a lot of maturing to do."

He watched as her eyes watered. Not a single tear fell.

"Shall I come back tomorrow?" she asked.

"Why not? Stephen still needs you. He isn't old enough to stay by himself yet."

chapter 5

Stephen had spent most of the evening gossiping with Grandma. He knew his mom and grandma used to do that every day, and he tried to fill the empty space so that Grandma wouldn't be sad. Grandma always warned him about telling tall tales about people, but she laughed and seemed so happy that he figured she really didn't mind the exaggerations. Dad had copped out of speaking to Grandma. Dad said he had work to do and he'd see Grandma in the morning when he drove her to work. Grandma seemed very disappointed, which made Stephen feel he had failed in his attempt to entertain. He wondered what sort of things Daddy could tell Grandma that he could not.

Stephen's socked feet padded over to the oak dresser, and he opened the top drawer. Inside under his T-shirts he dug out the few remaining articles his mother had left behind: a pair of pearl earrings which he himself had purchased for her the previous Christmas, a tortoiseshell comb with only one tooth missing (the tooth he kept inside a round locket Mom had worn around her neck), a missal from his mom's First Holy Communion, and a holy picture depicting the Assumption of the Virgin Mother. His prize possession was a chubby, naked goddess on a silk chord. Mother rarely wore that ornament, but when she did she became very serious and would rub it for good luck.

He took his mother's possessions over to his bed and lined each item up in a row. He rubbed the goddess' tummy in just the same way he had seen his mother do. He kissed the missal and holy picture and opened the locket, placing the tooth back into its appropriate spot on the comb. This was a nightly ritual for him starting two weeks after his mom's death. He grasped an earring in each of his hands and closed his eyes.

"Mommy, I miss you. I wish you never had gone away. Dad said you didn't have a choice, but couldn't you have begged for a few more years? I would settle right now for a few more months or even days. Maybe you could visit me once in a while. Dad and I come visit you out in the water. I send you flowers. I hope you get them and no one snatches them away from you the way stupid Gwen steals my candies. She never asks, Mom. She just takes them from my backpack or even my pockets. I know she is a girl and scrawny, Mom, but sometimes I just want to bop her in the nose. Is it a sin if I simply dream about doing something? I hope not, because I'll have a lot of forgiveness to ask for before I can be with you in Heaven."

His palms sweated. The earrings felt as if they were making indentations in the palms of his hands.

"And could you remind Dad that he needs to laugh more like before when you lived with us? He's not exactly cranky, but he could be nicer to Molly, 'cause I really like her and wouldn't want to have her stop babysitting."

Stephen dropped the pearls onto the bedcover and ran to his toy chest where he had left the wolf mask earlier in the evening. Quickly he put the mask on and raced back to clutch the earrings once more.

"I don't want to scare you, Mom. It's only me wearing a mask. I painted most of the colors, and Molly did the drawing and cutting. She says I'm getting better at staying within the lines when I color.

"Mommy, why can't Molly live with us all the time? Dad doesn't always have the time to color or tell stories, but Molly does. She tells me her time is mine whenever she's over here. And she wouldn't have to work or nothing, because Dad got a raise from Mr. Spectar. I don't think he's so mean. Mr. Spectar always gives me candy when I go to Daddy's office. And he's got a dog that he brings in on weekends. One of those big shaggy ones like in Peter Pan."

"Lights out in five minutes," Jacob yelled from the hallway.

Stephen gathered up all his mother's personal items and stored them back in the dresser drawer, pulling out a pair of pajamas before closing the drawer.

When Jacob rapped on his son's door five minutes later he found Stephen already tucked under the bedcovers. Stephen playfully pulled the cotton blanket over his head, forcing Jacob to have a tug of war with the boy before he could kiss his son goodnight.

"They've already bitten," squealed Stephen.

"What are you talking about?"

"The bedbugs. See!" Stephen pulled his right arm from under his blanket and pulled up the right sleeve of his pajamas, showing his father a large mosquito bite.

"Bad bedbugs?" yelled his father. "They hiding under the covers?" Jacob pulled down the cover and spluttered a raspberry into Stephen's tummy.

By this time Mom would have been telling them to quiet down, and Dad would be making a very serious face before winking goodnight to his son. Now, he and Dad would sometimes go on romping for another ten or twelve minutes before finally turning off the light and closing the bedroom door. Stephen missed his mother's stern warning.

chapter 6

"Rosemary's coming home this weekend. Wants to spend some time with Stephen, if that's all right."

"She should have given me more notice."

"Aw, come on, you and the boy can give up one day of fishing so he can spend time with his aunt."

Mabel glanced over at her son-in-law. He looked thinner, more hollowed-out in the cheeks. He had been spending every free moment with Stephen, attempting to make up for the fact that Cathy was dead. She wondered if he blamed himself at all. Didn't they all blame themselves? But the silly girl was always going in and out of her depressions. She had been the most sullen of Mabel's five children.

"Would Rosemary be able to change her plans and come the following weekend?"

"You're right, Jacob, she should have notified you sooner, but Rosemary can barely get away from her job these days. Next thing you know, they'll have her washing the windows at that stinkin' company."

"Rosemary's lucky if she remembers to wash out her underpants," said Jacob.

"I resent that. Rosemary is quite clean. She just looks disheveled all the time. Besides, she's not a clean fanatic the way Cathy . . ." Using the past tense when speaking of her daughter didn't sit well with Mabel.

"Doc said she went fast," Jacob said.

"All I know is she went too soon. What am I doing here, when my daughter's ashes have been dumped into the ocean?"

"You're going to work to teach a bunch of spoiled kids to read and write, just like you've done for years and will continue to do, although I hope it won't be for much longer." Jacob checked the rearview mirror and pulled into the fast lane.

Everyone assumed she would retire at fifty-five, but she hadn't. Each year she kept saying one more year, then it's off on a cruise. The last thing she needed now was a quiet cruise on the Pacific with time to think about Cathy as a little girl, as a pretty but awkward teen, as Jacob's tomboy wife. Getting married in jeans and sweatshirts–what the hell were they thinking? The best was seeing Cathy lying next to her newborn son at the hospital.

"Already smiling, thinking about what you'll do when you have the rest of your life off?"

Mabel shook her head and stared out the side passenger window.

"You having wild fantasies about me again?" Jacob asked.

Mabel swiped her hand against Jacob's shoulder.

"Rosemary can stay with Stephen and me," Jacob announced.

"You hate her guts!"

"She is Stephen's aunt, and I can tolerate her for a weekend. I think."

"She's not going to be cooking and cleaning for you guys."

"Would two guys like Stephen and myself try to take advantage of a guest in our house?"

"Yes, and I'm not permitting that to happen."

"Wouldn't she want to bond with Stephen over his jelly-stained T-shirts?"

"That's something *you* have to get used to," Mabel said.

"Either that or I'll be sending Stephen over to your house with the laundry. Ah, don't wince, Mabel, I'm joking. I've taken to buying him seven new T-shirts a week. If I'm lucky at least one is reusable."

"Try not to raise Stephen as a slob, Jacob," she said.

"So is Rosemary bringing Robin?"

"Not this time. She feels Stephen is going to need a lot of attention, and it would be hard to do that if she had Robin to take care of in the wheelchair."

"Too bad. Stephen was asking about Robin the other night."

"He was? What did he say?"

She heard Jacob chuckle.

"Okay, Jacob, what's the joke?"

"Nothing. Stephen was asking about why Robin was in a wheelchair."

"And what did you say?"

"I said she had nerve damage, that's all."

"No, you said more than that. I can tell by the way you can't keep a straight face. It's your job now to teach him to respect others, especially those disabled."

"That's always been my job, Mabel. Only now I have to do it alone."

"I'm sorry, Jacob, I didn't mean to make it sound like I didn't think you were doing a good job before Cathy died. But sometimes you forget things."

"Didn't forget Rosemary is coming this weekend. Shall I pick her up at the airport?"

"She'd certainly appreciate that, and maybe you could pick me up first so I get to see her for a little while before she goes back to Austin."

"You want to stay at the house too? We could have a pajama party. A night of 'thirties and 'forties horror flicks."

"No, thank you. And doesn't Stephen like some of the Disney movies?"

"Not as much as watching the Wolf Man. He may want to gather some techniques, since he'll be trick or treating as a wolf."

"They have some really cute costumes down at . . ."

"Mabel, the wolf wasn't my idea. He and Molly thought it up on their own. He's made his own mask, and Molly is making him a furry suit. He doesn't want to be dressed as a Harry Potter character or a fireman. He's an imaginative little boy and comes up with a lot of ideas on his own, which is what I prefer."

Mabel sensed that Jacob looked over at her, but she kept her eyes on the road in front of them. Sometimes he did make sense, however much she hated to admit it to him. Her grandson was small for his age, but was definitely not shy. She visualized his sandy hair and the brown eyes, exactly the same as his mother's. Cathy had taken the boy with her everywhere she went. He was her little shadow. He would sit attentively while she and Cathy held conversations over coffee. She swore that little boy could understand every word they said. He was attentive, especially to everything Cathy did and said.

"Okay, Mabel, I'm going to drop you off on the side of the road."

Mabel focused on where they were while Jacob pulled up next to the school. She looked over at her son-in-law.

"Did you say prayers with Stephen last night?"

Jacob's composed face stared back at her.

"I never wanted to be a nagging mother-in-law, and before Cathy died I would never have asked these questions of you. I guess because I knew Cathy would be taking care of all the little things."

"And my contribution would be minimal?" Jacob asked.

"No, you've always been a conscientious father." Mabel stopped and thought for a few seconds. "We got along better when Cathy was around. She kept me in my place."

"More than that. I can remember her actually throwing you out of the house," he said. "Not that I approved."

"You did by not contradicting her and driving me home."

"Trying to keep the peace."

"Did she really . . . Not hate, but . . ."

"Cathy and I were going to raise our son, and now I will."

Mabel nodded and stepped out of the car. Her legs felt shaky, and her hands trembled when she reached to close the car door.

chapter 7

Every day Molly picked Stephen up from school. She played a game of "mommy." Stephen was her little boy and Jacob was her husband. She and Stephen didn't look alike, but that was because he had the recessive genes. Molly and her husband Jacob both had blond hair, blue eyes, and long bones. At times she imagined carrying Stephen's little brother in her uterus and would pat her tummy as if quieting an active fetus. The babe would kick at the most awkward moments, and she had to be extra careful when she lifted Stephen in and out of the car. She never had given up on playing house.

"See what I made for Mommy?" yelled Stephen,

running down the steps of his kindergarten.

Or did he say, "See what I made for you, Mommy?" The sounds blended into one as the boy approached, his outstretched hand holding a brightly-colored piece of construction paper. Her own hand proudly took the gift from Stephen. Daisies, roses, and tulips bordered the length and width of the page. A big candle-lit birthday cake had been placed at the center of the page and written across the front of the cake were the words "Happy Birthday." "Mom" was barely readable, the letters were so scrunched together.

"Thank you, Stephen," she said.

"Don't be silly, Molly. It's not your birthday today," he said.

"Then it must be your mother's." Her right hand skimmed over the wax crayon marks.

"Not exactly."

She looked down at "her little boy" for clarification.

"It's this Saturday. Dad promised he'd go to the shore to visit Mommy, and he said I could bring a special gift for her." Stephen's eyes shined. His small hand reached to take back the drawing. "Do you think Mommy misses us as much as we miss her?"

"Definitely."

"I'm going to bless it tonight," he said, waving the construction paper in the air.

"What are you talking about?"

"I'm going to offer it up to the fat lady and ask her to bless it." Stephen pulled off his backpack and unzipped it. He carefully slid the construction paper inside.

"It'll get crushed in there, Stephen. Why don't you lay it on the back seat of the car until we get home?"

Stephen nodded and slipped the paper back out. He threw the backpack over his right shoulder, and several slender books fell out of the pack.

"I'll get it, honey. By the way, who is this fat woman you're talking about?"

"You don't know her."

"Does she visit your house often?"

"She lives there."

"That's silly. There is no lady living at the house."

"Yes, she does."

"What does she look like?" Molly lifted the books off the ground and guided the boy toward her beat-up car.

"She has a big tummy and keeps her arms up over her head."

"Why would she keep her arms over her head?"

"To show off her tummy, I guess." Stephen climbed into the passenger seat of the car.

Molly threw the backpack and books onto the back seat.

"Here, give me the drawing, and I'll put it in the back."

"No, I'll carry it."

"All the way home?"

He nodded while she adjusted his safety belt.

While slipping into the driver's seat, she asked Stephen whether he would introduce her to the lady. He became quiet. She insisted she'd like to meet the lady and discuss fashions with her.

"She's always naked," he answered.

Molly pulled out of the school parking lot and into traffic.

"Does your father like the lady?"

"No. I have her hidden away." Stephen paused. "You're not going to tell Daddy, are you?"

"Not if I get an official introduction."

Back home, Stephen ran upstairs to his room and came back down within a minute. He wore a silk chord around his neck and clasped his hands over whatever dangled from the bottom of it.

"This is the fat lady," he said, unclasping his hands.

"This is a goddess, Stephen, a fertility goddess."

"A what kind of goddess?" he asked.

Molly could tell he was rolling the letters over in his mind.

"A fertility goddess. She brings babies into the world."

"Like the stork and the cabbage patch?"

"Oh, she delivers far more babies than the stork or the cabbage patch could ever do. Where did you find her?" Molly asked, fingering the wooden sculpture.

"Mommy kept her down in the basement inside a wood box that's kinda decorated with all sorts of beasts."

"Do you have the box?"

"No, the box gives me the willies. Some of the beasts are so ugly."

"I'd like to see the box, Stephen. Will you take me down to the basement?"

"No."

"Why not?"

"Because that was Mommy's private place."

"You and your Daddy also go down there."

"Daddy never does. I'm going to put the fat lady back where she belongs." Stephen turned toward the stairs. "You finish my wolf costume yet?"

Molly thought about asking for an even trade: his wolf suit for a visit to the basement, but felt like a bitch for even considering the idea.

"It'll be ready by Halloween, don't worry."

"Good, because I already told Mommy all about it."

"You . . ." Molly watched Stephen run up the flight of stairs. When she heard his door slam shut, she went to the basement door underneath the staircase. The door was closed. She turned the knob, and the door easily opened, swinging way back on its hinges. Suddenly the front door opened, and she heard Jacob yelling out his son's name. Quickly she closed the basement door.

"You're home early," she said.

"Yeah. Got company coming this weekend, and I thought I'd better start cleaning up." Jacob dropped his briefcase on the hall table and called out to his son.

"Daddy!"

Jacob lifted Stephen when the child flew into his arms.

"So, what surprises have you and Molly cooked up for me today?"

"Nothing. You're home too early."

"Ah, didn't have a chance to plot behind my back."

"We never do, Jacob. If you mean the mask . . ."

"Shouldn't you be calling me Mr. Zaira?" Jacob interrupted.

"Sorry."

"Why can't she call you by your first name, Dad? Everybody else does."

"Because children should respect their elders, Stephen, and she should be a good role model for you." He looked at Stephen and then swiftly turned to face Molly. "I'll pay you the full amount of money, but you can leave a few hours early today."

"I'd like to talk to you, Mr. Zaira," Molly said.

"About?"

"Stephen, why don't you run upstairs and get the drawing you did today? I'm sure your father would love to see it."

Jacob put down his squirming son, and Stephen bounded off for his bedroom.

"I suppose we have to have this talk before you completely understand the consequences of our actions. Only I'd rather do it when Stephen wasn't around."

"This is about Stephen, Mr. Zaira. Not about us."

"Sure it's not just an excuse?" Jacob gave her a wry smile.

"Stephen is talking about naked ladies living here and—."

"Whoa, no naked ladies staying here, and even if there were, it wouldn't be any of your business."

"It's for Mommy's birthday. See?" screamed Stephen, racing down the stairs.

Jacob barely looked at the drawing.

"Wonderful. Tell you what, if you run upstairs and wash up, I'll take you out to eat."

"Chili! The really hot kind that makes the tears come."

"Your choice," Jacob said, and Stephen returned to his bedroom upstairs.

"I'm never sleeping with you again, Molly. Is that blunt enough? Our relationship caused Cathy to take her life."

"I don't believe that. Besides, Stephen has this fertility goddess he's been hiding from you. And he seems to think he's able to talk to his mother."

"Stephen is five years old. Of course he talks to his mother. People do that, Molly, when they lose someone close to them."

"Do you still talk to Cathy?"

"We didn't talk much when she was alive. Why would I spend my time trying to communicate with her when she's dead?"

"Stephen does."

"Stephen loved his mother."

"Did you love his mother?"

"Enough not to leave her for you."

"Maybe I shouldn't be babysitting for Stephen anymore."

"It's up to you. All I request is a few days' notice so I can find myself a new babysitter."

Molly wanted to resign, but didn't want to give up the opportunities to be around Jacob. He was almost sneering at her, his eyes cold, a slight rise in his top lip, and a calmness that frightened her.

"Is Molly coming with us?" asked Stephen.

"No, she can't come. She was just saying how she's been assigned a ton of homework for tonight."

"Come to dinner, Molly. I can help you with your homework."

Molly smiled at Stephen and thanked him for his offer, but said she didn't want to waste his night with her homework.

"So, have I been given notice, or what?"

"I'll pick up Stephen tomorrow."

"And the next day?"

"I'll continue babysitting, Mr. Zaira." She brushed a few strands of hair off the boy's forehead before heading to the front door.

"Hey, Molly, I'll be raising your salary, since you've lost one of the benefits of the job." Jacob laughed.

chapter 8

The basement was full of whispers. Full of condemnations. Voices audible only in the darkness. Voices with soft, melodic tones. Voices icy and determined. Voices grating and willful. Voices of spirits gathered to mourn. Gathered to complain. Peevish voices wanting revenge. And they all seemed to be centered around a long wooden table. A table with wax thick on the grain, wax in colors representing every emotion, every day that Cathy celebrated her rite.

A wooden box basked in the glow of the moon as the others in the house slept. The carved beasts quivered in the shine of the moon, in the magic of the moon. Writhing, almost escaping the confinement of the box, the beasts roared their frustration in silence. Their mouths open wide, their eyes bulging, their nasal cavities flaring, and the chords in their necks taut, they attempted to become flesh. To become something that could touch the angry world around them. To avenge the mistress existing now only in spirit. She hovered near but could not manipulate, could not sing her song of death for the world to hear.

The whispers spoke of her, spoke of her release. Still not satisfied, she longed for more than freedom. The hot voices worried the old wax, melting it into puddles of rainbows. Colors meshing together, forming new waves of color to harden on the table, and all the while the beasts remained trapped.

A slow, monotonous drip from a water pipe gave melody to the voices. Set the beat. Brought dampness to the basement. Paint swelled and flaked, leaving barren spots on the walls. Vermin climbed the walls seeking prey, seeking a mate, seeking a place to grow old and die, crawling unevenly over paint stains, ruptures in the wall, skeletons of families left to rot.

The floor covered with stains and dirt. Particles sticking to the baseboards. Every updraft swirled the specks into clouds that settled on tin cans, old furniture, and forgotten clothes.

The darkness couldn't hide the scene because

the moon spotlighted the rage embedded in the utensils Cathy once used. The dagger, the oil, the sea salt, the incense, the bell, the pentacle, always aware of their purpose, always aware of the failures and the conceits which flowed through them.

A rat sniffed at the window and pawed the glass. The lock on the inside of the window remained stuck, preventing the potential intruder from ruining Cathy's utensils. Protecting the spells from being broken, holding the curses in place until the little one found his way back. Shortly after his mother's death the child had slipped quietly into the basement, cautiously taking the steps one by one, directing his gaze to the box. Mommy's very special box where she kept her goddess guarded by fiends. The chubby goddess he took but left the fearsome box to await his return. But the forces of Mommy's power knew he'd come back, and when he did the simmering rage would explode into an unquenchable revenge.

chapter 9

The witch stumbled down the flight of stairs. Her oversized shoes didn't seem to fit properly on the narrow steps. Consequently she woke Brandy who had been snoozing inside a cage. The cage stood tall enough for him to stand and broad enough for him to take extremely short walks. He had fidgeted for hours with the padlock but never achieved anything more than a few splintered fingernails.

When he opened his eyes he saw a short young woman running up the steps of the basement until she reached the door. She pulled and banged on the door, but it didn't budge.

"Oh, rotten toadstools," yelled out the witch sitting upright on her fanny.

"Help. Help," screamed the young woman.

"Useless," he called up to her.

The woman either didn't hear him or ignored him, because she continued her frantic screams and banging.

"Serves me right," muttered the witch. "I should have never taken your shoes," she said, staring at Brandy. "Big feet. Enormous feet, that's what you got." She kicked off the shoes and rolled over onto her tummy, laid her hands flat on the floor, and walked her feet toward the front of her body to push herself up to a standing position. The sight of her bum covered with a flared skirt made Brandy cover his eyes.

The witch stooped, picked up the shoes, and threw them at Brandy's cage, forcing him to take a step or two backward.

"Oh, such a shrill voice," said the witch, covering her ears. "Young lady, please be still or at least quiet down."

Strangely the woman did quiet down a bit. She peered over her shoulder and saw the cage with the bare-chested man looking back at her. Glancing beyond him, she saw the witch twitching her fingers in invitation.

"No. I'll not allow you to take me prisoner." The woman's shoulders courageously stiffened. "Someone will hear my plea and save me." She glanced over at the male in the cage.

"Certainly I won't, miss," he said. "I haven't been

able to rescue myself, and I can fully assure you that I've not been waiting here to see to your rescue."

"Don't make me use my magic, deary," said the witch.

"Performing magical stunts gives her headaches," explained Brandy. "Terrible migraines that put her into foul moods."

"I should care about that evil woman's health?" said the young lady.

"Her grousing and moaning can be awfully irritating. Once she spent so long down here complaining about her headaches that I ended up with a terrible migraine myself."

"Part of her magic, no doubt," said the woman.

"No, just part of her overbearing personality."

"Sweetie, if you come down I'll give you a gift," the witch said.

"The only gift I want is my freedom," said the woman.

The witch jumped up and down on her stubby legs, taking on a terrible tantrum.

"Like I do sometimes, Daddy, when I can't stay up late?" asked Stephen.

"Now that you mention it, yes, very much like your tantrums."

"Only she doesn't have you to threaten to tan her hide."

"You're so lucky to have me, Stephen."

"*Calming herself, the witch closed her eyes and pronounced, 'Hocus-pocus, mucus . . .'*"

Stephen giggled. His father hushed him with a serious frown.

"Hocus-pocus, mucus, clueless, stewless,. . ."

Stephen stifled his laughter.

"Seize the woman, make her pencil thin, and slip her between the bars."

A flattened out young lady stood next to Brandy, her amazed expression frozen onto her face.

"Oh, yes, blow her up into normal weight."

And the woman suddenly puffed up into her normal shape.

"You can't put her in here with me," complained Brandy. "I have hardly any room as it is."

"You must share," said the witch.

"No, I refuse," he said.

The witch put her hands on her hips and walked over to the cage.

"I have nowhere else to put her. My other cage is in use. I have several large cats that I'm keeping for the circus."

"You'll have to tell the circus to come and pick up the cats."

"Can't. I need the money they pay for the storage."

"Why, you selfish witch. What about my comfort? You've already stolen my shoes and shirt."

The witch picked the shoes up and pushed them between the bars.

"I don't want them back now. You ruined them.

They were perfectly waxed and soled when I came. Now look at them."

"A little spit will do the trick," said the witch. "And as for the soles, they were almost worn down when you got here."

Brandy grabbed the arm of the woman and pushed her toward the bars.

"I want her out."

The witch shrugged.

"I have no place else to put her; either it's here or the furnace."

The woman glanced over toward the furnace and saw that it was red hot. She took several steps away from the bars and batted at Brandy's hand when he tried to stop her.

"Okay, okay," he said.

"Wasn't that nice of Brandy, Stephen?"

Stephen shrugged.

"Sometimes we have to make room for others, Stephen, and it means sometimes we must change our plans."

"We're not going to the shore this weekend, are we, Daddy?"

"Aunt Rosemary is visiting this weekend."

"On Mom's birthday. Doesn't she know this is a special weekend?"

"Aunt Rosemary doesn't get much time off from her job, and this is the only weekend she can get away. She wants to visit her favorite nephew."

"I'm her only nephew."

"That makes you her favorite."

"Is Robin coming too?"

"No, Aunt Rosemary wants to have some special time with you and is afraid Robin would be a distraction."

"But I like Robin better than Aunt Rosemary."

"It's better not to mention that, Stephen."

"I want to find out how it felt when the witch took out Robin's juice to make putty."

"Shush! That's a secret. Robin can't talk about that. Never ask her that question."

"Did you lie about making the putty out of nerves?"

"Maybe."

Stephen pulled his covers up to his chin.

"I still want to visit Mommy at the shore. Aunt Rosemary can come if she wants."

"I'm sure she will join us. Your mother and Aunt Rosemary were sisters, after all."

"Aunt Rosemary made Mom sad."

"What makes you think that?"

Stephen pushed the blankets away from his body. He felt a warm flush rapidly drive through his flesh making his skin prickle from the heat.

"When Aunt Rosemary visited, Mom hardly ever smiled, and when Aunt Rosemary left Mom would quietly sniffle like she was holding back tears."

"Could be your mom felt sorry for her sister. Here Mom had you, a healthy, active little boy, and Aunt Rosemary has Robin."

Stephen's held tilted to the side.

"You think Mom felt sorry for Aunt Rosemary?"

"Sometimes adults feel guilty when their own lives seem to be going so well and a close friend or relative is suffering a loss."

"If things were going so well, why did Mom go away?"

"Sometimes we don't get to choose when we leave."

"But I heard Grandma tell you that Mom was selfish to leave me now."

"I don't know when you heard that, Stephen, but Mom did not purposefully leave you."

"Then why isn't she here now?"

Jacob pulled his son close and kissed his mussed hair.

"She must have been in a lot of pain. When you're older you'll understand."

"I hate it when you say that." Stephen's muffled voice made Jacob smile.

chapter 10

Mom wanted to pry Jacob's arms from around her son. Stephen didn't try to break free from his father, instead he crumpled up into the embrace like the child he was. She sensed the warmth of the cuddle and writhed in the pain it caused her.

In these kinds of moments she couldn't touch her son. Couldn't call him back to her. His name on her lips meant nothing. The coldness of her fingers merely made Stephen shiver. Her breath stagnated in the air, having no way to reach inside the world of the living. Jacob blocked her spirit and strengthened the hold the tangible world had on her son.

THE WITCH

When father and son broke apart, Stephen slid down on the sheet and allowed his father to throw the blanket over him. His mother moved closer to Stephen's pillow so that she could whisper in her son's ear.

"Mommy is still here with you. I would never leave my little boy. I'm here to rescue you from the evil persons surrounding you. I will give you the strength to defeat those with evil purpose toward you, for they have destroyed me."

The boy appeared to flinch from her silent words.

"It's only Mom. Don't be afraid, Stephen. We can't hug yet the way you and Daddy do, but I promise we will be joined together again. I will fight for our union, Stephen. And you will learn how to take revenge for the both of us. Jacob, Grandma, and Molly drove me away from you, leaving you without my protection. Soon though we'll find our way back to each other. The spirits are waiting to help you in the basement. Listen to them call to you. Every spirit I have brought into your world, Stephen, awaits your orders. Such tiny lips as yours can command the devil's comrades. Your small hands can crush those who have hurt us."

The lights went out in Stephens' bedroom, but his mother still saw her son clearly. His fisted fingers grabbed the blanket up over his chin, and his teeth bit into the woven wool. He gave a half-hearted sigh and pulled the blanket out of his mouth to say his prayers.

Mom bowed her head, but she couldn't remember the

words to the prayers he recited. His long list of blessings tried her patience. She wanted to speak to him again. She wanted his full attention.

The last blessing called for peace for Mom's soul.

"Yes, yes, Stephen, you can bring me peace. But only when you meet with those waiting in the basement. They know of you. They call to you each night, but their voices never reach your ears. Open up to the world beyond your own, Stephen. Allow us to come into your heart and mind.

"Now I lay me down to sleep. I pray the Lord my soul to . . ."

She faltered over the last word. The Lord didn't have her soul, and He wouldn't have her son's.

chapter 11

The basement furnace exploded into action. For the next ninety minutes it would take the chill from the air of the house, then shut down until needed again the next day.

But there were denizens of the basement who loved the heat and wished the cranky furnace would never quit its job. A field mouse, who had burrowed in from the outside, sidled up close to the warmth. It sniffed the air, trying to sense food, its nose twittering quietly in the dark. The mouse sat up on its hind legs, the front legs stiff with anticipation, but it didn't like the odor in the air. Didn't like the chill that tried to wrap itself around the heat of the furnace. Didn't like the barely perceptible whine echoing in the basement. The field mouse's ears flicked several times before the mouse fell back down on all four legs to scurry for the hole through which it had gained admittance.

The box on the table pulsed, the beasts throbbing to the beat of their mistress' wishes, the grunts and groans verbalizing their frustration, energy igniting the tiny figures on the box.

A forked tongue pierced the air, stretching forth from the front of the wooden box, flicking the air, scenting for power. Finding none, the tongue popped back inside two thick lips that cut through pudgy scarred cheeks.

Gnarled fingers and blackened hands massaged the sides of the box, seeking to obtain the twisted fiends' release. But the tiny demons found themselves cemented to their prison.

The door at the top of the stairs opened, and a tiny voice called, "Mommy? Mommy?"

The jumble of bodies on the box quivered in joy.

"Yes, yes, come down here, little one. We await your commands."

With outstretched hands the beasts beseeched the child.

"Release us from our prison, and we'll obey only you."

One, two, three stairs squeaked from a child's feet.

"Mommy, are you down there?"

"Much better, we are here!" shouted the beasts, but their tiny voices couldn't carry to Stephen's ears.

"Mommy, are you hiding on me?" Stephen asked, his hands gripping the banister as he stared into the dark basement.

"Silly boy," called a bestial voice, its body rolling back and forth in agony.

"Another step," entreated a spindly demon who worried his hands constantly.

"Daddy doesn't want me coming down here, Mommy. He says it's dirty and cold and not very nice in the basement. I never tell him about us doing magic in the basement. I never talk about the colors, the sounds, and figures we played with. Especially not about the little uglies. They gave me the creeps like those movies Dad likes to watch." Stephen released the banister and sat down on the step, his knees pulled to his chest.

"Don't hesitate, little villain," snapped a misshapen bird, its beak slightly bent to one side, its beak firmly attached to the wood.

"I guess Dad wouldn't mind if I talk to you from the steps. It's warmer up here, and I only got on my pj's.

"Aunt Rosemary's coming to visit tomorrow. I told Daddy we should still go visit you, but now that you're back I guess we don't have to drive way out to the ocean anymore. Did you like Aunt Rosemary?

Daddy says you felt sorry for her because of Robin."

"She got the child she deserved." Mommy's harsh voice almost broke through the vacuum separating mother from son. She tried to take his hand and lead him down the steps but his flesh seemed too far away.

"Bring the babe closer, woman. Bring him to us, and we will fulfill your wishes." The beasts voices spoke in unison. *"We will sing to him the same lullabies that you did. We will cradle his soul safely in our hands. We will tend to his hungers and rub our own salve into his wounds."*

"Momma, why can't I see you anymore?"

"Your eyes can't see in the dark, my sweetness. The spirits I brought into this world can help you see, but you must go to them." Stephen's mother blew her son a kiss before the world of the dead retrieved her.

chapter 12

"Now look happy to see your aunt when she comes through the arrival door, Stephen."

"It's okay, Dad. We don't have to visit Mommy 'cause she visits us now."

Jacob looked down at his son and found himself feeling both proud and bewildered. Could this be Stephen's way of making the best of things? At some point he'd have to put a stop to his son's fantasies, but not now. Cathy had been dead only a short time. Let the boy find his own way through the grief.

"There she is now! Wave, Stephen." Jacob leaned down to whisper in his son's ear. "And don't forget to smile." Suddenly Jacob's face broke into a broad grin.

A woman with round spectacles and dyed charcoal-black hair squinted into the waiting crowd. Her ashen complexion appeared to be dotted with cherry-colored paste, and her lips nervously mumbled unspoken words. Her white teeth glinted when she caught sight of Jacob and Stephen. She rushed forward into Jacob's arms.

Jacob gingerly held Rosemary's frail body. He judged her to be about five feet ten and weighing all of one hundred pounds.

"I'm so sorry about Cathy, Jacob."

"You've mentioned that before, Rosemary. Stephen's been looking forward to your visit. Right son?"

Jacob's stomach tightened when he saw Stephen almost shake his head, but quickly the boy recouped and nodded with a big smile on his face.

Rosemary stooped and clasped her nephew to her chest. Her kisses wetted down most of the boy's face.

"Your mom is waiting out in the parking lot. We didn't find the best of spaces, and she worried I might get a ticket."

Rosemary stood and gripped Stephen's hand tightly. Jacob thought he saw his son wince.

"That's Mom. She worries about everyone and everything. She doesn't know how to mind her own business. But I don't have to tell you, Jacob. You've had far more patience with her than my Will."

"How is your ex-husband, Rosemary?"

"Still looking for a job. Trying to hit me up for money. I told him it's like trying to get blood from a stone. Every penny I make goes toward Robin's health."

"She staying with her father this weekend?" Jacob asked.

"And his hoochie-koochie."

"Dad, what's a hooey-kooye?" Stephen asked.

"We'll look it up in the dictionary later, son."

"Aunt Rosemary, what's a hooey-kooye?"

"It's the young girl your uncle is seeing."

"Then she's a who and not a what. Is she as young as Molly?" Stephen kept asking his questions all the way out to the car, and the adults stalled for answers.

Mabel swung open the door of the car and rushed out to greet her daughter. The two spent five minutes hugging, admiring, and questioning each other until Jacob reminded them that he didn't plan on paying for overnight parking.

On the way home, Rosemary and Mabel never stopped talking, and Jacob managed to tune out the shrill voices. He found his way home by rote and pulled into the driveway.

"What are we doing here?" asked Rosemary.

"You're staying with Jacob and Stephen," Mabel replied.

"Oh, Jacob, I couldn't intrude at this time. My goodness, you and Stephen must just be beginning to adjust."

"He volunteered as soon as he heard you were coming," Mabel said.

I did?

Jacob realized nothing had been said about where Rosemary would stay until he had suggested his own home. But he thought he hadn't a choice.

"If you insist, Jacob. I wouldn't insult you by refusing."

Insult me!

"It's going to be a wonderful weekend. We can take Stephen to the zoo and afterward stop to get that awful chili he so loves." Mabel ran her fingers through Stephen's hair.

"It's Mom's birthday," he said.

Jacob broke the moment of silence by offering to carry Rosemary's overnight bag into the house.

"Thank you, Jacob," Rosemary said, stepping out of the car. "Perhaps we should ask Stephen what he'd like to do today."

Behind Stephen's back Mabel violently shook her head at Rosemary.

"Hey, buddy, why don't you run up to your bedroom and get that special birthday card you made for Mom?"

"But, Dad, it's not meant for everyone to see."

"You showed it to Molly and me, didn't you?"

Stephen nodded.

"Then why not show it to Grandma and Aunt Rosemary?"

"Because they won't care."

"No, no, Stephen, we do care," said Rosemary, dropping to her knees in front of the boy. "Grandma and I got so excited about seeing you that we hurriedly started making plans. However, we also want to do something today to remember your mother. Can we sign our names to your birthday card?"

"Did you forget your card?"

"I think it would be more special if we signed your card; more likely she'd notice your hand-made card over anybody's else's."

"There's plenty of room on the card for everyone's name," Stephen said. "I'll go get it."

When the boy ran into the house, Mabel turned to Rosemary.

"Jacob and Stephen go to the seaside every weekend to visit Cathy. Just once I'd like to wean Stephen away from this obsession."

"There'll come a time soon enough, Mom, when he'll have such a full life he'll barely remember what Cathy looked and sounded like. Let him be. If he wants to go to the seaside we can stop on the way back at a nice fish restaurant."

"I'm shocked, Mabel." Jacob stepped forward.

"You always ask if he prays for his mother and whether he asks about her."

"I know, but a few minutes of prayer is different than spending a week planning for the weekend visit to his dead mother. And taking her own life. . ."

"I don't think Stephen remembers," said Jacob.

"My God, he found her hanging in the basement!"

"Mabel, calm down. He'll be back soon. I don't think he clearly remembers what he saw. He was only down there a few seconds when I called him up."

"But he's the one who told you," Mabel said in a hushed voice.

"He said he thought Mommy needed help. I didn't allow him back down in the cellar. Matter of fact, I put the cellar off limits."

"Is the door locked?"

"No, Mabel, locking the door would only draw attention to the basement. Next thing I know I'd find him in front of the basement door with a hand full of bobby pins trying to pry open the lock."

"He's right, Mom."

The front door opened, and Stephen came running with his hand-made card.

Inside the house everyone signed the card but were surprised when Stephen said it wouldn't be necessary to drive to the seaside to deliver the card.

"Mom's still here with Daddy and me. We don't have to go anywhere else to be near her," he announced.

chapter 13

Stephen slowly opened the basement door. The slight squeak made him pause for only a moment. He wore his heavy cable Irish sweater over his pajamas. The sheepskin slippers fit snugly around his feet. He kept one hand pressed against the sweater and used his other hand to hold the banister.

He didn't want to use the flashlight until he had managed to descend most of the stairs. Certainly he didn't want his father to catch him going to the basement. Midway down the stairs he couldn't wait any longer; he whipped the flashlight from under his sweater and pressed the button. The bright light cast some shadows, and Stephen turned to make a run back up the steps, but since he didn't see anything he expected, he stopped.

Mommy's spirit might be in the basement, but not her body. His shaky hand scanned the room with his flashlight.

"It's after midnight, Mom, happy birthday." He let go of the banister in order to pull his handmade card from under his sweater. "Everybody signed it. Dad, Grandma, and even Aunt Rosemary. She's visiting and sleeping upstairs in the guest room. Grandma went home after dinner, but she'll be back in the morning."

Stephen placed the flashlight on a step and folded the card into the shape of an airplane. Holding the card, he swung his arm far back before lurching forward, setting the plane free in the air.

"Air Mail." He giggled, moving his foot excitedly, sending the flashlight rolling down the steps one at a time.

Stephen stood in the dark and looked down at the floor where the flashlight rolled slowly toward the furnace before stopping.

"Drat!" his little voice muttered. He looked behind him and could see the open door and the moonlight lighting the hallway.

"Umm, Mom, I'm not supposed to be down here," he said turning back to the basement floor.

He held his breath for several moments, listening for the sound of footsteps. The bedrooms were all on the second floor, he thought; maybe they couldn't hear what went on in the basement.

"I should be getting back to bed, but I wanted to wish you a Happy Birthday."

He thought he heard a whimper, a sad sound that made his heart ache.

"Mom, is that you? I hope I didn't make you sad by telling you Aunt Rosemary is here. She doesn't seem so unhappy having Robin as her child. Robin may not be able to walk, but she's lots of fun and makes everyone laugh. I think Aunt Rosemary is lucky to have Robin. She's better at telling jokes than I am. Honestly, I think she may be a little smarter than me, even. Not a lot, but sometimes she understands things I don't. I know she's two years older, but I have the feeling she was smarter than me two years ago. Besides, I don't believe Daddy's story about witches making putty out of nerves. I don't think any witch has cursed Robin. She's too nice."

With his eyes he searched for the plane and saw that it had made a perfect landing atop the ugly box.

"Can you read it, Mommy? If not, maybe the uglies can read it to you." He thought for a second. "Can they read?"

The plane tilted and almost fell off the box, but it appeared glued.

"Come, read it to your mother, little man."

Stephen descended one step.

The furnace clicked off.

"Little man, don't make us wait."

Stephen quickly ran down the stairs and picked up the flashlight, almost toppling over into the furnace. His hand barely touched the furnace door, but he pulled back quickly while letting out a small cry: "Ouch."

The whimper started again.

"Don't worry, Mom, I'm not really hurt."

The plane wavered back and forth on top of the box but never fell. Stephen thought it might be taking off. Curious, he took a few steps closer.

"Mom, is that you or the uglies?"

Cathy broke free from the arms of death and instantly Stephen felt her presence. He sighed and smiled, knowing he was safe now. He even got up the nerve to move up close to the table.

"You are doing that, aren't you, Mom?"

"Make him hold us in his hands, Mother. Make him accept us."

"He is my son. He will know what to do. He has watched me often."

"But he hesitates. He fumbles with toys instead of taking up his task."

Stephen instantly took a step back, and his eyes widened when the plane burst into flames.

"Silly games. Silly toys. We are here for revenge."

When there was nothing but ash left of the plane, he closed his open mouth and swallowed.

"Didn't you like the card, Mom?"

"It was a beautiful card, sweetness. A beautiful card. Although ruined by the names that followed your own. Give me a better gift, Stephen. Give me your father's pride and handsomeness. His face, his hands, his body are too perfect. Too much temptation for the young, for the trollops that blindly sin for him."

"Mom, I'm getting scared. Something don't feel right."

Cathy stretched out her arms to hold her son, but as happened so many times before, she couldn't feel the solidness of his body.

Stephen shivered and wrapped his arms around himself.

"I have to go now, Mom. I'll visit again, I promise."

"Cowardly, child."

"Simpleton!"

"He mocks us."

Growls, groans, whimpers all filled the air, panicking Stephen and driving him up the stairs to slam the door shut behind him.

chapter 14

"Stephen has a charming babysitter to look after him, don't you, Stephen?" Grandma had brought over baked goods for breakfast, and Stephen, with a full mouth, couldn't reply.

"I've been thinking about getting another babysitter," said Jacob.

Stephen spit out his food into his plate.

"That's disgusting, Stephen. You know you shouldn't do that." Grandma grabbed her napkin and tried to wipe Stephen's chin.

"But, Dad, I like her. I think she should live here all the time."

"She can't do that, Stephen." Grandma slipped the plate from under Stephen's chin and threw the remains of his food in the garbage. "She's too young to move away from her parents and it wouldn't look proper. Now, upstairs, brush your teeth, and never spit your food out like that again. Go!"

Stephen looked at his father.

"Do what Grandma says, Stephen. We'll talk about Molly later."

"She hasn't even finished my costume yet." Stephen's small hands gripped the table.

Jacob laughed, but Mabel pulled the boys hands from the table.

"Upstairs, now!" she barked.

Stephen rose from the chair so fast it almost tipped over, except Jacob caught the back frame. Stephen ran out of the kitchen.

"Mom, did you have to do that?"

"What, Rosemary?"

"Discipline Stephen like that. I'm supposed to be here to make him feel better and loved. Instead, you're making it impossible to have any time with him."

"Rosemary, Robin is different than other children. She's . . ."

"In a wheelchair," Rosemary finished.

"No, I meant she's not as aggressive as Stephen. He needs to be taught how to behave."

"Could you leave that up to me, Mabel?" said

Jacob.

"I didn't hear you discourage his behavior. Rosemary and I are family but also company, and he must learn how to act when in social situations."

"When we were children Mom used to bat us in the head with her bag when she thought no one was looking. Once the mailman caught her and threatened to report her to Social Services."

"He should have been minding his own business."

"What did you carry in that bag, Mom? Lead?"

"Rosemary, I barely touched you with the bag. I meant to make you more alert to your surroundings. You and Cathy would drift off into dreamland and paid no attention to what happened around you."

"Cathy one time emptied Mom's bag into a drawer, and for some reason Mom didn't notice how light it was. Boy, Mom was really embarrassed when she couldn't pay the bill at the grocery."

"Cathy always came up with little spiteful things like that." Mabel's eyes watered.

Jacob reached over and held her hand.

"Mabel, promise you'll never hit my son with your monster of a bag."

"Jacob . . ." Tears flowed down Mabel's cheeks.

"Mom, Stephen is Jacob's problem, not yours. You're the grandma. You're supposed to have fun with him. He's supposed to look forward to your spoiling him. Okay?"

"I'm sorry, Jacob, I'm doing it again."

"Yup; at this point I should be sending you home."

"Like Cathy did."

Jacob nodded.

"Don't go home, Mom, just lighten up." Rosemary stood to walk over to her mother and give her a hug.

"Stephen will forget all about this," said Jacob.

"But not about his babysitter," said Rosemary. "Why are you thinking about changing sitters? I always thought Molly was conscientious."

"I think he's gotten too close to her. You heard him talk about having her live here."

"Yeah, but that's because he misses the mothering Cathy gave him. That's where you can come in, Grandma." Rosemary patted her mother's shoulders. "Instead of being the bad guy, why don't you give Stephen unconditional love? He already has Jacob to boss him around."

"But—"

"A grandma's unconditional love," interrupted Rosemary.

Mabel nodded her head.

"I'm going upstairs to make up with Stephen and find out what he wants to do today. I promise I will not try to affect his decision even if I think it unhealthy." Mabel stood.

"Going to visit his mother at the ocean isn't unhealthy, Mom. Cathy's only been dead a short time."

Mabel nodded and left the kitchen.

"Thanks," said Jacob. "I didn't think you approved of my fatherly techniques."

"Mom's going to alienate Stephen the same way she did Cathy. I don't want that to happen. I'm afraid she sees a lot of Cathy in him.

"As for you, you creep, I never said you made a bad father. A bad husband? Yes. You fool around with Stephen's babysitter?"

"Rosemary, why would you think that?"

"Because I was stupid enough to sleep with you the night before you married Cathy."

"Ah, but Cathy and I were not officially married yet."

"Come off it, Jacob. You're a male slut."

"And you, Rosemary?"

"Stupid."

Rosemary shivered.

"Is there a window open?"

"No. It's me giving you the shivers," Jacob said, smirking while picking up the breakfast dishes. He placed the dishes in the sink and ran the cold water over them, getting his own hands wet in the process. Shaking off his hands, he turned to see Rosemary looking out the window and softly walked over behind her and settled his wet fingers on the back of her neck.

Rosemary jumped to her feet.

"What the hell do you think you're doing?" she asked, turning the full force of her anger on Jacob.

"Stop being so jumpy, Rosemary. You used to have nice soft curves, but now you look like a scarecrow. Divorcing Will certainly didn't help matters. How much do you weigh now?"

"None of your business."

"Don't blow up at me because you can't find a decent boyfriend to soothe your nerves. When's the last time you went to bed with anyone? Should we count in months or years?"

"Between you and Will, I've had my fill of low-life men. Obviously Cathy felt the same."

"We don't know what was going on with Cathy. She went in and out of her depressions. When we first married, she'd go for days without talking. With the arrival of Stephen she seemed better."

"That's because she had lost a previous baby."

"The one she aborted?"

"She didn't want to. Mom dragged her into the clinic."

"If I count from the date you married Will to the arrival of Robin, I come up with six months."

"Will was willing to marry me. The scum who got Cathy pregnant wasn't. I shouldn't say that. He and Cathy were both underage. I believe she had just turned sixteen, and the guy wasn't much older. Everyone except for Cathy wanted the baby gone.

She'd remind me yearly of how old that baby would have been."

"Stephen served as a replacement?"

"Never a replacement but a second chance."

"Tell them, tell them." Mabel pushed Stephen into the kitchen in front of her.

"Let's go to the zoo," said Stephen. "And eat chili after we see the animals."

"This came from Stephen. I didn't say anything."

Stephen looked up at his grandmother. "You mentioned there's a new baby gorilla."

"But I didn't say we should go to the zoo to see the gorilla," Mabel said, looking back and forth between Jacob and Rosemary.

"Before we gorilla *aficionados* go to the zoo, I'd better call Will and make sure Robin is all right."

chapter 15

"Is Robin going to be all right?" asked Stephen.

"Sure. Her dad probably fed her something greasy and she has a sensitive stomach."

"You feed me greasy food."

"Yeah, but you've got a tummy of iron," Jacob said patting his son's stomach.

Stephen scratched his head.

"I don't believe that a witch stole Robin's nerves, but . . ."

"Hmmm?"

"But if she had, would that make Robin's tummy upset?"

"Nah, I think her father's bad cooking could, though."

Stephen sat on the oak floor and rested his head against his father's leg.

"How come we never see Uncle Will anymore?"

"Because he's no longer married to your Aunt Rosemary."

"Why not?"

"Ask your Aunt Rosemary."

"But she's gone to pick up Robin from her daddy. Aunt Rosemary didn't even get to go to the zoo with us."

"Hey, what did you think of that baby gorilla?"

"Couldn't even see him 'cause his mom kept him so close to her."

"That's how moms are."

"Do you think his mom will go away from him someday?"

"More likely he'll leave his mom. Maybe even go off to another zoo to begin a brand new life. Some of us do it sooner than others."

"But I'm too small to leave home."

"Yes. Someday, though, you'll break my heart and leave to have a family of your own."

Stephen shook his head.

"I know how sad it would make you. I wouldn't hurt you the way Mommy hurt us."

"I keep trying to explain, Stephen, that she

didn't do it on purpose. She had problems."

"Then why didn't she come to us? We would have helped her. You always say I should come to you and you'll make things right."

"I may not always be able to make things right, but I will be there to give you support." Jacob ran his fingers through the boy's tawny hair.

"I would have helped Mom. She always did stuff for me. There must have been something I could have done for her."

Cathy's shadow fell upon the room, her chilled spirit almost numb from the coldness of death's hand. Her ravaged soul ached for peace, but she fought the quiet that beckoned to her beyond the world she once knew.

"Help me, Stephen. You can still help me. I can't rest until you've avenged me. Your small hands and lips carry the magic to bring the fiends to life."

She spread her arms to enfold her little boy, but Jacob scooped up his son to wrap him in a bearish hug. Her fingernails scratched at air, her stagnant breath poisoned the air around her, and her little boy appeared to flinch away from her.

"Tell you what, Stephen, if you go upstairs and get ready for bed, I'll tell you some more about Brandy and the witch."

"Don't forget the new lady that's sharing Brandy's cage."

chapter 16

"We must escape from here," said the lady standing next to Brandy in the cage.

"Fine. You come up with a plan and I'll be most happy in assisting you to escape. I'll even escape with you."

The lady frowned at Brandy.

"You expect me to rescue us?"

"Why not? Obviously I haven't been successful at getting away from the witch. Maybe you'll have a better plan."

"Witch! Witch!" screamed the lady.

The witch, who had been sorting her garbage, stopped and toddled over to the cage.

"We're terribly thirsty and hungry. You must feed us."

"Nonsense. You ate up all my jams, bread, and tea just fifteen minutes ago when you were in my sitting room."

The lady turned toward Brandy.

"Tell her you're hungry," demanded the lady.

"That might not be a good idea," said Brandy.

"When did you last eat?"

"This morning."

"Well, it is easily the middle of the afternoon now. You must be hungry. What did you have for breakfast?"

"Frogs' legs and bats' feet."

The jam and bread in the lady's stomach sloshed around dangerously.

"Eew!" shouted Stephen. "What did Brandy have to drink for breakfast?"

"Drink?"

Stephen nodded his head violently.

"I believe it was a puree of snot."

Stephen let out a scream of disgust.

"Luckily the lady didn't ask what Brandy had had to drink because she surely would have lost her lunch."

Stephen giggled.

"The witch can't treat you that cruelly," the lady said to Brandy.

"Cruel!" shouted the witch. "They were the freshest frogs' legs and bats' feet I had in the house. You'll get nothing of the kind, young lady."

"I certainly wouldn't eat it if you served it to me," the lady indignantly said.

"I wouldn't antagonize her," warned Brandy. "She serves much worse meals when she is out of sorts."

"Like what?" asked Stephen.

Jacob sighed.

"It's much too gross to repeat, Stephen. You might never be able to eat again. Especially not that chili you like so much."

"The chili?" Stephen frowned. "What's in the chili?"

"Let me just say that eating steak, potatoes, and vegetables are the safest foods. It is obvious what they are. A nice fried or poached egg would not be served by this witch because it wouldn't be interesting enough. She can't mix vegetables with frogs' legs and bats' wing—"

"Bats' feet," corrected Stephen.

"Because the vegetables would wilt and the legs and feet would be glaringly obvious."

"What about green vegetables? Wouldn't they match the frogs' legs?"

"Naw. Totally different shades of green."

"But you cook the meals at home, and you're not a witch."

"That's right, and I would never serve disgusting foods, even though sometimes you think I do."

"Witches might be cooking at the chili place and

putting in snot and all kinds of icky things. Maybe even nerves and ground bones."

Jacob himself started to be put off by eating out. He figured he may have taken this too far. He wanted Stephen to eat healthier meals, but he enjoyed the occasional luxury of going out.

"There are people who inspect restaurants, and they wouldn't permit a witch to cook in the kitchens."

Stephen wrinkled his nose.

"Maybe I don't like eating chili anymore."

"Once in a while it's okay. Sometimes we have to be brave and adventurous."

"I'd rather take my chances on the jungle gym."

"Then who will I eat with when I want chili?"

"Dad, remember how Mom made you stop smoking, and you finally told her that you were glad she did, even though you were cranky for a while?"

"No, Stephen, you're not going to ask me to stop eating chili."

"Well, at least don't eat witch's chili. Maybe we can make chili at home. That's what we can do tomorrow, make chili."

"The last time we cooked together all we made was a mess, and we ended up going out to the chili place. Remember?"

"Mom said people have to practice over and over again before they can do anything well. She made me . . ." Stephen paused.

"She made you what, Stephen?"

"Help her in the basement."

"You mean cleaning the basement?"

"Sometimes," he said, avoiding answering the question directly. He remembered the box covered with uglies and the candle wax that when dripped on each ugly brought them to life.

"I guess I should go down and clean up the basement myself. No one has been down there in ages. Maybe we could sweep out the basement tomorrow."

"No, Dad. Mom wouldn't want that."

"You're right. Tomorrow we should go outdoors and enjoy the day. Maybe even live dangerously and have chili again."

Stephen shrugged.

"Oh, Stephen, I didn't mean to turn you off chili completely. I just wanted to suggest that you eat more of the meals I make and not pick at your plate so much." Jacob used his fingers to quickly squeeze the tip of Stephen's nose. "And if you want to try making chili sometime, that's fine with me. We'll make a big pot and invite Grandma over. How 'bout that?"

"I don't think she'll clean up after us, Dad."

"If she wanted to, I wouldn't stop her."

Stephen laughed.

chapter 17

The demons in the basement tried hard to stretch their limbs, but they could only reach so far, and then the box pulled them back. One demon moped in a far corner, depressed by how slow-witted the child appeared to be. The mother may have been wrong to pass her powers on to the child. The demon felt the coldness of death and knew the mother had returned. Her shadow passed close to the box, and the demon could feel her eyes rest upon him.

What a shame she had not produced better stock, the demon thought.

"He is strong. He will free all of you, but he needs

time. Time to understand my death. Time to recapture the dizzy feel for magic. Time to cut himself off from those who grip him tightly in the base world in which he exists."

"Time is not our friend," said the lone demon. "We need action now. We need a taste of his blood to give us strength. A taste of his flesh to gain in wisdom. Instead we are dusty and slow. We are in the human's world but not free to experience the terror they have of us."

"He is too young," shouted out a malformed bird of prey who had pushed his way closer to the lone demon. "He is not sincere. He merely played at learning. He copied you, Mother, only by rote but didn't feel the exhilaration and sweetness of the evil we carried with us."

"Don't speak of my son. Speak of your new conjuror."

"He can't conjure one of us. He may be able to free us, but he'll never bring another of our kind into his world. He carries too much fear with him. Too much goodness. His magic would only destroy us."

"He is the only one left to follow me. He misses me and will do what needs to be done to bring me back."

"A mamma's boy who is manipulated by the dead. A stunning promise for us," screeched an older dwarf on the farther corner of the box.

"It is because you don't believe in him that he doesn't come to your aid. You must call to him softly. Let your pleas sound like invitations, not empty sounds that drive him away. Hurling angry invectives will ensure failure," the mother said.

THE WITCH

"She is right," hissed a snake that had wrapped itself around the dwarf. "Pretty words and empty promises will turn the child's head. We all know how that works."

"Especially you," said the dwarf, freeing both his arms from the snake's tightening hug.

The snake hardened his grip on the dwarf, forcing a guttural sound from him.

"Don't argue among yourselves, for it will only bring a final defeat," the mother cried.

The snake let go of the dwarf and fell at his feet. The dwarf lifted a foot to stomp the snake, but he felt the cold hand of his mistress flick his shoulders. He gently rested his foot against the wood of the box.

"I was a warrior dwarf once. I killed thousands."

"Not you alone, I'm sure," muttered the snake.

"Wrong you are. I swept across battlefields."

"Hardly imagine you able to sweep across a playground."

"I was not this size. At one time I inhabited the body of a fleshly dwarf. A stupid fool who fell easily to my possession of his soul. A filmy, thin soul who collapsed almost instantaneously to my will."

"And did you join the battles of his people?" The snake coiled into a circle, its head swaying in the air.

"Before I took over he had never been in battle. He had lurked back in caves and woods, always promising to care for the womenfolk and children. Every day his

fellow warrior dwarfs spat upon him. Meekly he would cower and turn away. But I changed it all."

"Did you suddenly send his body wildly into battle?"

"Worse. I killed every dwarf that crossed my path with foul words or derogatory names. Finally he gained respect."

"Not he," Cathy whispered. "You!"

"Yes, yes, I bloodied flesh and stole lives still blooming."

"How many battles have you fought?" Cathy's cold breath made the air shiver with her words.

"Countless," the dwarf shouted. Pride filled his eyes, and his chest swelled out so that a tear broke the seam of his shirt. "This ax I carry is merely a slight symbol of the weapons I wielded. I never feared death."

"Why should you?" commented the snake. "You are a spirit. You lose one body and seek out another."

"But you know how difficult it is to gain access to this world," Cathy said, hoping to massage the dwarf's ego. "Master dwarf overcame many obstacles to win a tangible life."

"And look at me now," groaned the dwarf. "A mere clay figure, tiny and not perfectly formed." He held up his hands to show all twelve of his digits.

"Mistress did the best that she could," the snake fawned. "Look at me; I was molded into shape by the hands of a child, but I've never complained." The snake shook the tip of its tail in the air. "I would have so loved having a rattler, but I'm not complaining."

"I watch you playing your tail in the air," said the dwarf. "You dream every day of having a rattler. A silent complaint like your silent tail." The dwarf laughed.

The snake wrapped itself around the dwarf's ankle.

"I often wonder how you'll be able to wield that ax with so many fingers. Isn't it awkward?"

The tiny dwarf's hands tightened around the ax.

"Haven't I met you before?" the dwarf asked.

"How could you have? Were you in the Garden of Eden?"

"A big claim for such a meager snake." The dwarf sniffed the air. "You smell more of piles of manure than of any Garden of Eden."

"It does not matter where each of you originated. You are here now because I brought you back to be my revenge. Slowly my son will gain the confidence to pry each of you free from your prison."

"It is you," barked out a dog with a man's head, "who bound us to this wooden box. If you wanted revenge, why not have let us run free?"

"Because I have targets that you might have missed in your chaotic rush for blood."

"Does that mean after we do your bidding we shall be free to continue the dark deeds for which we have such pride?" asked the dwarf.

A silence fell heavily on the basement. Death's coldness seeped between the cracks.

"She refuses us an answer," said the dwarf.

"No, no. Death merely stole her back to its bosom." The snake uncurled, leaving a bruised ring around the dwarf's ankle.

"She cheats us," said the dwarf. "She robs us of liberty, of our powers, and of our proper shapes. Each of us has a malformation, and I believe it is on purpose to debase us."

"Not all snakes have rattlers," muttered the snake.

"But a snake of your caliber would definitely be able to rattle, instilling fear into the quarry before death. No, you give her too much power over you."

"You want us to rebel while still glued to this horrid bark of a tree?" The snake slipped its body across the smoothly polished wood.

"I say we wait for a moment of weakness. But we must keep our eyes open and our senses acute."

chapter 18

"Where is it?" shouted Stephen as Molly walked into the house.

"My son has been waiting for this day, Molly. I hope you won't disappoint us."

It had been a long time since Molly had seen Jacob smile. She smiled back and faltered a bit before she spoke.

"I have it in the car. Stephen said he didn't want you to see the costume until he put it on."

"Yeah, yeah. Go, go, Dad." Stephen pushed against his father's hip, trying to steer Dad into the living room.

"What if I just close my eyes?"

"No. You'll peek, Dad."

"But I'll cover my eyes like this." Jacob covered his eyes with his fingers but spread the fingers so that there were obvious big gaps.

"That's not fair, Dad. You can see."

Jacob uncovered his eyes.

"Okay, I have errands to run. You and Molly can scheme behind my back if you like. But don't scare me too much when I come home."

Jacob lifted his son and kissed him goodbye. He blew a soft kiss in Molly's direction.

"You're supposed to catch it," said Stephen.

Molly reached out a hand but knew there was nothing to be captured in the kiss.

Molly followed Jacob out to retrieve the costume from her car. By the time she returned to the house, Jacob had driven away.

She held the costume up in front of her, and Stephen clapped his hands in delight. He especially liked the pointy claws she had attached and the tail that looked so real.

"I've brought fangs too," she said holding up a wax image.

Stephen grabbed the fangs and inserted them into his mouth and growled menacingly. Molly let out a very feminine shriek when Stephen grabbed for the costume.

"Can I try it on now? Can I?"

"Sure. We'll go up to your room, and—"

"No. I want to put it on myself and surprise you."

"I think you'll be needing some help getting into the wolf suit." She showed him the snaps and zippers, and he declared that he could dress himself. "Okay, I'll wait here for you, but if you need any help, call."

Stephen rushed up the staircase.

Molly waited a few seconds before walking down the hall to the basement door. Even if he had some difficulty getting into the suit, she knew he would keep trying. He hated asking for help.

She turned the knob on the basement door which opened easily. Stepping onto the landing of the basement stairs, she began feeling around the side wall for a light switch. The bulb lit up immediately although the wattage couldn't have been high, since it didn't offer much light.

Her eyes adjusted to the dimness quickly. The wooden stairs were painted white and the banister matched. Before descending the staircase she pushed the door open as wide as it would go.

The stairs creaked a bit but not as badly as her parents' basement steps, which were old and half-rotted away. When she reached the bottom, she paused to look back up the stairs and to listen in case Stephen should call. A slight background noise buzzed in her ears, but she couldn't tell where it came from.

As soon as she passed the furnace she saw the table with the box Stephen had talked about. Candle wax surrounded the box and the multiple colors brightened the scene. She walked over to the table and touched the hardened wax. A rush of voices echoed in her ears, but no one appeared to be in the room. The voices sounded like a maddened mob calling for an execution, only the words were not easy to understand. The garbled words rang out in the room but from no particular direction.

Molly spun around, attempting to catch sight of a television or radio that might have been left on. Nothing but the cacophony of reflected panic.

"Stephen?" she called. Could he be playing a joke on her? she wondered. "Stephen!" Her voice rose into a yell.

A hiss quieted Molly as she zeroed in on the wooden box. The images on the box flowed, wave-like. A savage dance ringed the box with unattractive beings.

"The uglies," she said remembering what Stephen had told her.

"You're not supposed to be here," a muffled voice said.

She turned and saw the shadow of an animal moving down the stairs. When she caught up with the real being she realized it was Stephen dressed in his costume with the mask fitted tightly over his face.

"You scared me, Stephen." Her nervous laugh seemed too high-pitched.

"Dad said no one should come down here."

"I didn't know that."

"Yes you did 'cause I told you."

"I'd forgotten. I came down to see the box you told me about."

"If you remembered the box, then you should have remembered the warning."

Molly realized the voices had stopped, but she didn't know whether it had been before or after Stephen entered the basement.

"Stephen, do you ever hear voices down here?"

"Go upstairs, Molly. I don't want to have to tell Dad that I caught you down here."

"You're down here too." She turned her back on Stephen and lifted the box. "I could have sworn the images were circling the box a few minutes ago."

"They're bound to the box."

"By a spell?" she asked, holding the box up to the dim naked bulb that hung from the ceiling.

"That's my mother's box. Put it down."

"Your mother doesn't own anything in this world anymore." She turned and faced Stephen with the box still in her hands. "Did you inherit the box? Are you supposed to continue your mother's witchcraft? Did she leave you a book of spells?"

"Please don't take the box, Molly. It belonged to my mother."

"I'm not a thief, Stephen. I'm simply curious as to what use you could put this box to."

Stephen pulled off his mask and walked closer to Molly. When she handed him the box he took a step backward.

"You're afraid of the box. Why, Stephen? What kind of power does this box have?"

"Dad is talking about replacing you with a new babysitter. I like you and don't want him to do that, but if you don't put the box down I'm going to report you to Dad."

"I bet your father doesn't even know about this box. He'd be upset if he knew you came down here and played with the box."

"I never touch the box, Molly, and you shouldn't either. Momma knew how to control the uglies; you don't."

Molly squatted down to Stephen's level.

"Show me how to use the box, Stephen."

He shook his head.

"The uglies don't like people."

"Did they like your mother?"

"They did what she told them to do."

"And what was that?"

Stephen shrugged.

"Did you ever see the uglies do bad things?"

"They fought among themselves a lot, and Mom would have to quiet them down."

"Why did she want them around?"

"She said one day they would serve a purpose, but she didn't tell me what the purpose was. She wanted me to touch them and talk to them, but they're too ugly and nasty."

"Do you want me to take the box away?"

"No! Momma would be mad. She likes having them near her."

"But she's not here anymore, Stephen. If you're afraid of the box we can throw it away. We can even throw it into the furnace."

Molly felt the images on the box turn to sludge. The box fell to the floor. Stephen walked past Molly and found a candle lying near a leg of the table. He brought the candle to her and asked her to light it.

"I don't have any matches."

"Lift the lid of the box."

The images looked frozen on the box, but she hesitated, recalling the ooze that had dampened her fingers a short while ago. Bravely she reached down and lifted the lid, spying a set of matches inside. She removed one and struck it on the underbelly of the box. Stephen lit his candle and knelt next to the box. He paused to look up at Molly before lowering the candle to the box. He allowed several drops of melted wax to fall on a blackish snake. The color blackened to a shine and the snake throbbed and twisted until it finally fell from the box.

Molly let out a sharp yelp.

"He can't do very much, Molly. He's slow and doesn't have wings or legs, so he can't go far."

The snake flexed its body, obviously enjoying the longed-for freedom. It raised its head, and two tiny fangs slid out of its mouth.

"Is he poisonous, Stephen?"

Stephen shrugged.

The snake inched its way toward Molly.

"Stick him back on the box, Stephen."

He reached for the back end of the snake.

"Don't let him bite you," she warned.

"He won't bite me, Molly." Stephen lifted the snake and slipped him back inside the box before closing the lid.

"Why didn't you attach it to the box?"

"He can't get out. He's the weakest of the uglies. He'll complain, but that's all."

Molly heard the faint sound of a snake hiss.

"Pick up the box, Molly, and put it back on the table. We should go upstairs before Dad comes home."

Molly visualized the snake slithering around inside the box, and her fingers tingled with the thought of how the box had last felt while in her hands.

"Maybe we can just—"

"Momma always said that equipment must

always be stored in its proper place, Molly. Don't make Momma mad."

Goose bumps broke out on Molly's flesh before she could remind Stephen that Momma didn't live here now. But did Stephen's mother still prowl the house?

Molly's fingers touched only the edges of the box when she returned it to the table. She turned to see a small face, half-shadow, half-frightened little boy, standing behind her. She bent to blow out the candle he still held in his hand. He let out a big sigh and placed the candle on the table.

"Momma doesn't want us down here."

"You mean she doesn't want me down here."

"Why don't Dad and Momma like you? I do." Stephen's quizzical expression melted Molly's heart.

chapter 19

"He's free. He's free, I tell you. I saw him fall to the floor but a few feet from the harlot."

"Then why isn't she dead?" a deep voice asked.

"It's the child. He protected her. Stupid child. Weak child."

"What can we do if he won't free us?" asked a whiny voice.

"She promises us that he will come round, but he doesn't trust us. I sense it in the way he won't touch the box. He never touches the box."

"Too big a temptation we are for him."

"No! No!" screeched a bird. "He's merely a stupid

child. A pathetic progeny that will fail his mother. When will she learn? When will she destroy him herself and give us a new master?"

"Hush!"

Every demon held his breath and listened.

The furnace kicked on. A spider softly wove its web. A termite burrowed its way out of the wood into the midst of a moonbeam and immediately flipped itself over and rushed back into the wood. Otherwise nothing stirred.

"Don't let her hear us arguing, or she will banish us back to hell."

"I don't want to go back to hell," said the dwarf. "I haven't done anything wrong. I've been waiting like she told us."

"Waiting. Waiting. An eternity of waiting will not do." The big beaked bird tried to spread his wings but couldn't.

"At least we are out here and not inside the box." said a miniature satyr.

The other demons turned to him with looks of curiosity.

"I saw the little one put the black snake inside the box. Yes. He locked him away."

"If more of us were inside the box we could push the lid and climb out," said a hopeful demon.

"Will he grow?" said a demon pulling on his beard.

"Who? The boy?"

"No, no. The black snake. Can he grow fatter and longer now that he's not attached to the box?"

The demons looked at each other, not knowing the answer to the question. They wished they could communicate with the black snake.

"I already miss the snake," said the dwarf.

"How could you? You hated each other." A malformed bird twisted his head around to face the dwarf.

"He misses someone to argue with," another demon said.

The dwarf threw his ax from one hand to the other. "We could sally forth and free him."

"Master dwarf, you are not in a fable. This is the real world. We are limited by the woman's power. If she grants us the right than we will . . . oh, such a crude, archaic word . . . sally forth. Until then we are glued to this box and the black snake, although free, wanders in circles inside the box."

"Snake! Snake! Can you hear me!"

"Incorrigible dwarf, your yelling isn't going to achieve our own freedom and I'm sure the snake can't assist us even if he hears you."

"But if you listen quietly you can hear the drag of his body against the wood. If I can hear that why couldn't he hear my voice?"

"And what would you have him do? Lift the lid, slip out, light a candle, and drop a bit of wax on you? And remember he must feel the hunger now. Once free our bodies need nourishment. Need blood and flesh. He may dry up and shrivel for all we know. The spirit animating his

clay body may once again find itself homeless."

"Horrible fate," whispers a demon.

☆ ☆ ☆

Inside the box the black snake tumbles back to the floor of the box after crawling up to the lid. He shakes his entire body to right himself. The darkness is consoling but the freedom is futile without a way to touch the earthly world.

It hears the dwarf call from far away. Far away is merely the other side of a wooden wall, but the dwarf's voice is muted by the differences in their status, for the snake truly is of the boy's world now.

Foolish boy, thinks the snake, remembering the rough feel of the boy's fingers lifting his tail. A tail without a rattler, but, hey, the fangs made the girl cringe. The snake takes comfort in playing the girl's frightened face over and over again.

In a former body he had teased and provoked royalty into bringing about the death of . . . little dwarfs. As difficult as it was the snake managed a smile. Hundreds of thousands of dwarfs were tortured, burned, and hanged. And one dwarf in particular had a fitting end.

chapter 20

Stephen sat in the darkness of his room surrounded by his ritual utensils, holding his mother's earrings tightly in his fisted hands.

"I'm sorry, Momma. I know you want me to make peace with the uglies, but they aren't nice. And Dad doesn't want me in the basement. And I couldn't stand to bring the uglies up here to my room. I wouldn't be able to sleep thinking of them running around.

"Molly thinks I should throw the box in the fire, but I don't think you'd like that. If she goes back into the basement what will I do? I don't want a new babysitter, and Dad will send Molly away if I tell him she went down into the basement. All of this confuses me. I wish you were here."

"Don't wish, Stephen. Make it happen. Use the power inside your little body to bring me back. I will care for the 'uglies'. But you must bring me back soon, or they will tire of waiting and will take revenge on you instead of the others."

Stephen covered his ears with his fists. He thought he heard words spoken in a familiar voice, but they were far away.

"Momma, come back to me. Help me, Momma." Tears drifted down his cheeks, and he used his fists to wipe them away. Some of the teardrops touched the pearls of the earrings, making the pearls cry their own salty tears.

His blurred vision caught a shadow moving. A shadow with outstretched arms and hands whiter than ivory.

"Momma?"

The shadow passed into the darkened end of the room and waited in silence.

"Is that you, Momma?"

The pearls dropped from his hands, and the room became frigid, the chill filling it with loneliness. He fumbled through the bedclothes trying to find the pearls, tossing many of the ritual utensils aside. He must find the pearls, he thought. The power to reach his mother lay in the pearls.

Finally Stephen reached over and turned on his bedroom lamp. He got out of bed and shook out the blanket, wrapping himself in the chaos of the wool.

His tears stopped and were replaced by frustration and anger. How could he have been so stupid as to lose the pearls? The very pearls he had bought for his mother. He tripped on the blanket and fell, but to his happiness there under the bed lay the pearls, leaning upon each other. He reached under the bed and clasped the pearls inside his right hand.

Quickly he shifted one of the pearls into his left hand and shut his eyes tightly, visualizing his mother. Not as he had last seen her, but as he remembered while she was still alive.

Someone touched his hands and folded them together as if in an act of prayer. He didn't dare open his eyes.

"Momma?"

He felt a kiss gently touch his cheek. He smelled petals of her perfume and almost the solidness of her body as she hugged him.

But when he opened his eyes she left, and he remained alone in the small bedroom.

chapter 21

"Mr. Zaira, I need to talk to you."

"Not again, Molly, I can't take these talks. Is this about the fat, naked women running through my house?"

"No, the fertility goddess is minor in comparison to what I've seen."

"I am so close to firing you. The only reason you still work here is that I can't think up an excuse to tell Stephen. 'Sorry, Son, but I've been fucking your babysitter. I've grown tired of her and let her go.' Do you think at five he'd understand?"

"I think you should wait until he is twenty-five."

Jacob laughed.

"I believe you like my son. I know you're trustworthy. You've never cancelled out and you're punctual. It's just that I look at you, Molly, and I can't help seeing Cathy swinging from a beam in the basement."

"The basement. You haven't cleaned out the basement, have you?"

"The basement never appealed to me. It appeals to me even less now."

"Did you know your wife was a witch?"

Jacob turned stern.

"This could get you fired. Have you been putting wild ideas into my son's head?"

"No, his own mother did. She practiced witchcraft, Mr. Zaira."

"You've been watching too much television. Try dating one or two boys instead."

Molly hesitated. If she told him the truth he wouldn't believe her, unless she could bring him down into the basement.

"Let me show you what's in the basement."

"No!" he shouted. "I have a meeting to go to." He started for the door. "And I'm giving you a week's notice." He slammed the door behind him.

"You promised not to tell Dad." Stephen's somber voice carried down to Molly from the top of the staircase.

"What your mother left behind isn't right, Stephen.

The uglies should be destroyed. They're demons."

"They belong to Momma." At a slow pace Stephen descended the staircase. "She wanted me to keep them safe for her."

"But she's not coming back, Stephen."

"Momma's back."

Molly looked into his icy stare. The boy's features seemed carved of stone. His eyes had lost the little-boy brightness that had been there just a few days ago.

"If she's back, where is she?"

"She's in every room all the time. She's tapping you on the shoulder now, but you don't know it."

Instinctively Molly used her hands to brush off both her shoulders. Immediately she sought a sly grin on Stephen's face or listened for a giggle.

"You're serious, Stephen. You believe your mother is with us right now?"

"I only see her shadow, but someday she'll be flesh again.

"She doesn't like you, Molly. You'd better go away."

"I can't leave until your father gets home."

"Momma wants me to send you down into the basement to play with the uglies."

"I'm sure they don't play very nice games." Molly's skin itched, she smelled something sweet, and she tasted something coppery like blood.

"Tell her to go away, Stephen. Please. I'll only be working here one more week. Your father just fired me."

"I heard. You and Daddy hurt Momma, didn't you?"

"We didn't mean for her to go away and leave you, Stephen."

She took several steps toward Stephen, but he backed up the stairs.

"I didn't mean to hurt either of you. Believe me. I didn't even mean for you to hear the conversation I just had with your dad. I'm trying to help. I don't think what your mother did in the basement was right."

"You don't know what we did."

"She had you help her?"

"Sometimes."

"Don't continue what your mother was doing. Make the uglies go away. You know how, don't you?"

"Momma doesn't want them to go away." Stephen shivered, and Molly immediately moved to embrace him, but he pulled away.

"Momma's hugging me."

Molly touched Stephen's hand.

"You're cold." Molly pulled back and started for the basement door.

"No," he yelled.

She opened the door and flicked on the light before going down the stairs and rushing to the table. But the wax-covered table had nothing on it.

"You've hidden the box." She faced Stephen, who had followed her down the stairs. "You wouldn't take it up to your room because you're afraid of the uglies. It must be down here somewhere."

Stephen ran into the back of Molly's legs, forcing her to grab hold of some old boards that toppled sideways, hitting Stephen across his brow. He lost balance and ended up on the floor.

"Oh, Stephen! I didn't mean for you to get hurt." She kneeled down next to the child and saw the blood dripping down into his left eye. He rolled away from her and under the table, setting his back against one of the far legs.

"Let me wash that for you. I don't think it's too bad."

Stephen sulked against the leg, and when she tried to pull him out he batted her away with his hands.

"You can't stay under there. Please let me look at the cut."

Stephen shook his head and used his right hand to mop his brow.

"I'll stop looking for the box if you agree to come upstairs with me. I'll wash the cut, and we'll have a bite to eat. I know you love the restaurant that serves the spicy chili. We'll go there."

"You're trying to poison me. They might have

frogs' legs and bats' feet in that chili."

"What?"

"I'll come upstairs if you promise never to search for the box and you won't try to ever feed me that chili."

"Agreed. No box or chili."

"Promise."

Molly had never seen Stephen this angry or aggressive.

"I promise."

"And you won't say anything to Dad about what happened down here today?"

Molly hesitated.

"If you tell Dad I'll ask why he was 'fucking' you."

"Don't ever use that word, Stephen."

"I will if you go to Dad, and he'll be even madder at you 'cause I'll tell him you told me that word."

"You overheard—"

"I'll tell him you said it!"

"All right. Come upstairs." She reached out a hand to the boy, but he chose to crawl out from under the table in the opposite direction.

Hours later when Jacob came home Molly had already decided this would be her last day in the house.

"What happened to you?" Jacob asked his son as soon as he saw him.

"I bumped my head when I was playing. Molly

washed the cut and put a Band Aid on it. It's fine."

Jacob looked at Molly who hovered near the door.

"Something I should know about?" he asked.

"I'm not coming back. I can't after the talk we had this morning."

"I need you to finish out the week. Old Stephen here needs your first aid. Right?" He squeezed his son's shoulders.

"If I find someone to take my place, would—"

"No, Molly. I'm not going to dump my son with a complete stranger. I'll get started looking for someone else tonight, but I'll expect you to finish out the week."

She looked down at Stephen and noticed how complacent he looked. Usually he looked forward to seeing her; now his eyes looked dull with indifference.

"As soon as you find someone I'll stop coming," she said, noticing a sudden coldness filling up the room.

chapter 22

"She didn't find the box, Momma."

"*Good boy.*" His mother kissed him lightly on the wound.

His father had pulled the Band Aid off earlier in the evening to check the wound and left it uncovered, saying the air would heal it.

"I feel bad that I pushed Molly. She really didn't mean for me to get hurt."

"*But, Stephen, you managed to get her away from the box. Exactly what I wanted you to do.*"

"I know, but I still kinda like Molly. Only she's too nosey. She doesn't keep a secret. I hope she doesn't tell Dad how I pushed her and made her knock over the boards."

"She won't. She just wants to get away now, but not before we give her back the costume she made."

"But, Momma, she made that for me to wear to school on Halloween."

"You can't keep her present, Stephen. She's been mean to us by telling Daddy our secrets. What if Daddy found the box? If he went down into the basement he'd clean everything out, including the box."

"I know the uglies would be safer here in my room, but they scare me, especially the stupid dwarf who keeps smiling at me. I wish he'd stop. I don't think he has a nice smile, and besides, he looks like he carries a little ax."

"But it's very tiny, Stephen. Besides, he knows he will have to obey you."

"Because I can send him back to where he came from?"

"You will give him freedom."

"What happens when he is free? Will he hurt anyone?"

"Only bad people."

"I don't think he should be allowed to hurt anyone. He's bad too."

"Bring the costume and mask over to the bed, Stephen."

The boy obeyed his mother. He tried to tease his mother by holding the mask over his face and growling.

"Do I look scarey, Momma? I don't want to look scarier than the uglies. I just want to make people laugh."

"What did I say, Stephen?"

"That I had to give the costume back to Molly. But I painted the mask. She drew the face and cut it out for me, but I did all the painting, so it's kinda my mask too."

"Lay the costume and mask across the bed, Stephen."

He hesitated, his fingers rubbing the furry costume.

"Don't disobey me, Stephen. I'll have to go away if you do."

Sadly Stephen spread the costume across the comforter on his bed. Slowly he placed the mask at the top of the costume, visualizing what he had looked like in it.

"Remember what the wolves at the zoo looked like, Stephen. They skulked across the grass and jumped up on some rocks. One of them growled fiercely and showed his teeth. You grabbed onto me and felt your own teeth that were so much smaller than the wolf's. Can you see it again?"

"I was smaller then. I wouldn't be as afraid now."

"I want you to feel the fear all over again. Imagine that wolf coming for you. Saliva dripping off his teeth. Crouching in readiness to spring. Your small neck vulnerable. Meanwhile all the wolf can see is the whiteness

of your neck. A weak victim for his dinner."

"Momma, I'm not sure I like this."

"I need you to do this for me. Please, Stephen."

He closed his eyes and saw the big wolf that had frightened him. He watched the animal circling around him. The circle kept getting smaller, and the eyes of the wolf grew until, hypnotized by the dark eyes, Stephen couldn't move. He thought he heard a throaty noise, low, intense. The smell of earthen dung stung the air. Under his hands he felt the costume move. When he opened his eyes a wolf sat on his bed for only a moment before deflating to the costume Molly had made.

"Perfect, Stephen. Now you give the costume and the mask back to Molly. Tell her you can't keep it because she hurt you."

"But I'm not all that mad at Molly, honest."

"Stephen, she wanted to destroy my box. She wanted to take your daddy away from me. Instead she took me away from you."

"Did she make you very sad, Momma?"

Cathy felt the ligature mark on her neck.

"Yes, Stephen. It would hurt me if you accepted a gift from Molly."

"I never want to hurt you, Momma. Not the way Molly and Daddy hurt you." He heard his mother chuckle. "You believe me, don't you, Momma?"

"You've never hurt me before, Stephen, and I'm sure

you will obey me now."

"It would hurt if I didn't obey?"

"It would cause me great sorrow. I would cry for days if you should ignore my wishes."

"I never want you to cry, Momma. I want you to laugh again and give me your special kisses." He felt his mother's embrace and her kiss pressed against his cheek, but the kiss wasn't the same as when she had lived. Instead of warming his tummy the kiss made his shoulders shiver and his skin broke out in goose bumps. "Will you someday be like before? Will I be able to hold your hand? Will you be able to climb into bed with me and warm me on stormy nights when the lightning is booming over our house?"

"There'll be a day when we can rejoice in our unity, Stephen. However, if you fail to obey me I will have to go away and will never come back."

"Don't scare me, Mommy."

"There's nothing to be afraid of unless . . ."

"Momma. Momma. Are you still here with me?" Stephen pulled the blankets together into a ball and searched the dark room with his eyes. "Momma, I'll protect the uglies. Molly and Daddy won't be able to destroy them. I promise. And I won't keep the silly costume. I'm a big boy; I don't have to dress up anymore. Halloween is for babies. I'm not a baby. Momma, answer me. Please." His little heart pounded, his skin flushed with the rising temperature of his body. He wanted to be cold again. Cold and in his mother's embrace.

"I'm here, Stephen. But if you ever doubt me or refuse anything that I want I'll have to go back to the ocean."

"Is that why it feels so cold to be near you? Are you still cold from being in the water? Are you mad at Daddy for throwing you into the water?"

"Death makes me cold, Stephen."

"Can I bring you back? Dad says you can't come back. Grandma says God wanted you near him."

"I left too soon, Stephen. You must help me to return to you."

"How?"

"You'll know when the time is right. First you must accept me back inside your heart."

"You've always been inside my heart. I've never sent you away."

"But we must be closer than ever before, Stephen. We must be one."

chapter 23

"He touched us today," the dwarf cried out gleefully.

"Only briefly and certainly not with any love or respect," said the gargoyle.

"But she's winning him over. I can feel it. He is protecting us."

"But now we're stuck under a pile of tarp," said a big bird.

"Still, he'll come back. He won't leave us here forever. At least I don't think so," said the dwarf.

"We should find our own way to break free."

"The black snake is free."

"And imprisoned inside the box."

"He can move about."

"He goes from one end of the box to the other. Hardly much in the way of freedom."

"The gargoyle says the black snake is growing."

"How would he know?"

"Sometimes the snake bangs against the lid. The last time he raised the lid ever so slightly," said the gargoyle.

"He needs blood. He needs flesh. There's none inside the box. The boy didn't share."

"We'll grapple the boy, pin him down, and take his blood and rip apart his flesh," shrieked the bird.

"She wouldn't like that," whispered the dwarf.

"The witch is caught within the bonds of death. She is as limited as we are. Without the boy we are all shades in this world."

All the figures on the wooden box agreed. The boy had to live because the witch hadn't given them any other conjuror.

"She brought us here with promises. Enticed us with the smell of fresh blood and the soft squishy taste of human flesh. Her flesh. Her blood. Promised more if we did her bidding. And we wait."

"The boy is small. Too small perhaps to satisfy all of us."

"All we need are a few drops. Once we have tasted of him we can attach ourselves to larger prey."

"A fat, juicy, chubby baby," dreamed the gargoyle.

chapter 24

"Time for another adventure of Brandy and the witch," said Jacob walking into Stephen's bedroom. "What's this, your wolf costume laying in wait for me?" Jacob patted the furry costume Stephen had carefully laid out on his dresser.

The boy nodded.

"You look unhappy." Jacob brushed his hand over the top of his son's head. "I think you need to be cheered up with stories of snot, frogs' feet, and bats' legs."

Stephen sighed.

"Frogs' legs and bats' feet, Dad."

"Whatever suits your taste." Jacob smacked his lips. He almost caught sight of a smile, but Stephen turned it into a heavy frown. "Serious, are we, tonight?"

The boy lay back on his pillow and resigned himself to another bedtime story.

"Usually you love the Brandy and witch episodes. Why's tonight different?"

Stephen shrugged.

"Remember the lady?"

Stephen nodded.

"It so happens that Brandy and the lady grew to like each other. They played checkers, chess, and poker together."

"Did Brandy cheat?"

"Of course not. The lady did."

"Dad, Mom won't like this story."

"Okay, neither cheated and they were fairly matched. Is that better?"

"Yes."

"I wonder where the witch went this afternoon," said the lady crowning her own king.

"Brandy scratched his head and meditated on his next move until he heard the witch clomping down the basement stairs. She was wearing the shoes the lady had come in, but they were too big for her, and the heels were much too high.

"Good news," the witch said.

"You never bring good news," said Brandy.

"Maybe she's going to pitch herself into the furnace," suggested the lady.

"Hardly," said the witch. "That's what I should have done with you when you first arrived. Now all you two do is plot against me. I see it in both sets of eyes. Plot. Plot. Plot."

"Tell us your news so we can get on with our game of checkers."

"Ruin the game, I will." The witch cackled. "I'm selling the lady to a troll."

"A troll? Dad, what's the troll going to do with the lady? He brought her there, didn't he? Now he wants her back?"

"He fell in love."

"But she's not in love with the troll."

"Wait a second. It so happens that the troll is really a prince."

Stephen groaned.

"A black prince with evil intentions."

"What's intentions?"

"Let's just say the troll repents and wants to take the lady back to her home."

"What about Brandy?"

"The troll doesn't care about him. Anyway, the witch would never give Brandy up because she's grown fond of him. And truthfully Brandy is a bit fond of her too."

"Really?"

Jacob nodded.

"They've spent months and months together. Frequently she comes down to the basement just to chat with Brandy. She's still sorry about using the giant spider. Turns out the spider's legs weren't at all useful to Brandy."

"Is the witch jealous of the lady?"

"Shh! She'd never admit it."

"Does she hate the lady?" Stephen said very seriously.

"The witch would rather be rid of the competition. I don't think the witch cares about the lady at all."

"Then why did she capture her?"

"Because she was bored that day and had nothing else to do."

Jacob saw his son make a face.

"Don't you sometimes do things just to take up time, Stephen?"

The boy thought about what his father had said.

"No, Dad."

"Oh! Good boy." Jacob patted his son's head.

"She must leave now before I change my mind," said the witch.

"But we haven't finished our game," said Brandy.

"I'll take over her pieces," offered the witch. "Who is winning? I do like to win, you know."

"I'm losing," stated the lady, brushing the pieces onto

the floor.

"Really the lady was winning, but she didn't want to give the witch the advantage.

"*The witch magically brought the lady out of the cage.*"

"You mean she flattened her out the same way as when she put the lady into the cage."

"Exactly. This, of course, made Brandy very sad."

"Dad."

"Yes, Stephen?"

"I know why Molly has to leave. She let me hurt myself and you don't want to have her around anymore."

"How do you feel about that?"

"It's okay. Momma doesn't want her around either."

Jacob searched his son's eyes for traces of tears but there were none.

"I'm sorry, Stephen. I know she and you got along well."

"I still like her, Dad. But if you and Momma would be happier with her gone, then it's all right. Can I go to sleep now?"

Jacob turned off the light and kissed his son.

"Did Momma ever tell you she didn't like having Molly around?"

"I'm tired, Dad."

Jacob would have to wait for his son's answer.

chapter 25

"This is Molly's last day as Stephen's babysitter. He's taking it better than I thought he would." Jacob eased up on the gas when he saw traffic ahead.

"He's a good boy. Never gave Cathy any problems. I don't know why I'm so harsh with him at times," said Mabel.

"Rosemary seems to think it's because he reminds you of Cathy."

"Did she say that?"

"I'm not making it up. He does look a lot like his mother."

"So what if he does remind me of Cathy? There

has to be some Cathy in him."

"But Rosemary said you could be hard on Cathy when she was a child. And from what Cathy told me . . ."

Jacob let the thought linger in the air.

"I exercised a great deal of patience with Cathy. Far more than anyone can believe. She did the opposite of what I wanted her to do."

"From what I hear, Cathy didn't always know what you expected."

"It's true. I wouldn't tell her what I wanted her to do. I felt like I needed to write a manual for her, because she always did what I didn't want her to do, even when I was sure she had to know enough to do the right thing."

"Like when she got pregnant?" Jacob wondered whether he might be pushing this too far.

"When Cathy was pregnant with Stephen I was delighted."

"I'm not talking about Stephen. You forced her to have an abortion before I met her."

"She told you about that?"

"Why be surprised? Did you think she'd keep it a secret from her own husband?"

"I was hoping once the baby was gone she'd . . ."

"Forget?" Jacob glanced at his mother-in-law.

"At least keep it a secret. What good did it do to tell you?"

"I didn't think less of her, if that's what you're saying."

"You thought less of me, though, didn't you?"

Jacob planned on letting the conversation drop there.

"Why bring this up now, Jacob? The baby and Cathy are both gone. You and Rosemary don't gain anything by pointing fingers at me."

"More like talking behind your back. Maybe that's what made me uncomfortable."

"Bullshit!"

The car veered slightly when Jacob turned to look at Mabel.

"What, you don't think I know how to curse?"

"Ah, but can you spell it?"

"Listen, Cathy hadn't even finished high school, and I certainly didn't want to be responsible for raising her bastard child."

"Two curse words within five minutes. Is this a record?"

"Hypocrite. That's what you think I am."

"Now that you brought up the subject. You were the one lecturing me about church. I don't believe the church approves of abortion."

"I teach young children. What do you think the parents of those children would feel about a woman who couldn't even teach her own children right from wrong?"

"You pushed Cathy into getting an abortion so you could keep your job?"

"You have no idea how complicated the situation was."

"Yes, I do. You didn't want to face the embarrassment of having a grandchild out of wedlock."

"Jacob, if you're going to continue like this, I'd rather you didn't drive me to the school in the morning."

"You're not perfect, Mabel. You didn't bring up perfect children, and your grandchildren aren't perfect. Robin has a disease that keeps her in a wheelchair, and Stephen gets into mischief. We all have failings. Live with your own, Mabel, and don't worry about changing other people."

"What did Molly do that was so wrong you couldn't forgive her, Jacob?"

"Like I told you, Mabel, you have to stop worrying about everyone else's sins."

"Stephen loves Molly."

"I told you he took it surprisingly well."

"Did she do something to him?"

"He hurt his forehead. Not much. Doesn't even need a Band-Aid."

"What was he doing?"

"Not clear to me, but I know he was under Molly's supervision at the time."

"You should have told me, Jacob."

"Why?" Self-satisfied, Jacob pulled over in front of the elementary school.

"You think I'm intruding again."

"Nah, I know you are."

chapter 26

Molly picked up Stephen from school, and both remained silent during the ride home. Stephen spent the entire time staring out the side window, and Molly kept her radio going, even raised the sound level.

At the front door of the house Molly had a sick feeling she shouldn't go inside. She wanted to run away, but Stephen couldn't be trusted to stay by himself. Inside Molly noticed how cold the house felt. Unusually cold. Perhaps the furnace had gone out. Should she go into the basement to check? she wondered. No, she decided they could both keep their jackets on instead. But Stephen didn't notice the cold; he pulled off his jacket immediately and dropped it on a hall chair.

"Do you want something to eat?" she asked.

"No, I'm on a diet."

"What for?"

"I eat only food prepared by Dad now." He crossed in front of her to enter the living room.

"You used to always be hungry."

"You can't tell me what to do anymore," he reminded her as he sat down on the carpet in front of the television.

"Excuse me, Stephen. I'm not about to force food down your throat, but I am still in charge until your father gets home this evening."

Stephen sat in silence for a few minutes.

"Why do my father and mother not like you?"

"I never had any problems with your mother. She hired me."

"But she doesn't like you anymore."

"Let's not talk about your mother."

"Are you afraid of her?"

Molly walked past the living room to the kitchen. The counter had cereal boxes and breakfast dishes sprawled across the tiles. She spotted a container of milk that had been left out on the table. She lifted the container, and despite the coldness of the house the container felt warm. She popped open the container and smelled the contents. Since the milk didn't smell sour she returned it to the refrigerator.

"You didn't answer my question, Molly."

Startled, Molly almost dropped the container. She placed the milk on a wire shelf and searched for something to eat.

"You can have the leftover chili if you want," Stephen said.

"It's from your favorite restaurant. Is this a parting gift from you to me?"

Stephen walked over to Molly and pushed her aside to reach inside the refrigerator. He lifted out the brown bag containing the chili and carried it off to the waste can where he disposed of it.

"Don't eat it. It's not good for you," he said.

Molly slammed the refrigerator shut and declared she could wait until she got home.

He left the kitchen. She heard his feet swiftly climb the stairs. When he returned he carried the wolf mask and costume.

"I can't wear this," he said presenting the items to Molly.

"I don't want them back. What am I going to do with them? Toss them in with the chili if you like."

Molly walked past him and plopped herself down on the living room sofa. Fifteen minutes later Stephen entered the living room, still carrying the mask and costume.

"Please take them away, Molly. I can't wear them

and I can't throw them out. Momma won't let me. She says you have to take them. She'll be angry with me if you don't." Tears brimmed his eyes.

"Why does she want me to take them?"

" 'Cause you made them. She doesn't want me accepting gifts from you."

"Stephen, you have to tell your father about the basement. I don't know whether that snake act was a trick, but you have to let your father know how you feel about your mother."

"Please, Molly. Momma says if I keep them I might be tempted to wear the costume on Halloween. Maybe she's right. I do think it's neat." He stroked the furry costume.

"Your mother wouldn't have acted this way before."

"She's different now. She's mad."

"Like crazy?"

"No. Momma's not looney. She doesn't like anything."

"Including you?"

"She says she loves me but needs my help."

"To do what?"

Stephen shrugged.

"Come here."

Clutching the costume he walked over to Molly who lifted him up onto her lap for a hug.

"I'll take the costume. I'm sorry you won't wear it on Halloween because I would have been very proud to see you in it. But if it makes you unhappy to have the costume, then I'll take it back home with me. I'll keep it until after Halloween. If you change your mind I'll bring it back to you."

"I don't think Momma will change her mind."

"I said if you changed your mind, Stephen. I don't care what your mother thinks. Do you understand?"

"Is that why she doesn't like you now?"

Molly smiled at him.

"That and maybe . . . But never mind. This is our last afternoon together; why don't we play some games?"

"Ladders," Stephen shouted.

chapter 27

Jacob paid Molly an extra week's wages since she had been forced to leave on short notice. She refused the money, but Jacob insisted, saying she had been worth every penny. She wanted to slap the smirk off his face, but Stephen stood by Jacob's side.

"Goodbye, Molly," Stephen said. His sad eyes could barely look her in the face.

"How about a kiss?" She squatted so Stephen could give her a final hug and kiss.

"Hey, you two will be seeing each other around. No one is moving out of town as far as I know," said Jacob.

"Your father's right," she said, giving Stephen a final kiss on the nose.

As she walked over the threshold she kept wanting to turn back and tell Jacob about the fears his son had and how he insisted his mother had returned. But Stephen would make a scene and Jacob would think she merely wanted to make trouble. Perhaps she could write a letter, but no, Jacob would probably toss it in the garbage.

Molly knew Stephen's grandmother taught at the local elementary school. That might be the answer. She had only met the grandmother once, but it was worth a shot, even though the grandmother looked very schoolmarmish and might not take kindly to being told her daughter was a witch.

Molly threw the costume on the passenger seat and sat down behind the steering wheel. Jacob had worked late, and no moon lit up the night. She turned on the car's bright lights since she didn't expect to encounter much traffic on the way home. When she adjusted the rearview mirror she spotted Stephen at the living room window. Instinctively he must have known she saw him because he gave a weak wave to her. She stuck her hand out the open window and waved back.

There had to be a way to help Stephen. Jacob should have gotten the child therapy right after his mother's death. Stephen had been pathologically close to his mother, and given the circumstances, any child would need some professional help.

She pulled out of the driveway and closed her side window. Driving at night made her nervous. Not only did she worry about thieves, murderers, and rapists, but her vision seemed poorer at night. The trees along the road leaned too far in over the car, their bulky stumps standing grimly on each side, daring her to lose the slightest bit of control of the steering wheel.

Quickly she lowered her brights when she saw another car rounding the bend. She wished the town would invest in street lamps. A few more stop lights would help also.

A low, steady, deep sound hummed in the background.

"Please don't let it be the car," she whispered to herself.

A chill in the air forced her to turn on the heater. Usually at this time of the year she wouldn't ordinarily need to, but her hands felt almost numb. Initially more cold air blew out at her. After a block, when it didn't get any warmer, she sped up hoping to get home sooner.

Something moved against her right thigh. Only a slight movement, but enough to attract her attention. Looking next to her she saw that the costume, mask included, had fallen to the floor.

The car went over a bump, but Molly thought she might have run over some animal, because the car filled up with a foul odor. She wrinkled her nose and tried to open the windows, but the electrical system didn't work.

"Damn! Don't give out on me now," she said to the car. "We only have another few miles to go. You can make it."

A growl sound came from under the dashboard.

The traffic light turned red, and she stepped on the brake, hoping the car wouldn't stall. No one walked the streets. Men, women, and children were either home in bed or watching late night television.

Something flicked against her right calf; looking down she caught the movement of the tail on the costume.

"What the heck?" She peered down on the floor but could see only a furry ball of fiber. There seemed to be a sudden sheen to the cloth, and in the shadows the mask looked filled out, the snout longer, the ears perked forward; even the eye holes caught the reflection of light coming from someplace. The costume pulsed with deep breaths.

Molly recalled the episode with the black snake in the basement. Stephen's mother hated her. As she reached for the door a full-grown wolf sprang from the floor; its hot, stale breath struck her face before the teeth sunk into her flesh.

chapter 28

The cruel witch took away all of Brandy's games. He had beaten her once too often in Poker. Why, she had even considered mortgaging her home, except the bank didn't seem very interested in using her house for collateral.

"Dad, what's colla . . . whatever?" asked Stephen.

"It means that the bank would loan the witch money to pay off the debts she owed to Brandy, and if she couldn't repay the bank, then the bank would take away her house."

"That doesn't sound very nice."

"We're talking banks here, son."

"From now on we'll make up our own games," said

the witch.

"You mean you'll decide what the rules are, don't you?" asked Brandy.

"I've been very nice to you. I'm still waiting for that stupid wart to grow. It never gets bigger."

"Ah, it was probably just a piece of dirt you saw."

"No!" screamed the witch. "I've been using warts for years. I know what they look like."

"You said yourself that you could barely see it."

The witch scratched her dirty hair.

"Let me see the hands." The witch moved closer to Brandy to peer between the bars.

"What hands?"

The witch jumped up and down.

"Your hands, fool. I want to see your hands."

"Why should I show them to you?"

"Because I want your wart."

"Dad, didn't the witch want to use Brandy's whole hand?"

"He talked her out of it. Yes, he did. Brandy could have been a salesman."

"That's what the witch thought he was when he first knocked on her door."

"Actually, he's a student."

"Like me?"

"A little further along. A college student."

"That's why he wanted the giant spider."

"Exactly."

"What if I want to keep my wart?" Brandy asked.

"Why would you want to do that?" asked the witch.

"I would have asked him that too, Dad. There's a boy at school who has a big wart on his thumb."

"Oh, I hope no one makes fun of him."

"No, he draws funny faces on it. Some of the other kids think it's cool, but I don't."

"Maybe I want to cast my own spells," says Brandy.

"Don't know how." The witch stood as tall as she could and folded her arms across her chest, raising her chin high into the air.

"I've been watching you. It doesn't seem difficult to cast spells. A little wiggle of the nose. A snap of the fingers. A wave of a hand. Or even some muttered gibberish words under one's breath, and poof." Brandy clapped his hands. "Spell complete."

"Not that simple," said the witch. "Takes years to know what to use and say. I have many books upstairs."

"I've never seen you read from a book."

"Have it all memorized."

"Then you don't need the books anymore," said Brandy. "Why don't you bring some down here for me to read, for I often get bored."

"She'd have to be a really stupid witch, Dad."

"I never called her a scholar."

"What's a schla?" asked Stephen.

"Scholar," corrected Jacob. "A scholar is someone who is very smart."

"Is Brandy a schol-ar?"

"He was captured by the witch. That does put his smartness into question. Let's say he's a so-so student."

"I'm better than that, right, Dad?"

"I'd say you were closer to scholar."

Stephen grinned broadly and Jacob smiled back.

"The witch said, 'If you're good I might bring one book down for you to read.' "

"And which one would it be?" asked Brandy.

"WITCH ZELDA'S BOOK OF MANNERS," said the witch.

"I doubt you've ever read it," said Brandy.

"Don't need to. I'm a witch."

"Isn't it written for witches?"

"No. For prisoners."

"A manners book for prisoners? Isn't that silly? Why should a prisoner have good manners?"

"Why should a witch? Besides, it will explain how you must provide warts."

"Even if I don't have any?"

"It's there! It's there!" shouted the witch while jumping up and down.

"She sure throws a lot of tantrums, Dad. She's worse than me."

"Than I," corrected Jacob.

"I never saw you throw a tantrum, Dad."

"No, Stephen. If you're going to be a scholar you

have to learn proper English. She's worse than I, not she's worse than me."

"Or I'm better than she is."

Jacob laughed.

"That works too."

Stephen's eyes twinkled with pride.

"What do you need the wart for?" asked Brandy.

"I'm making chili," the witch said.

"Aw, Dad. Not chili again."

"I'm just fooling with you. There's nothing wrong with eating chili."

"As long as a witch isn't preparing it," said Stephen.

"Not many witches sit around making chili."

"Momma made chili."

Stephen's expression turned very serious.

"Mom would never feed you anything icky except for maybe creamed spinach."

Father and son made a face at each other in memory of the creamed spinach dinners.

"It's getting late; better bundle up under the covers and get some sleep." Jacob fluffed Stephen's pillow and lifted the boy in the air for a goodnight kiss.

"No school tomorrow."

"And so?"

"I could watch some late movies with you so you won't be lonely."

"Got work to do, Stephen. Besides, scholars need their sleep."

"But I'm not a schol-ar yet."

"You're in training." Jacob shut off the light.

chapter 29

At the end of the school day Mabel hurried out of the school to catch her ride home with Jacob. He arrived just as she reached the curb.

Opening the passenger door, Mabel commented about his punctual service. Jacob pulled away from the curb without answering.

"Hello, Jacob?"

He nodded without saying anything and without looking at her.

"What is wrong? You look way too serious for a pleasant afternoon like this. Has your boss been on your case again about the hours you keep?"

"No, Mabel, that's been straightened out for a while now."

Several minutes of silence followed.

"Why are you ignoring me, Jacob? Is this another complaint about how I raised Cathy, or did I say something wrong to Stephen the other day?"

"Molly's dead."

Mabel's breath caught for but a moment.

"How?"

"She seems to have been attacked by an animal. The police aren't sure what kind."

"Where was she?"

"In her car driving herself home after leaving Stephen and me."

"Oh, you're not feeling guilty?"

"Mabel, it was late. I could have offered to drive her home or at least follow her home to make sure she was all right."

"Instead you pitched her out the door."

"I fired her, remember? It was her last day babysitting Stephen. I paid her the money I owed her and was glad there was no major scene. Actually, I recall sighing when I closed the door behind her."

"What did Stephen do?"

"He ran to the window to watch her drive away and then went up to his room to brood until I came up to tell him a bedtime story."

"I thought you said he had taken her being fired

well."

"He did. He didn't throw a tantrum, didn't spend hours sulking or crying. I thought I was home free until I heard about her death this morning. Shit! What do I tell Stephen?"

"Certainly don't tell him when and how she died."

"He'll find out at school. He stayed with our next door neighbor today. I hope they were sharp enough to keep Molly's death from him."

"You'll have to tell him something," Mabel said, watching the muscles tighten in Jacob's face.

"I'm going to tell him she died in the car on the way home. That's the truth. No one can figure out how the animal got into the car. Seems the front windshield is totally smashed, but what kind of animal could be that powerful?"

"Perhaps it was rabid."

"This is the second person to die on Stephen. I don't know how he'll take it."

"Do you want me to be there when you tell him?"

"Thanks, Mabel, but I don't think it would help. It might make him more nervous. If he wants to cry or scream and yell, I don't want you there to censor him."

"Oh, Jacob, I have more sense than that. He's a little boy; of course he'll be upset. I would expect him to be."

"Is there some bad karma or black cloud following

Stephen and me around?"

"People die, Jacob. You know catastrophes often happen in three's."

"What does that mean, Mabel? Should I be especially wary when I cross streets?"

"The way you cross, yes. No. I don't know why I said that. Actually, Molly's death gives me the creeps. Probably because she died in such a strange fashion. We don't live in the middle of the woods. Where the heck could this animal come from?"

"Could have been someone's pit bull broke lose. I don't know."

"What street was she on when this happened?"

"Matilda."

"But that's a major thoroughfare. There's nothing there but stores."

"She had stopped for a red light, and whatever it was rushed the car."

"Makes no sense, Jacob. Are you going to take Stephen to the burial?"

"What for? He's five. He's been around enough death. I'm not dragging him to a cemetery."

"You're right, Jacob, but he may need some form of closure."

"We'll buy a mass card to send to the family. I'll let him sign his name."

Mabel shook her head, knowing she'd never be able to win an argument with Jacob.

chapter 30

Stephen jumped up and down on his mattress.

"It wasn't so bad staying with Grannie Smith."

"You mean Mrs. Rosen," Jacob corrected.

"No, she said I could call her Grannie Smith, since she makes the best apple pies in town."

"Okay, that's fair. What did you and Grannie Smith do today?"

"Eat!" Stephen screamed. "When you dropped me off she had my favorite breakfast waiting for me. And guess what?"

"What?"

"The waffles were in the shape of Mickey Mouse's head. She used berries for his eyes, a slice of pear for his nose, and whipped cream to give him a broad smile. Then she showed me how to feed her fish, and we watched some stupid show where she kept covering my eyes every time there was a bedroom scene. I told her I've seen that stuff before when I watch TV with you."

"Good. I'm glad you clarified that." Jacob grabbed his son to stop the bouncing.

"The worst part of the day was when she expected me to take a nap."

"You weren't tired?"

"I don't take naps anymore, Dad. At school we work right through nap time. Instead of napping we usually go out to the yard and run around for a while. Napping is for babies."

"You didn't tell her that though, right? You were polite."

"Yeah. In Grannie Smith's bedroom I waved to Mom 'cause she was standing at my bedroom window wishing I were there."

Jacob rested his hand on his son's head.

"Momma can't wave at you anymore. You know that."

Stephen quieted down and stared up into his father's eyes.

"Do you have something to say, Stephen?"

Stephen shook his head and continued with the day's schedule.

"We made apple pies and brownies and Jello in the afternoon. The Jello was for her. The pie and the brownies were for me and her son who was coming for dinner."

Jacob sat down on the bed and lifted his son onto his lap.

"I have something to tell you."

"Is it about Brandy and the witch? Did the lady come back? Did she miss Brandy? Did she fall in love with Brandy? That's what everyone seemed to be doing on Grannie Smith's television show."

"No. This is a true story." Jacob hesitated, not knowing how to begin. "After Molly left our house last night she . . ."

Silence burdened Jacob's thinking. How to tell his son?

"Was she unhappy about leaving us?"

"Yes, I think she was."

"You told her that we could still see each other since we live in the same town. She's not going away to college for another year."

"She's not going to college."

"Molly's not a scholar?"

Jacob sighed.

"Molly died in her car last night. It was an accident."

Stephen's body stiffened in his father's arms.

"How did she die, Daddy?"

"The police aren't sure yet."

"She didn't want to die; that's why she was afraid of Momma."

"Stop talking about your mother as if she were still alive, Stephen." Jacob heard his loud voice echo in his own ears. "I'm sorry. People don't understand when you talk about Momma like that. They don't know that you're playing make believe. You even frightened Molly a bit."

"Momma scared Molly, not me."

"You're right. The only way you could scare people is in that wolf costume."

"Did they find the costume in the car?"

"I don't know, but we certainly can't ask about it. Let it be. We'll come up with an even scarier costume for you."

"I don't want to scare people this Halloween, Dad. I want people to smile."

"I know, we'll dress you as a belly dancer."

"Ugh! I'm a boy!"

"That's why everyone would be smiling."

"Laughing at me," said Stephen, a heavy frown forcing his eyebrows to almost meet.

"What do you want to be?"

Stephen shrugged.

"Maybe you can dream about what you want to

be," said Jacob laying his son back on the sheet and pulling up the covers.

"Dad, where's Molly?"

"I told you she died last night."

"No, I mean where did she go?"

"Your grandmother would say to heaven."

"Where do you think she went?"

"Honestly, I don't know. Your grandmother's guess is as good a guess as anyone could make."

"You don't think she'd want to stay on earth like . . ."

Jacob's breath halted.

"You don't think Molly would want to haunt us, do you?"

"Why would she do that?"

" 'Cause she might be mad about the way we treated her. When I cut my forehead it wasn't Molly's fault. It was mine. I pushed her, and she grabbed some wood boards 'cause she didn't want to fall."

"Why would you push her?"

Stephen shrugged.

"Listen, Molly died in an accident on the way home. She loved you. I know she would never hurt you on purpose. Or even haunt you." Jacob tweaked his son's nose. "Now go to sleep"

chapter 31

"Momma, maybe we upset Molly too much. She had an accident."

"*No accident.*"

"Dad said it was. Dad wouldn't lie."

"*He lies when it suits him.*"

"Momma, you're not going to let Molly come back to haunt me, are you?"

"*She'll never see you again.*"

Stephen felt cold fingers brush back his tawny hair. Cold lips placed a kiss on his forehead right next to the wound.

"*It's almost all better.*"

THE WITCH

"Dad says I heal fast."

"The little people are waiting for you in the basement, Stephen."

"You mean the uglies."

He heard his mother laugh.

"They're beautiful. Tiny and wispy, finely fashioned. A little blood and flesh and they can grow strong."

"Are they very old, Momma?"

"Older than this world."

"If they are older than the earth then where did they come from?"

"From the dark pits where fear and vengeance are born."

"Do they hate people?"

"No, they don't know hate. They're little savages that have never felt hate or love or friendship. They only serve. If someone wishes revenge, they will fulfill the wish."

"Do you hate, Momma?"

The odor of flowers and earth filled the room. The covers no longer offered warmth to Stephen's small body. And the shade of his mother pulled away from the bed.

"Don't go, Momma," Stephen shouted out. He sat up and tried to reach out to the shade, but it became wispier, blending in with the shadows clinging to the bedroom.

"Don't go, Momma. Please. I don't want to be alone. What if Molly comes back?"

Jacob opened the bedroom door and flipped the switch for the light.

"Are you okay?" Jacob lifted Stephen up into his arms. "You having bad dreams? How about we bunk together tonight?"

Stephen gripped his father's T-shirt tightly and bit into the skin of his father's neck.

"Ow. What are you doing?" Jacob raised Stephen's face to his and saw that the boy bit his own lip so hard he had drawn blood.

"Come on, Stephen, take a deep breath. It was a dream. Molly is not here and neither is your mother. It's just us two guys." Jacob carried his son out of the bedroom.

"I was just getting ready for bed myself. You can keep me company while I brush my teeth. I'll even let you turn on the TV. Would you like some water?"

Stephen remained stiff in Jacob's arms and wouldn't let go of his father when laid on his father's bed.

"I'm so sorry, son, that all this has happened to you. I wish I could have prevented it. But there was nothing either of us could do." Gently Jacob opened Stephen's tiny fingers. "I'm just going to brush my teeth and wash up a bit before bed; won't take more than five minutes."

Jacob left the room.

The blanket covered Stephen's shivering body and cold lips touched his.

"Don't believe him, Stephen. He caused it all to happen. He made us all sin. He's to blame and must suffer for it. Help me, little one. Help me."

Stephen slowly nodded his head.

chapter 32

"It's not my fault," said the troll sitting next to Brandy's cage.

"Yes, it is. You sent me here and never warned me that the witch would take me prisoner."

"You wanted the spider, and I merely brought you to the place where the spider was kept. How was I supposed to know she used it in one of her potions? You think she keeps me informed?"

"She admitted you purposefully brought me to her house because she wanted a wart."

"What's a wart?" the troll asked.

"It's a viral bump that grows on skin."

"I got lots of growths, and the witch never asked me for any of them. See?" The troll flipped up his shirt, showing a chest with various sized growths with black thread-like hair growing out of some of them.

"Please," Brandy said covering his eyes. "Put your shirt down."

The troll let go of the shirt, and very bad body odor filled up the basement.

Brandy sneezed several times before he grabbed hold of the bars of the cage and demanded, "Get me out of here, you . . . you . . . kidnapper!"

"I didn't kidnap you;, the witch did."

"Herbal brews and stews. I hear voices in the basement." The witch's voice carried easily down to Brandy's and the troll's ears.

The basement door squeaked open, and the witch attempted to tip-toe onto the landing without being heard. Unfortunately, the troll had left his sack of rocks on the landing, and the witch tripped over it and tumbled down the stairs in an unsightly display.

Brandy and the troll covered their eyes as gentlemen should.

"Beetle brains! Who left that sack at the top of the stairs?" Silence filled the basement. The witch picked herself up and hurriedly smoothed her skirt down over her hips. Catching sight of Brandy and the troll with their eyes covered made the witch pause.

Did they know she was there? Did they think they

were hiding from her? Or were they playing hide-and-seek and were confused about who was it?

The witch marched over to the troll and kicked him in the shins.

"Ow!" yelled the troll, moving his hands from his eyes to his shins. His eyes were tightly closed, but hearing all the fuss, Brandy had dared to peek.

"The troll is taking me away," announced Brandy.

"He is?" said the witch.

The troll opened his eyes and looked at the witch.

"Well?" The witch tapped one foot on the basement floor and put her hands on her hips.

The troll shrugged.

"That is not an answer," said the witch.

The troll looked at Brandy. Looked at the witch. And shrugged again.

"He's here to rescue me," said Brandy. "He knows he was wrong in bringing me here. Don't you?"

"Who do you wish to help, troll? I have been like a mother to you all these years."

"I could be a father to you. If you need one." Brandy's attempt to compete with the witch sounded weak even to Brandy. What would this giant, ugly troll want with a family? Brandy wondered.

"I really didn't plan on making anyone unhappy," the troll said. "I thought Brandy would get his spider and you would get your . . ." The troll looked at Brandy.

"Wart," Brandy reminded him.

"Yes, yes, exactly. But Brandy doesn't seem to be happy and you've been terribly angry ever since he arrived," the troll said to the witch. "I wonder whether I did the right thing?"

"Fool! You must go with the magic. Haven't I taught you little tricks to make ingrown nails disappear? I've taught you how to use herbs to make headaches go away. And when you were sick with a tummy ache I spooned my magic potion into your mouth and made you all better. I even blew your nose and patted your forehead dry when you had a cold and fever. You think Brandy would do that for you?"

"Why not?" asked Brandy. "I could baby this oversized child just the same as you. So there!" Brandy faced the troll.

"You have both been kind to me in different ways. It is hard for me to make a choice. Please don't make me hurt one of you for the benefit of the other. Please," pleaded the troll.

Stephen woke up to the morning sun that sprayed his father's bedroom. Dad peacefully snored to the right of Stephen.

"Dad," whispered Stephen. "Dad, I love you."

His father must have heard the words even in his sleep, because he reached out and drew Stephen into a hug.

chapter 33

"Has Stephen said anything about Molly?" asked Mabel.

"He hardly speaks for some reason. I don't know whether he feels guilty about Molly's death or whether he is overwhelmed by so much death."

"Have you thought about getting him therapy?"

"For my little trooper?"

"He's a little boy, not a soldier in your army, Jacob."

"Yeah, but where would I find an appropriate doctor?"

"You could ask Rosemary."

"Robin's doctor would be too far away."

"But her doctor might be able to suggest someone local. If you don't want to ask Rosemary I can do it for you."

"Mabel, I'm thirty-eight and still on speaking terms with Rosemary. I can do it myself."

"Then do it and don't wait until Stephen is in serious trouble."

"You make it sound like Stephen will become a juvenile delinquent."

"Just a few months ago his mother died. She committed suicide. Now his babysitter is dead from some strange animal attack. Your little man has a lot to work out there."

"And so do I," Jacob mumbled.

"What did you say?"

"I was hoping Stephen and I could lean on each other for help."

"You're an awful big load for little Stephen to carry."

"I let him sleep in my bed last night, and we woke enmeshed in a tight hug."

Jacob drove slowly down the road where Molly had died. He saw a wreath of flowers and a grouping of toys heaped to the side of the road in her remembrance.

"Molly said Stephen talks to his mother. I didn't pay much attention because I figured he would grow out of it. Maybe I'm wrong. She also said Cathy was a witch."

Jacob waited for a sharp rebuttal from Mabel.

"Did you hear me? I said Molly claimed Cathy was a witch."

"I wouldn't permit her to keep her ritual utensils at home when she lived with me. However, I did find them hidden in her closet during a spring cleaning. She had a fit when she got home from school and found out I had pitched everything. The whole neighborhood heard her. She actually started screeching spells at me as if she were going to send me to hell or at least make me disappear forever."

"She practiced witchcraft?"

"She did as a teen. I don't know what she did when she went off to college."

"And I bet you didn't want to know," Jacob said.

"I couldn't stop her from engaging in the behavior, but I wasn't going to condone any of it by seeming to accept her silly practices."

"Molly wasn't making this stuff up. Damn, I wish I had listened."

"It wouldn't have saved Molly's life," Mabel said glancing out the side window.

"Are you sure?" Jacob asked.

chapter 34

"What did you and Grannie Smith do today?" Jacob helped pull off Stephen's jacket.

"We prepared more food than anyone in the world could eat. I got tummy aches just watching her." Stephen bent over and put his hands on his abdomen. Jacob pulled Stephen's hands higher.

"The tummy is in the middle," corrected Jacob. "I guess you're not hungry then."

"Naw, she already fed me dinner and two desserts."

"Two?"

"Her son had a lot more than I did."

"At six-two he's a lot bigger than you too."

Stephen raced up the stairs.

"Whoa, where are you going?" asked Jacob.

"Up to my room."

"What, don't you want to spend some father-and-son time together?"

"No, Dad. I mean, I've got some stuff to do up in my room."

"Okay. But you have . . ." Jacob checked his watch "two hours before lights out."

Stephen continued on to his room. Jacob was glad that for once he didn't hear the door slam.

Walking by the basement door on the way to the kitchen Jacob stopped. The door stood open a crack. He went to close the door but decided to take a look at what was down there instead.

Why was Molly so upset about the basement? Maybe she wasn't just trying to lasso Jacob back into her arms. He should have cleaned out the basement immediately after Cathy died.

Heaving a heavy sigh, he turned on the basement light and started down the stairs. He didn't like the coldness or the smell of the basement. Going full force, the furnace emanated heat, but the basement still retained a chill.

"What the hell!" Jacob caught sight of Cathy's work table. On some parts of the table the wax had to be an inch thick. What a mess she had made of the antique dining table. He remembered the sheen he put on it when they used it as their own dining table. Cathy had to have matching table and chairs in the dining room, and the old table went down into the basement. She said that she could use it. And used it she must have.

"Hell, were you practicing candle magic, Cathy?" His voice sounded sad to his ears. "Why couldn't you have just divorced me? Did you think killing yourself would make me feel guilty? Instead it made me see how little I knew you and how weak you really were."

A chirping noise came from the far corner of the room. A fast-paced worrisome chirp that confused Jacob's thoughts.

"He's here."

"What are we to do?"

"Kill him. Kill him."

"With what? We are all stuck to this box."

"Where's the little one?"

"The boy. The young conjuror. He could free us."

Jacob walked to the corner of the room where a tarp had been shaped into a ball.

"Silence," called out the dwarf.

Jacob lifted the tarp, figuring he could start his clean-up by throwing the tarp into the garbage can already at the curb. The sharp edge of an object hit his big left toe causing him to hop for a few seconds. He was about to kick the object when he noticed the unusual designs on the box. His fingers stung when he lifted the box as if the box were covered with nettles. He placed it on the wax-covered table.

"Why are you down here?"

Jacob turned to see his son standing at the bottom of the stairs.

"I decided it was time to clean the basement. Lots of garbage down here and some things for the charity shop," he said nodding toward the box.

"The box doesn't belong to you. You can't give it away."

"To whom does this ugly box belong?"

"Momma. She sent me to get you away from her stuff."

"How did you know where I was?"

"I told you. Momma sent me."

"Go upstairs to your room, Stephen. I have to clean up all this left-over crap."

"You can't throw out the box."

"Do you want the box, Stephen?"

The boy made a face.

"Not really. That's why I keep it down here. Momma wanted me to keep it in my room, but it's way too creepy."

"If it frightens you, Stephen, we can throw it out."

Stephen stood staring at the box before he put out his hands.

"I want the box, Dad. Give it to me, and I'll take

it up to my room."

"But if the box frightens you, why take it to your room? You won't be able to sleep."

"It's Momma's box, and I swore to take care of it."

"When did she make you swear?"

"I don't remember." Stephen's bottom lip pouted out.

"I bet you remember the exact moment." Jacob lifted the box, and the prickly feel of nettles burned his fingers again. "Show me what you're supposed to do with the box, Stephen."

With his hands still extended outward the boy said, "I want to keep it so I can always remember Momma. I never want to forget her."

"I can re-wrap it in the tarp and put it back where I found it."

His son shook his head.

"I'll keep it in my room. Then it won't tempt you."

"So you think your old man would give the box away behind your back?"

"The box tempts people. It tempted Molly."

"Molly found it?"

"And something bad happened to her."

"I don't think it was because of this box, Stephen."

"Give it to me. Momma said they won't hurt me."

"Who?" Jacob took a closer look at the shapes on the box. Each figure was uglier and crueler looking than the next. "Is there anything inside the box?" Jacob went to open the lid.

"Don't, Dad." Stephen ran to his father who held the box out of his son's reach.

"How about we have a compromise? I won't open the box and I'll leave it on this table if you promise to let it stay in the basement."

"You won't throw it out or give it away?"

"I swear. The box will be here in the morning."

Stephen agreed and Jacob placed the box amidst the wax on the table.

"Look at your fingers, Dad."

The tips of Jacob's fingers were raw. On some fingers it looked as if the skin had been scraped off.

"What the hell is on that thing?" Jacob asked. He looked at his son for an answer, but he got none. "It's as if the box had been dipped in acid. Come on, let's go upstairs where I can understand what is going on."

The boy climbed the stairs beside his father, and the uglies swelled with excitement.

"Why didn't the boy let him open the box?"

"Too soon."

"We must all be free to take her revenge."

"We can't fail her, or she will send us back to where we came from, and I couldn't abide that limbo anymore. Not when I know what this human world is like."

"The boy will come tonight to set us free," the dwarf

THE WITCH

wisely pronounced. "He has no more time. The father has marked the time for his own punishment."

chapter 35

Stephen sang a nursery rhyme to himself as he walked down the basement stairs. Momma had awoken him with the song. She had just left Dad, who slept deeply. It was time to free the demons before Dad destroyed them.

The boy looked at the odd shapes covering the box. The smiling dwarf stood out as the most ugly because he seemed not at all trustworthy. The little ax he held shimmered in the moonlight, and when Stephen lit a candle, pearls of water—or was it blood—shined on the ax.

He spilled a small amount of wax on each figure,

and each swelled and pulled until free of the box. Being the last figure imprisoned by the box, the dwarf became agitated. His smile weakened. He fought the frown that knitted his eyebrows.

"You be good," Stephen warned before allowing a drop of wax to touch the dwarf.

It was less wax than the others received, making the birth of the demon more difficult. Finally when freed, the dwarf's smile returned, and he waved his ax in the air like a mighty warrior.

The rest of the uglies had built an upward chain to open the lid of the box. The black snake lethargically crept out. His black skin was mottled and his fangs seemed dulled.

"He needs some blood," shouted a bird. "Give him some blood." And all the uglies stared up at Stephen.

"You want my blood?"

"Just a little. A few drops will take care of all of us." The bird became the spokesman.

"But I have nothing to prick my finger with."

The dwarf ran forward holding the ax high in the air.

"But you'll cut off a finger," yelled Stephen.

"No, just a little slash across your creamy, baby flesh and we are happy," said the dwarf. "Why would we want to cut off a finger? It would be much too much for us."

Stephen began to lay out his right index finger in front of the dwarf, but almost instantaneously pulled it away when he noticed the sharpness of the tiny ax.

A cold ache engulfed the boy, and he felt his mother wrapping her arms around him. The smell of her perfume calmed his breath. The rhythm of the nursery rhyme she sang mesmerized his thoughts, and he allowed her to move his hand back to the table, where the dwarf waited with raised ax.

The sting of the cut made his body quiver with the knowledge of what had been done.

"Close your eyes, my sweet baby. Lean back on my breast and rest."

Uglies swarmed his hand, fighting for a taste of his precious blood. The tiny tap of their feet and claws kept his hand from going numb. He thought he felt something bite but couldn't come out of his dreamy haze to check. Another bite followed and another.

Stephen swooned on his feet, held tall only by the hands of his dead mother.

"Enough!"

His mother's voice cut the fog, and he looked down to see his hand terribly mauled.

"By morning it will almost be healed. Their mouths take some of your power but also give you some of theirs."

"What will I tell Dad when he asks why my hand looks so awful?"

"Hide your hand. By midnight tomorrow he'll not be

asking that question of you."

"Why not? Will the hand be completely healed by then?"

"We'll both experience the healing magic these little friends have to give."

☆ ☆ ☆

The fiends watched as the mother guided her son up the basement stairs. She'd put him to bed, kiss him, and hurry back to death's embrace.

"We're free," one of the demons whispered.

"No," said the dwarf in a grumpy voice. "In the morning we will be clinging again to that accursed box. They gave us freedom only in the night." The dwarf squatted down, holding his ax between his legs. "She doesn't trust us."

"Can you blame her?" asked the snake.

The dwarf rose to his feet and whirled on the black snake.

"You ate more than the rest of us."

"I'd been free longer and without sustenance. Of course I would have a greater hunger."

"I think you desire to be stronger than the rest of us." The dwarf squinted down at the snake. "I think you would do us in if it benefitted you. Your skin is wet and shiny. Even in the dark I can make out where you are."

"All of us have perfect night vision, Master Dwarf.

It is part of being a creature of the night." The snake looked to the other demons for agreement, but the others only stood and stared at him. "I can't help that you don't like me. Perhaps it should be you that we worry about deceiving us."

"I need no one else. In battles I bloodied a goodly share of the enemies but never sought protection from others on my side."

"Did you have any allies, Master Dwarf, or did you kill and maim indiscriminately?"

The dwarf's brow furrowed.

"What right do you have to question my actions? Have you fought at all in battles, or have you hidden behind trees and bushes, voyeuristically feeding on the pain?"

The black snake did not reply.

"I know you from somewhere, but not in battle. I sense the battlefield is not your domain. Your treachery seeks dark crevices where you cannot be seen employing your brand of misery."

"I can't think of any more miserable position to be in than here listening to you brag on about your victories."

"Not all my battles were victorious, but they were bloody," said the dwarf, bringing his ax dangerously close to the black snake.

"Cut me, Master Dwarf, and you had better have a good answer for the witch and her progeny."

"I certainly don't fear the child."

THE WITCH

"Maybe we all should take extra care when around the young one. I fear that our existence is in his hands."

chapter 36

Stephen found that he didn't have to worry about his father noticing his injured hand the next morning because his father slept late and didn't have time to notice.

"I can't believe I slept so late. I must have been more tired than I thought," said Jacob trying to whip some breakfast together for his son.

Stunned, Stephen sat in the kitchen, examining the hand the uglies had tortured the night before. Most of the wounds had healed perfectly without any scars. Some damage was still visible but little enough that he managed to keep his hand inside his pocket through the hurried breakfast of cereal.

"I'm going to do without and have a big lunch instead. The only reason I woke up this morning is because your grandmother couldn't get to her school. Boy, did she yell. She's late once in thirty years, and you would think the school board was about to fire her. Maybe she's afraid they'll make her take forced retirement. I don't think she'd be able to sit home and relax for more than a month or two. Even now she teaches summer school."

Stephen's wide eyes followed his father around the kitchen. He himself had awakened early but hesitated to disturb his father, hoping the hand would heal more and more with each passing minute.

"Mrs. Rosen will pick you up from school. I might have to work an extra hour or two. I certainly don't have to worry about her stuffing your face. If she keeps babysitting, you'll weigh at least twenty pounds more by the end of the year.

"Hey, you don't mind Mrs. Rosen, do you?"

"Grannie Smith, Dad. She's not Molly but she's kind. I don't think she'll be making me a Halloween costume."

"Damn, I forgot all about that. Do you want me to pick up something on my way home?"

"Naw, I'm going to school as me tomorrow. That's probably scary enough," Stephen said.

Jacob brushed his son's hair.

"I'll let you borrow some of my old work clothes, and you can be a tramp."

"Really, Dad, I'm not worried about Halloween."

"Don't you want to go door to door and mooch off the local neighbors?"

"Grannie Smith will feed me enough candy." Stephen had a difficult time eating since he had to use his left hand to spoon the cereal into his mouth. He hoped Dad wouldn't notice. But Dad hardly looked at him.

The doorbell rang, and Jacob rushed out of the kitchen to answer it.

Stephen slid his hand out of his pocket to check his right hand. Only a few bruises and scratches were left; the open wounds had all disappeared. Momma must have been right. The uglies must have some magic healing power in their saliva. Stephen quickly sat on his hand when he heard his father's footsteps returning to the kitchen.

"That was Mrs. Rosen. Grannie Smith to you. She noticed my car and worried that something may have been wrong over here. I told her not to worry because her assistant chef would still be keeping her company today."

Stephen watched his father walk out of the kitchen in search of his briefcase. Stephen slid off the chair and followed, remembering to slide his hand back into his pant pocket. His father stopped at the basement door, put his hand on the doorknob, shook his head, and released the knob before going on to the living room.

Stephen knew the uglies would again be glued onto the wood box unable to cause any problem. The uglies could use their magic only at night. Wherever they were, at dawn the uglies would be swept up in a chill breeze and returned to the box. During the day they would also be unable to defend themselves.

The boy wondered whether his allegiance to his mother or to his father should take priority. Momma couldn't touch things in her son's world. She needed Stephen's help. Dad was fine but seemed at times to be working at odds with his mother's wishes. And why was Momma so angry? She'd never talk about it. But she didn't like his dad anymore, and that made Stephen sad.

"Let's go," shouted Jacob, halting at the door to see his son standing in the hall without shoes or socks. "Didn't you bring all yours clothes down into the kitchen like I asked?"

Stephen nodded.

"Then where are your shoes and socks?"

"In the kitchen with my jacket."

Jacob swept the boy off his feet and into the kitchen.

"I can't let you go to school half naked."

"Dad, I'm only missing my shoes and socks.

During the summer you always let me walk around barefoot."

"The teachers wouldn't approve. Think about what your grandmother says when you're barefoot."

Stephen giggled.

"She calls me Lil' Abner. You still haven't found that cartoon strip so's I can know what I look like."

"Look in the mirror and you'll know what you look like."

"Nah, I want to see the way Grandma sees me."

Jacob finished tying the laces of Stephen's shoes and lifted the boy off the kitchen chair.

"Do I really look like a cartoon, Dad?"

"You look like your mom. And that's good. That makes you . . ."

"Pretty?" Stephen made a face.

"Handsome." Jacob stood back to view Stephen and lifted a brow. "Very handsome. All the hearts you'll break."

"I don't want to break anyone's heart, honest."

"Then you won't. Let's go."

chapter 37

"The boy is very stupid," said the giant bird.

"Innocent, not stupid," corrected the gargoyle.

"Stupid. Innocent. They are both the same," said the bird.

"He's but a child," hissed the snake, wishing he were still inside the wooden box instead of stuck to the outside of the box. He could move even during the day when he lived inside the box.

"A stupid, innocent child," murmured the dwarf. "And all of you have been quite cruel to him."

"What? You were the first to break his flesh." The gargoyle hated hypocrisy.

"I only helped. Someone had to do something. We couldn't all stare at him and wait 'til he stabbed his own hand. He wasn't about to do that. Oh, no, not he. Momma's boy he is."

The uglies facing the window were uncomfortable. The sun rose strong that morning and would grow warmer and brighter as the day wore on. Already several uglies squinted. A quiet bird with two heads had tucked each head under a wing. The uglies away from the window remained bored.

"I scented the father this morning at the door of the basement." The dog with the head of a man sniffed the air again. "But he's gone now. The little one must have stopped Father from coming down to destroy us. I worried just before the sun came up as I was drawn back to the box that we might be destroyed before we did our mistress' bidding. We are here for her."

"Who is she?" said the dwarf. "A third rate witch. I've worked for better. I worked with witches who had a true passion for blood and killed or maimed entire families. Entire countries even."

"Don't lie," hissed the black snake.

Indignantly the dwarf tried to raise his ax, but it was firmly glued to the box. The black snake managed to stretch up to the dwarf's ear.

"Entire countries, comrade? Your ax can barely bloody a little boy."

"If I were free you'd be in tiny bits." The dwarf

snarled.

"The fire. We must stoke the fire tonight before Father comes home." The gargoyle had been sitting, planning the task that would be theirs tonight.

"Better than this idiot's ax." The snake flicked out its tongue to tease the ear of the dwarf.

"We are one tonight," the gargoyle reminded the other uglies. "We work together. No one can say he did more or less. The work is divided equally."

"And who will keep the boy out of trouble?" asked the bird with the large beak.

"His mother will care for her progeny. We need not ask her to. She'll keep the boy close to her so he doesn't hear the screams. She will pull him into her own world."

"She will take her son to the world of the dead?"

"Only briefly."

"Death is not brief," the bird with the large beak said. "Death is forever."

"Do you care whether he comes back?" asked the gargoyle.

The uglies chuckled with delight except for the dwarf.

"We need the boy more than the witch now. I care where the boy is and will protect him for my own sake."

"Even against his mother?"

"Especially against the woman who rules us."

"How? We owe our existence in this world to her."

"I owe her only revenge. Then I am free to rule my own conjuror."

"The boy's soul is not black enough to listen to you," said the gargoyle.

"We'll see. Yes, when the night comes the boy's soul is frail. Already the mother has confused his world with her petty pleas. Her revenge is but a token. We are capable of much more." The dwarf's eyes flashed briefly.

"We'll not follow you," the snake said, and hissed softly in the quiet of the basement.

"Who would you follow?" The dwarf's head dipped slightly toward the black snake.

"The gargoyle leads us this night," said the dog with the head of a man. "There'll be no arguing. You two should work out what problems you have separate from us. You both drain our energy, leaving us frailer than we should be."

"You're a mystery to me," the dwarf said to the dog with the man's head. "What were you before coming here?"

"A god," answered the dog.

Gasps flooded from the mouths of the demons.

"I've heard of the Anubis having the body of a man and the head of a jackal, but never have heard of a god looking like you." The dwarf used his ax to gently scratch his head.

"I didn't look like this, fool."

The dwarf puffed up and blustered out several curses. If a snake could shake with laughter, then the black snake quivered his skin in that same manner.

The gargoyle dragged its body over to the fracas.

"Be still. It doesn't matter what any of us were in a former life. Now we are spirits residing in the shape our mistress chose for us."

"Do you think she gave much thought to what she was doing?" asked the snake.

"She gave us a way to exist. I'm sure none of us want to return to nothingness."

"Not me," said the dog.

"Certainly not you," said the dwarf. "A god turned into nothingness. Whoever heard of that? After all the sacrifices and gifts which were laid at your feet, you had to be very lonely in the limbo from which we came. Were the virgins truly virgin? Did the hearts taste as sweet as they're supposed to? Or were you a minor god satisfied with chickens and sheep?"

"Quiet!" The gargoyle's voice stayed low but hard-edged.

The demons settled back into their own private thoughts and slept the day away.

chapter 38

"Don't worry; the boy can sleep over if you're going to be really late," said Grannie Smith over the telephone.

Stephen rushed over to the woman and begged to speak to his father. She handed him the receiver immediately.

"I can't stay over. I gotta be back with you tonight."

"Wow! You must have been standing right next to Mrs. Rosen. You eavesdropping on our telephone calls?" Jacob asked.

"No, Dad. Grannie Smith doesn't mind my listening to her calls. At least she never said she did."

Mrs. Rosen chucked the boy under the chin.

"Yeah, well, some things you don't have to be told. It's just polite to give people some privacy."

Stephen hunkered close to the phone to whisper. "Do I have to apologize?"

"I'm sure Grannie Smith knows you didn't mean any harm. I should be able to pick you up just about at bedtime. That okay with you?"

"Sure. I can't stay over here. I want to be with you."

"Don't worry, son, I'm not going to leave you."

Stephen spent the rest of the afternoon worrying. The uglies could now peel themselves off the box when the sun went down. The wax from his candle had melted their bond to the box, and his blood and flesh had given them the incentive to seek out more nourishment. He didn't trust his dad not to go into the cellar to remove the box from the table. What if the box were thrown into the garbage can at the curb? The uglies would be able to rampage the neighborhood. Pets and small children would be their favorite victims.

That evening Grannie Smith and Stephen were the only two at the dinner table, although the amount of food didn't seem decreased. She tried to coax the boy into eating, but he noticed nothing but the clock. Each minute brought them closer to the night.

While Stephen pushed his food around on his

plate the sun went down. He dropped the fork into the plate and ran to look out the study window which faced his own house. He wondered what the uglies would be doing. Would they be hungry again? Would Momma make him feed them with his own flesh? He looked down at his small hand and saw that even the bruising had almost disappeared. There were a couple of areas on his palm that still had a yellowish tinge, but other than that his right hand looked unmarred.

"Momma?"

He heard a noise behind him and caught himself before he could say anything else.

Grannie Smith knelt down next to him to give him a gentle hug.

"I could use help with the dishes," she said. "Want to give me a hand?"

Stephen nodded and followed her into the kitchen, but through all Grannie Smith's jokes Stephen remained somber, his mind on the uglies the entire time.

Later, Grannie Smith attempted to get the boy interested in television shows, but when a car passed Stephen jumped up from the couch to see if his father had come home.

Finally, he saw his father's car pull into the driveway. Stephen excitedly ran to the front door and waited. He could hardly breathe, and he danced about so much Grannie Smith suggested he might need to use the bathroom. The idea inspired his little bladder, and he ran off to the powder room.

He expected to find his father waiting for him when he returned, but Grannie Smith sat alone on the couch watching the news on television.

"Where's Dad?" he asked.

"Hasn't come for you yet. I suppose he may have a few things to take care of before picking you up."

"No, he can't. I have to be there."

"What are you talking about?"

"He wants to throw out Momma's box. He said he wouldn't, but what if he does? The uglies need to be able to go back on the box."

Grannie Smith stood.

"I have no idea what you're talking about, but I'll take you back home so you can settle down. Okay?"

Stephen nodded but was disappointed that Grannie Smith had to put on her shoes and sweater before leaving the house. He scrambled about the living room, helping her to find the shoes. The sweater at least hung from a hook by the front door.

chapter 39

After pulling into the driveway, Jacob got out of the car and walked to the trunk where he had put Stephen's gift. He slipped the box under his arm and searched his pocket for the house key.

As soon as he opened the door a wave of heat struck him.

"What the hell?"

The house felt like a pizza oven. Perspiration broke out on his body before he reached Stephen's room.

He placed the box on the bed, thinking his son might enjoy playing a pirate on Halloween. He certainly had enjoyed the ride Pirates of the Carribean at Disneyland, forcing his parents to take the ride five times in a row. Not that Jacob didn't secretly enjoy it. Cathy became a bit bored though. Must be a guy thing, Jacob said to himself. He remembered he had an old bottle of rum in his den. He'd empty the bottle and fill it with Coke for Stephen to imbibe while trick or treating. He couldn't wait to see a smile on his son's face, but before picking up Stephen he'd best go down into the basement and turn off the furnace. The house had enough heat to last them the rest of the fall.

He quickly ran down the stairs and checked the hall thermostat. Ninety-five degrees! The damn thing must be broken. He couldn't complain, though; for five years the furnace had worked without any repair.

Jacob opened the basement door and flicked on the light. The bulb stuttered but finally came on full force.

"Guess this basement needs a good fixing up," Jacob mumbled out loud.

The banister gave a bit when he touched it. The steps seemed to creak more than he remembered. Could be the heat causing the problems. The temperature in the basement made him think of all the forest fires he had heard of in the area.

Jacob did a double-take when the furnace came into view. He thought the damn thing had actually turned a bright red. Funny what an imagination can do.

The switch was too hot to touch with his bare hand, so he searched for some old rags. Conveniently a stack of old clothes had been piled under the staircase. He grabbed an old ripped pair of jeans, and while folding them over he walked back to the furnace. He stopped in his tracks when he noticed the box on the table. The demons had disappeared. He walked over and picked up the plain wooden box that no longer burned the tips of his fingers. Could Stephen have managed to pry the figures off during the night while Jacob was asleep? But there were no marks on the box to indicate anything had once been attached to it. He flipped the lid open. Empty. He'd ask Stephen about the box later. Now he had to take care of the furnace. He put the box on the table and turned to take a step when he tripped over something. The furnace door flew open, and riding it were the figures that had been on the box.

Something liquid was splashed on him. He shut his eyes, smelling the strong odor of rum. The rum he had kept in the den. He opened his eyes to the sight of a ball of flame reaching out to embrace him. His clothes instantly caught fire.

His hands tried to smother the flames that ignited his hair. He tried to rip the cloth from his flesh but felt the melted material tear at his skin. Someone wetted down his trouser with rum and the fire spread.

He tried to roll against the cement floor, but every time he turned he felt a new splash of rum hit his body.

"My handsome Jacob with those classic features and tight muscles. I lusted for you. And so did so many other women."

In the midst of the chaos Jacob heard Cathy's voice.

His screams filled the cellar but Cathy's voice rang in his ears.

"No one will want you now. The classic features are melting off your face. The long lashes have disappeared into ash. The blond locks that Molly fondled will grow no more. Your athletic body will be shrink, wrapped inside your flesh. You will know why I sought death."

chapter 40

Stephen hurried Grannie Smith out the door. She had the key to the front door of his house and he wanted her to use it.

"Now, Stephen, we can take a minute or two to be polite and knock." She rapped lightly on the door, but Stephen pounded with his small fists.

"He'll answer. He'll answer. Give him a minute," she said.

When Jacob didn't answer Stephen ran around to the side of the house to peek in the basement window. Immediately he saw the bulb had been lit. He also caught the flash of something on the floor.

Screaming, Stephen ran back to Grannie Smith and begged her to open the door. When she did, Stephen ran to the basement, not noticing the heat or the smell of cooked flesh. He found his father shivering on the floor with most of his clothes burnt off. The flesh sizzled as small plumes of smoke rose from his body. He touched his father's face in an attempt to put the skin back together but had to raise his hands when his father groaned in pain.

"Stephen," Grannie Smith called. She stood at the top of the staircase. "Is your father down here? It stinks. What's been going on?"

Stephen's whimpers turned into genuine tears, bringing his babysitter down the stairs. Her scream pierced his small ears. A splash of vomit hit his right hand as she tried to turn away in disgust. He listened to her heaves until he began feeling ill himself.

Cold embraced him. Momma's cold arms. Her frigid lips touched his cheek, and he wanted her to sing to him again.

This wasn't his father. The man didn't have the same features, the same unmarred flesh. No, this is a stranger. A man who broke into the house. Dad hadn't come home yet.

Stephen decided to wait in his room until Dad came home. He stood with the support of death, the cold numbing his body and his heart. But then he saw the dwarf peek out from behind the furnace.

The galling smile plastered on the ugly dwarf made Stephen's insides turn. Leaning on his little ax the dwarf seemed cocky.

"Come upstairs," Grannie Smith demanded. "We have to call for help." She dragged the boy several feet but couldn't get him to climb the stairs. Giving up, she let go of his arm and ran up the cellar stairs.

"Why aren't you on the box?" Stephen asked the dwarf.

"What? You forget that it is night. I run free at night. Thank you." The dwarf offered Stephen a gracious bow.

Two warm arms circled the boy's body.

"An ambulance is coming. We can't do anything here. Come upstairs. You don't want to be in their way when they come for your father."

"He's not my father. I'd never let this happen to my father."

"It's not your fault, Stephen. The house is too hot. There must have been something wrong with the furnace. It was an accident."

The dwarf dramatically mouthed along with Grannie Smith's words and finally did a little jig.

"Daddy won't like this when he gets home from work," Stephen said.

"Come upstairs, please. Your grandmother should be here soon."

"It smells bad here. Grandma won't like it. She'll blame me and Daddy. It's my fault, not Daddy's." Stephen looked up into his babysitter's eyes. He saw tears. They rolled down her chubby cheeks, cutting into the lines and wrinkles. He reached up to her face to wipe away the tears and wrinkles, but they kept coming back. He looked back down at the stranger lying on the floor. The man's blackened hands twitched, the fingers playing silent music on the air. A soot-covered ring had become enmeshed in the flesh. Daddy's ring? The man stole Daddy's ring?

Grannie Smith picked Stephen up and slowly climbed the stairs, the weight of the boy causing her to grab the banister to keep her balance.

"Momma? Why?" Stephen thought he had whispered the words, but Grannie Smith's shoulders rose with the sound of his voice.

"Shhh! Grandma will be here soon." She patted his back, her warm hand breaking the chill of his mother's kiss.

chapter 41

After the ambulance left the house Stephen turned to his grandmother and asked when his father would be coming home. She had no answer to give and crushed him closely to her breasts. She carried him up to his bedroom and left a small light lit in case he should awaken during the night. The firemen had declared the house safe. They found no cause for the fire. Perhaps the man would survive and could be questioned as to what happened.

Stephen hadn't wanted to leave the house, and Grandma decided she'd make do with what little she had with her and stay in the guest bedroom.

Stephen had his eyes tightly shut when Grandma looked in on him.

"Stephen," she whispered but he didn't answer. As soon as she left Stephen opened his eyes and searched the room for the shade of his mother. He knew she didn't like the light, and he reached over to shut off the switch.

Blackness filled the room until his eyes gradually adjusted.

"Momma, something bad happened." He listened for her voice.

"Momma, some man got hurt in our house."

He felt the cold arms and the still, cold feel of his mother's breasts as she pulled him close.

"Momma, who was that man?"

Her frozen lips softened enough to form a kiss on his brow.

"I'm here, Stephen. I won't leave you. I'll always be here with you."

"The man . . . Do you know him?"

"He cheated."

"Does that make him a bad man?"

"That makes him a liar. He'll never be tempted to lie again."

"Because you taught him a lesson?"

"There will be no opportunities for him to lie. Who will want to look at him? His words will be as distorted as his lips and face. He'll inspire pity instead of lust."

"Where's Daddy?" The boy's voice quivered with the cold and the fear that enveloped him.

"You know where Daddy is, Stephen. You saw Daddy yourself."

"In the basement?"

"Yes."

"That man wasn't Daddy. He didn't look like Daddy."

"He'll look different now. Be kind to him. Don't let him know that you find him frightening to look at."

"I'll never be scared of Daddy."

"Yes, be brave, Stephen. I want a strong little boy who can aid me."

"But Daddy . . ."

His mother silenced him with a kiss that filled his mouth with a fetid poison as he breathed in the augur of death.

chapter 42

Mabel paid the cab driver in change. She had found a large jar of quarters, dimes, and nickels in the utility room of her son-in-law's house. What a waste, she thought. The jar had been overflowing with coins. Some had probably fallen behind the washer and drier, never to be seen again. At least she'd put them to good use. However, the cab driver didn't seem to agree with her plan. He grunted as she slowly counted out the exact amount of the fare. Since he had shone no patience, she kept the tip to the bare minimum.

"I hope you got someone to pick you up, lady," were the cab driver's parting words.

Shaking her head, she walked to the front entrance of the hospital. Over the telephone the doctors had informed her Jacob was stable. There were burns over seventy-five percent of his body. She shivered thinking about it. They'd pumped him full of drugs to alleviate the pain, and he might not make much sense when he talked, but the doctors thought he should have a family visitor.

Jacob had no local family. Both his parents were deceased, and his sister lived in Australia. Mabel didn't know how to reach the sister and hadn't wanted to go through his address book without his permission. He had never been close to any of his other relatives, and he acted disdainful of them.

The doors automatically opened for her, and she entered a busy lobby. Several visitors carried bunches or baskets of flowers. Should she have brought some? Would he notice whether she had or not?

At the reception desk she had to wait several minutes while a volunteer helped an elderly patient into a wheelchair. The volunteer placed a hospital green blanket over the patient's knees and turned to help Mabel.

"Sorry, the regular receptionist had to potty. Can I help you?"

"I'm looking for Jacob Zaira."

The volunteer, a man of about sixty, plopped himself down in front of the computer.

"Let's see if I can get this right," he said, tapping the board lightly with his fingers. "Last time I sent someone off to the wrong room and well. . . you don't want to hear the names that visitor called me."

"I promise to be more understanding," she said.

He smiled up at her and returned to his tapping.

"Here it is. Zaira, Jacob."

"That's him. He had an accident."

"Must have been pretty bad. He's in the burn unit, intensive care. Got a good doctor watching over him, though."

"I've spoken to several. I'm not sure which is his primary doctor."

"Dr. Stall. Been here for twenty-five years."

"That's comforting."

"This your son?"

"Son-in-law."

"I wish him the best and you too. He's in room 110. It's a private room."

"Thank you. Which way do I go?"

The volunteer gave her directions, but Mabel had a hard time following them. She tried to follow the yellow arrows, but they disappeared somewhere between the elevator bank and the nurses' station.

"Excuse me."

A nurse dropped the clipboard she was holding on the desk.

"I'm looking for room 110."

"Are you a relative?"

"Mother-in-law."

The nurse smiled.

"Does that count? I hope no one lets my mother-in-law in to see me if ever I'm in intensive care. Just joking."

Mabel gave the nurse a weak smile.

"Two doors down on the right. He's groggy and goes in and out of sleep, so don't stay too long. By the way, you'll have to put sterile garments over your street clothes."

Mabel wanted to run out of the hospital. What to say to him? Talk about Stephen, she reminded herself. As long as she talked about Stephen, she wouldn't have to worry about what to say.

"Are you all right?" the nurse asked.

"Just trying to get my courage up," Mabel replied.

"He'll appreciate your visit. I'm sorry I said what I said before."

Once Mabel was gowned and gloved the nurse added a puffy green paper cap to cover Mabel's hair and helped to slip a mask over Mabel's face. Mabel nodded a thank you to the nurse and walked down the corridor as if she were going to the electric chair. She opened the door to the room and felt intense heat. The temperature had to be in the nineties. A curtain hid part of the bed. As she walked around the curtain she saw lamps placed around the bed;

the intense heat of the bulbs was directed at the bandaged form lying still on the mattress. Over the phone a doctor had indicated they were trying to stabilize his body temperature. Bandages wrapped his face, hands, and arms. Edema made him look uncharacteristically pudgy.

She leaned over Jacob, and the smell of burnt flesh turned her stomach.

"Mabel."

Her name sounded distorted, and she noticed that his lips were not whole.

"Jacob." She didn't ask how he was because it wasn't necessary. "Stephen has been praying for you."

"Is he staying with you?"

"Yes. Actually, today I sent him over to Grannie Smith. I didn't think he'd be up for school. I thought a day or two at home might help him . . ." Help him what? The words weren't coming easily.

"You took him by cab?" He winced as he turned his head to see her better.

"Cab? Oh, no. I'm staying at your house; I didn't want to upset him by taking him away from his home."

Jacob's eyes grew wider and his breath seemed to falter. He tried to talk, but the pain grew worse with the effort.

"Relax, Jacob. Should I call the nurse?"

"Mabel."

"Yes." She leaned closer to hear him, all the while feeling she might faint.

"Take him out of the house."

"He's at Grannie Smith's now, I told you."

He moaned and shut his eyes tightly.

"Stephen will be fine. I'll tell him I talked to you. He's worried that you might not come home. But I told him you would."

Was it a lie? She hoped to God it wasn't.

"Mabel, I want him to stay at your house."

"He doesn't seem to want to leave his home. I can't drag him off to my house."

"Drag him, Mabel. I beg you, drag him kicking and screaming." Jacob tried to raise his head. He appeared to black out for a few seconds.

"All right, Jacob. I'll do what you say."

"Don't humor me. Do it."

"Oh, Jacob, all of this is so horrible. I don't know how the child can stand it. What did happen with the furnace?"

Jacob closed his eyes, and Mabel thought he had fallen asleep until he spoke.

"Demons, Mabel."

"Demons?"

"Cathy's demons. She sent them after me."

"Jacob, you know that isn't true. The doctors said there might have been some alcohol involved. Had you been drinking?"

Jacob opened his eyes and raised his right hand as if to grab hold of Mabel.

"I want Stephen out of that damn house. I want him cut off from his mother's influence."

"He loved Cathy."

"I wish she had loved him."

"That's a terrible thing to say. No one loved him more than Cathy did. She'd do anything for him."

"Including killing herself?"

Mabel worried her bottom lip. There was no answer to Jacob's question.

"I'm going now, Jacob. I didn't come here to upset you. I want to help. May I come back tomorrow?"

"Please. I do nothing but sleep, count the hours to my next dose of medications, and stare up at the ceiling. The lights are so strong. The lamps give me a headache."

"They don't want you to go into shock. They're trying to keep you warm."

He acknowledged her words with a slight nod of his head.

"Is there anything you'd like me to bring?"

"Someone. Stephen."

"The doctors won't let him see you. Visitors have to be at least thirteen. They're afraid he'll bring in some germs. I don't know. I'll keep trying to talk them into letting me bring the boy."

"Then I can expect to see Stephen soon." The

raw meat of his lips could almost form a smile.

"At least I'll be here tomorrow." She took a deep breath, held it, and leaned over to gently kiss his bandaged cheek.

chapter 43

Jacob lay on his hospital bed envisioning little demons sliding up and down the curtains. Remembering the balls of fire coming at him and the smell of the rum.

Is this what you wanted, Cathy? But why use our son?

Every emotion swept over his body in waves of pain that attacked every nerve ending. He couldn't find peace even in his sleep.

The visit from Mabel had been a brief respite from the smell of hospital antiseptics and burnt flesh. She wore her favorite perfume. The one he used to hate. Now he tried to keep the smell alive to hide the rude hospital odors.

Would Mabel listen to him and take Stephen out of the house? What could he say? *Quick, take him out of the house before the little demons get him.*

"How are we feeling?" asked a volunteer.

"You're feeling better than I, I'm sure."

The volunteer nodded.

"Do you need anything?"

"A new sheath of skin."

"The nurse will be coming in with your medication in about fifteen minutes. You'll be able to sleep then."

The volunteer fussed around his bed. He couldn't be certain what the woman thought she accomplished. She placed the call button closer to his hand.

"Would you like me to read to you until the nurse comes?"

"Do you know the story of Brandy and the witch?"

"Is that a fairy tale I missed while growing up?"

Jacob swallowed hard several times before he could speak again.

"Brandy is being held prisoner by the witch. She's a kindhearted witch. All she did was put Brandy in a cage. Some witches are viler. Some. . ." He stopped. Tears came to his eyes, and the pain shot through every nerve ending of his body.

"Maybe I can get the nurse to come in sooner. Hold on."

THE WITCH

The volunteer vanished. Only the pain shared Jacob's room.

He looked toward the window and saw the shadings of the end of the day. Yesterday at this time he had been whole. Tonight he was supposed to have taken Stephen trick or treating in the pirate costume. And the rum should have been dumped down the sink.

The pain clung to his body, slowly hugging the life out of him. He panted for air. Against the bed curtain he saw the shadow of his hands waving, clutching for life.

Stephen, I love you. I would have never touched Molly had I known what would happen. I love you so much.

His heart pounded to the beat of the pain. He wanted to crumble into a fetal position, but the pain wouldn't let him. The bandages tightened against his skin.

A nurse's hands began to change the IV bag beside his bed.

"Mr. Zaira. I'm changing the bag. You'll feel better in a few minutes."

She kept droning and he fled to a dark world.

chapter 44

Stephen's head turned to his right when he noticed the red brick buildings of the hospital. Men and women dressed in white lab coats and jeans circulated on the lawn. An ambulance sat at the street curb with paramedics standing to the side, talking. He tried to get Grannie Smith to stop the car, but she didn't hear very well today because the battery was out on her hearing aid. The battery was one of the items on the long list she had made before starting out.

They had just passed the hospital when Grannie Smith had to stop for a red light.

"Grannie, I need to go to the bathroom. Can we stop here?" he shouted.

"Bathroom?"

"I really have to go. The hospital must have a bathroom."

"Can you hold it 'til we get home? We only have one more stop to make, and then we can return to home base."

"No, Grannie Smith, I gotta go now." Stephen bounced up and down in his seat.

"All right. There's a McDonald's up ahead . . ."

"No! The hospital has cleaner bathrooms."

"Stephen, the doctors won't allow you to see your father right now."

"No! I need to go," he yelled, screwing his face into a pained expression.

"Okay."

When the light turned green, Grannie Smith made a U-turn and pulled into the lane leading to the hospital driveway. She had to wait a minute for the oncoming traffic to clear before turning.

Stephen clutched his hands together and his breath almost stopped. He sunk back into his seat while Grannie Smith pulled into the parking lot.

"Let's not take too long, Stephen. Your grandmother will be wondering where we've gone, and I don't want her worrying about you."

Grannie Smith helped Stephen out of the car.

Immediately he headed for the front doors. She had to call out to him to wait for her while she locked the car.

His little eyes took in the massive size of the buildings. He couldn't imagine how he would find his father. He didn't know where to start.

Grannie Smith grabbed his hand and yanked him to her side, pulling him along.

"Are all these buildings full of sick people?" he asked.

"Some people are sick, some are visitors, and some work here."

"How can you tell what the people are?"

"Let's just worry about getting you to the bathroom," she said, nodding her head to the receptionist at the information desk. "It's just down the hall here."

"Look!" shouted Stephen. "There's a girl like Robin. A witch must have stolen her bones." He watched a girl on crutches pass in front of them.

"Shhh! Stephen, you have to be quiet in hospitals. You don't want to wake the sick people. Okay?"

Stephen nodded.

"Here now." Grannie Smith began taking him into the ladies' room.

"I can't go in there."

"It's all right as long as you're with me," she assured him.

Stephen crouched down.

"I'm a boy!"

"Shhh. What did I say about keeping your voice down?"

"I want to potty in the boys' room."

"But I can't go into the men's room with you."

"So?"

"I don't like letting you go in the bathroom alone."

"Why? I know what to do. I go every day at school, and the teacher never comes in with me."

"This is different. You know who is using the bathroom at school. Here you don't know who will be in there with you."

"Yes, I do. There'll be other boys."

"And men."

"Dad sometimes uses the bathroom when I do."

"Exactly. He wouldn't let you go in alone."

"At home he does."

"Oh, Stephen, we're just going round in circles. If you really need to go, you'll use the ladies' room this one time."

Stephen shook his head.

"What are you going to do? Wet your pants?" Grannie Smith stood with her hands on her hips.

"It'll be your fault if I do." Stephen pouted and covered his crotch with both hands.

"Okay. Go, go but make it fast," she said.

Stephen ran into the bathroom. The chill of the room hit him hard enough that he really did have to pee. He used a stall and washed his hands after he was finished.

How could he loose Grannie Smith? he wondered, wiping his wet hands against his denim jeans.

"Hey, can't you reach the towels?" A young man dressed in white entered the room. "Need a hand?" The man grabbed several paper towels and handed them to Stephen.

"Do you know where my father is?" Stephen asked.

"I don't know; we have lots of patients."

"His name is Jacob Zaira. The . . ." Stephen hesitated, trying to find the right words. "The furnace set him on fire."

The young man nodded.

"I'm afraid I don't know your father, but he wouldn't be in this building. Most of the patients here don't stay overnight."

"Oh, my dad did stay last night, and Grandma says he'll be staying here for a while."

"Is that your grandma waiting for you outside?"

"She's not my real grandma. I'm helping her to go shopping."

"That's nice of you. I think she may be getting a bit anxious to continue her shopping. Last I saw her she was pacing back and forth in front of the men's room."

"Which building would my father be in?" Stephen

asked, trying to forget the guard outside the door.

"Are you with someone else who's visiting your father?"

"My real grandma is visiting Dad, but she isn't with us. She's in the building where Dad has to stay. We came here so's I could potty."

"Have you finished?"

Stephen nodded.

"Okay, let's go see your fake grandma." The young man offered his hand, but Stephen wouldn't take it.

"First I've gotta know where my dad is."

"I'd say he's not in here. Wouldn't you?"

Stephen checked the empty stall before agreeing to leave the men's room.

"There you are. I was getting worried."

"He couldn't reach the towels and I gave him some."

"See, you should have used the ladies' room. I could have helped you."

"But I don't need any help to potty."

"Thank you for returning him to me. I wouldn't know what to say to his grandmother if something happened. The family has had enough bad luck."

"So I heard." The young man shook Stephen's hand and returned to the men's room.

"I want to see Daddy."

Grannie Smith squatted down to Stephen's level.

"Your father isn't feeling very well. He needs lots of sleep so he can get better."

"He can't sleep all the time," Stephen retorted.

"Give your dad some time to get better."

"What if he never gets better? What if I never see him again? If I'd told Momma that I loved her, maybe she wouldn't have gone away. I need to tell Dad that I want him to come home."

"He knows, Stephen. I'm sure he's trying very hard to get better so he can come home to you. I bet if you ask your grandma what your father said today she'll tell you that he sent his love."

"That's not good enough. I have to tell him how I feel." Tears blurred Grannie Smith's face. Stephen fisted his hands and tried to clear his vision.

Grannie Smith leaned forward and gave Stephen a kiss on his cheek.

"Let's go home. Your grandmother may be waiting to talk to you. Tell her how you feel and see what she says." Grannie Smith stood and took Stephen's hand, guiding him slowly down the hallway and to the front doors. He kept looking around, seeing strangers. Outside he tripped when he stepped off the curb; he almost fell except Grannie Smith had a tight hold on him.

"Did an ambulance bring Molly here when she had her accident?"

"I really don't know, Stephen."

"Do a lot of people die here?"

"Hospitals make people better."

"Does everyone get better?"

Grannie Smith sighed.

"I think these are questions for your grandmother to answer."

"Why? Don't you know? Did Mr. Grannie Smith die here?"

"His name was Fred, child. Fred Rosen." She quickly ushered him into the car and tightened his safety belt before closing the door. As she circled around the car she took a last look at the hospital. She remembered the emergency room so well.

When she got into the car she felt Stephen's eyes on her.

"My husband Fred was very ill when he came to the hospital. The paramedics took him to the emergency room where the doctors and nurses did the best they could." She turned her head to look at the boy's small face. "Fred barely got to say good-bye to me."

"What if I never get to say good-bye to Daddy?"

"I pray that you won't need to say good-bye."

"Is Dad in the same building that Fred died in?"

"No, your father is out of the emergency area."

"Does that mean he won't die, then?"

Grannie Smith took hold of his hand and kissed his fingers. A jumble of platitudes passed through her mind, but she couldn't bear to lie to him.

"He's made it through the night, and what we have to do is pray for him each day."

"If I pray hard enough, will he live?"

"That's up to God."

"Daddy didn't believe in God. Will God punish him for that?"

"No, Stephen. Your father is a good man, and that's what is important. Let's make our last stop at the pharmacy, and then we can return home and see what your grandmother has to say. Okay?"

Stephen pulled his hand away and turned his face forward.

"Does that mean Momma was bad?"

"Heavens no! God called her to him. She's with Him now."

"No, she's not."

"Stephen, don't say that about your mother. Do you hear?"

He shook his head and worried that he had been bad to ask his mother to come back. Maybe she would have been happier with God and not so angry. Then no one would have died or gotten hurt. But he had missed her so much that he couldn't let her go.

chapter 45

"He's ours now." The gargoyle giggled quietly while stretching his talons.

Night had gripped the day again and the demons were set free from the wooden box.

"I'm not so sure," said the bird.

"But he has only us now." The gargoyle's giggle turned into a loathsome chuckle.

"He has his grandmother," the black snake reminded.

"Easy it will be to rid ourselves of her," the dwarf pronounced, wielding his ax at the black snake, who glided quickly out of the way.

"He doesn't protect us properly." The bird pecked at

the box to sharpen its bill. "He doesn't worry about our safety. He only tolerates us because of his mother. That worries me. What if he should turn on us?"

"Then we turn on him," said the dwarf, waving the ax in the air. "Did you see how I took his flesh and blood? How we all took his flesh and blood. Sweet flesh and salty blood." The dwarf smacked his lips. "More. We shall have more, and my ax will again make the first cut."

"Our appetites must not make an enemy of him. Too much of his flesh and too much of his blood will sour in our mouths if we cause him to turn against us." The snake wrapped its body round the dwarf, forcing the dwarf's arms to his sides.

A sly pig with a filthy snout and a stench that kept the others a distance away from him sidled up to the dwarf to snort his view.

"In a way we are his prisoners. We return to the box at dawn and must remain still during daylight. We are made to feel embarrassed about our sins. At night our sins melt away and we are cleansed."

"You've never been cleansed in your life," said the dwarf, raising his nose into the air. "No, no, we are not cleansed. Sins become pure in the dark, that's all."

"Pure nonsense," grunted the pig

The black snake moved away from the pig and the dwarf, seeking less polluted air.

"I am a snake at night. What am I during the day? Only decoration? Do all my powers vanish in the day-

light? No. I merely suffer temporary restrictions. Your ax looks dull when the sun hits it, but under the moonlight it glistens."

"We must have eternal night," shouted the dog with a man's face.

"No, we must overcome the sun," said the dwarf, waving the ax in the air.

"You are very stupid," said the black snake. "We must join forces with the light. Make the sun our friend."

"Impossible," said the dwarf. "I don't even like the heat the sun produces. It causes the color of our flesh to fade. It takes the boy away from us. It drives our mistress deeper into the land of the dead so that we can't call upon her for assistance. I hate the sun."

"And because of that the sun will always rule over you." The black snake coiled its body and raised its head so all could hear him. "We are handsome at night. Why can't we be the same during the day? The boy is beautiful under the sun and under the moonlight. We must get him to show us how to survive in both worlds."

"But it is natural for a child," said the dwarf.

"We are children too," said the dog.

"We are centuries old, fool." The dwarf turned his back on the dog, who immediately ran up to the dwarf and bit his rear end.

"Ouch!" The dwarf dropped his ax and fell forward.

"Stop!" hissed the black snake. "We can't bicker among ourselves if we expect to win over the boy."

"He hates us for what we did to his father," spoke a timid voice. An old woman with a staff came from behind the box. "He knows it was we who burned his father alive."

"But we spared the father's life," said the dwarf.

"We cannot be certain of that. He could still die." The old woman leaned heavily on her staff. "And what will the boy do then?"

All the demons looked at each other. Gradually they all bowed their heads in thought.

"We kill the boy," snuffled the pig, its head buried into rainbow-colored wax.

"The mother's loins will not abide by that," said the old woman. "She'll rage."

"And we'll destroy her too," shouted the man/dog.

"If we are to survive, someone who links to both worlds must also survive."

"Then the mother is useless."

"The boy is our charm, and we must prey on his weakness."

"The fact that he is human?" asked the bird.

"No, the pity he feels for others who are in pain." The old woman shuffled over to the dwarf. "He hates you. I can see it in his eyes. If we can make him pity you, then we have won."

The dwarf looked around at all the other demon faces. "He doesn't hate me."

"He merely despises you," said the old woman. "You

try to wield power over the boy. He knows that. Your eyes tell all."

"Small and beady," added the black snake.

The dwarf's eyebrows crouched down over his eyes.

"Listen, the mother doesn't understand the boy. He'll break under too much evil. He should be introduced gently, slowly." The old woman leaned heavily on her staff.

"No!" shouted the dwarf. "Enough of this babysitting. We must force him to our will."

"Shhh!" The old woman spun in a circle and covered her lips with an index finger. "She's here."

Each demon bowed as gracefully as he or she could. The black snake reared up and dramatically bowed his head.

"The boy is mine," the mother said. "He is of my flesh. He takes my place while I cannot reach into his world. But through him I'll become stronger and will take material shape."

"You have no body," reminded the dwarf.

"I have my son."

The demons all began whispering to each other.

"The boy!"

"She'll take the boy's body."

"She'll be with us again."

"His will is frail."

"He'll have no defense."

"He has a soul," the tiny old woman stated. "A pure soul."

The mother blew her breath on the demons and all were silenced while she spoke.

"He has killed in my name. Under my instruction. Stephen's soul is no longer free of sin. His father is maimed. All because he set you free."

The black snake coiled into a ball, and the old woman used her staff to return to the box.

The rest of the demons cheered.

chapter 46

"Momma, they won't let me see Daddy. I begged Grandma to sneak me in the way you and Dad did when Grandma was in the hospital. But she said this was different, that Daddy was very sick, and he might get sicker if I brought in germs. I promised not to bring any germs with me, but Grandma laughed. Why did she laugh? Doesn't she know Daddy needs me?"

"Of course she does, Stephen. Every night you say your prayers with her. She always hears you mention your father, but sometimes you forget me."

"I never forget you, Momma. Even if I don't say

your name I still pray for you. I always pray for you. I pray that you come to me every night."

"And don't I answer your prayers, Stephen?"

"Could you make Grandma take me to see Daddy?"

"Grandma can be so unfair. She makes you suffer so."

"Not really. She just won't let me see Daddy. I asked her to let me stay in this house like you asked me to do and she has. She brought over several suitcases of clothes. I don't think she likes the way you kept the utility room. I heard her complaining and spraying and wiping. It's really clean in there now."

"Grandma is tedious."

"What's tedus?"

"She's finicky. Nothing I ever did made her happy. She was very cruel to me."

"Did she spank you?"

"She tortured me with her words."

"Bad words?"

Stephen felt a wave of coldness and knew that his mother hugged him. A soft kiss on his cheek gave him goose bumps.

"Don't you like Grandma anymore?"

"She hurt me very much, and she's never said that she was sorry."

"Did you ask her to say she was sorry?"

"I shouldn't have to, Stephen. If she loved me she'd know when I hurt. She'd cuddle me the way I embrace you."

Stephen's shoulders shivered with the cold. He

looked at his hands and saw they had turned red. His breath came out in puffs of smoke, and his toes curled inside his slippers.

"I would feel at peace if only she once said she was sorry for all she's done." His mother sighed and let her arms fall away from Stephen.

"Maybe I can help," Stephen said. "I could tell her how you feel and she'd . . . But she'd never believe me. She'd think I was telling lies."

"Of course she would. She has no imagination."

"Are you just my imagination?" asked Stephen, searching the room with his eyes. He saw a wisp of a shadow pass through the moonbeam spread across his bedroom carpet. From out of the dark white hands reached out for him. He almost pulled away from them but understood they were his mother's hands, and he reached out his own in greeting.

"Take my hands, Stephen, and pull me back into your world."

"I'll pull real hard, Momma. I won't let go until you're here with me again."

"I'm proud of you, Stephen."

His hands passed through the white hands. The only time his hands had ever felt this cold was when he made snowballs to throw at his dad. The boy slumped back onto his haunches, remembering his father.

"The demons hurt Daddy. We should get rid of them."

"It was your father's fault that I went away. Do you think he cared how you would feel?"

"Daddy wouldn't hurt me." The boy's bottom lip puckered out and quivered in the darkened bedroom.

"Be a brave boy."

A shapeless form spun like cotton candy in front of him. A sweet odor filled his nostrils, and Mother's soft voice said his name.

His heavy eyelids left him squinting in the dark as his body floated back down on the bed. His stuffed lion rested against his cheek, and the covers slid noiselessly across his body. The flannel shirt barred the coldness of night from touching his flesh, but the coldness of his mother's love could not be rebuffed.

chapter 47

"What is that itchy thing you just rubbed against my cheek?" asked Brandy.

"It's one of the giant spider legs," replied the witch. "Belongs to the spider that brought you to me."

Brandy began sneezing.

"Take that thing away. I'm allergic."

"If you had but known you were allergic you would have never visited me. And I would have been lonely pining for you."

"You old hag, you'd have someone else as your prisoner instead of me."

"No. Only you could make me happy. I know. I've

had many guests. Only you excite my emotions. You make me angry. You make me laugh. Sometimes in the privacy of my bedroom you make me cry."

"I've never been in your bedroom, madame."

"You come to me in my dreams. Not every night, of course, but at least twice a week."

"Without fail?"

"Hmmm." The witch thought long and hard. "One week you failed. That's when my insomnia ruled my nights."

The witch shook the spider's leg at Brandy. He sneezed again.

"I've told you I'm allergic. Why must you wave that ugly thing at me?"

"You didn't expect it to be so ugly when you first came into my house, did you?"

"I thought I would find the mummified spider in one piece. You've ruined it. I have no further use for it. It is now ugly."

"It was ugly when it was whole," the witch shared in a whisper. "Almost as ugly as your father is now."

"How would you know what my father looks like?"

The witch shrugged her shoulders and replaced the spider leg on a shelf.

"Don't go," called out Brandy. "What do you know of my father? I've never spoken of him."

"But I know him all the same. Don't you recognize me?"

"I know you only as the witch who is holding me captive."

"I'm more than that." The witch gave a little dance and then headed for the staircase.

"Do I know you from someplace else?" Brandy asked.

The witch paused with her back to Brandy.

"Think on it. I do love having you back."

"I've never been here before, and my father never would have been either. You are playing games, madame, and the games are cruel and childish."

"No, no, this is no game. This is very, very serious."

The witch faced him, and suddenly he thought her features had melted and reformed into someone else, but when he rubbed his eyes he saw just the old witch staring back at him.

"You are the one who is ugly," said Brandy. "My father is a handsome man."

"Yes, once he was handsome, but no more. You can't even stand to look at him."

"No, it is the others who stop me," cried out Brandy, his hands gripping the hardness of the bars.

"Your fault. No one else to blame."

The witch toddled up the long staircase.

chapter 48

Stephen awoke from his dream hearing the screams of his grandmother coming from downstairs. First he grabbed his stuffed lion tightly before pushing the covers to the side and jumping out of bed. The sun temporarily blinded him until he reached the door and entered the hallway. His foot almost slipped on the first step, and he had to let go of his stuffed lion to grab onto the banister.

"I can't believe this." He heard his grandmother yell.

"Sabbatical. I pulled some strings and have four months off all to myself."

He recognized the voice of his Aunt Rosemary and the giggles of his cousin Robin.

"Robin," he yelled, tearing down the stairs to end up in Robin's lap.

Rosemary lifted him up into the air.

"Hey, you're getting a mite heavy to be sitting in your cousin's lap."

"Isn't it wonderful, Stephen? Rosemary and Robin are going to be living with us for a while."

"He's gotten so big," Robin said. "You're not a baby anymore."

"I wasn't a baby the last time you saw me," said Stephen. "I haven't been a baby for a long time. Daddy says I eat like the Big Bruiser."

"Who's the Big Bruiser?" asked Mabel.

"Mom, I get the feeling Jacob and Stephen have spent some time watching wrestling."

"Oh, no. I wish Jacob would have some common sense."

Rosemary's cold stare stopped Mabel from continuing.

"Come into the kitchen. I was letting Stephen sleep late, but I do have coffee on, and I can make some waffles with fresh strawberries."

"And whipped cream?" asked Robin.

"Do you think your grandmother would forget whipped cream?" Mabel pushed Robin's wheelchair into the kitchen. "There's a little room between the kitchen and the basement door. It was probably meant to be used as a pantry, but right now there's nothing in it. We could move the cot into that room, and Robin could sleep on the first floor."

"No!" Stephen's emphatic tone stopped the procession.

"Excuse me, Stephen, but where do you think your cousin should sleep?"

"She can have my room, and I'll sleep on the cot in the little room."

Mabel and Rosemary looked at each other and smiled.

"Don't be silly, Stephen, I can't go up and down the stairs. How will I sneak into the kitchen for midnight snacks if I'm sleeping upstairs in your room?" said Robin.

"I'll bring them up," he suggested.

"It's quite warm in there, and the window looks out at the garden." Mabel continued with her conversation ignoring Stephen's suggestion.

"I don't want her sleeping near the basement," Stephen said.

"We're not putting Robin in the basement."

"It's all right, Mom. Robin will sleep upstairs in my room. I think he'd like that better, wouldn't you?"

Stephen nodded his head.

At the table Stephen sat next to his cousin.

"So, are you going to go to my school while you're here?"

"No. Mom home-schools me."

"Huh?"

"Mom teaches me at home and I have a tutor."

"A what?"

"A teacher comes in and teaches math and English. Mom takes care of the rest of the subjects."

"Wow! Don't you miss your friends?"

"My friends visit me after they're finished with school."

"Are you going to teach me too, Aunt Rosemary?"

"No, you'll have to go off to school."

"You could come to school with me, Robin, but I'm not in your grade. You might get bored."

"That's okay; we can play games when you come home."

"And after you do your homework." Mabel began blending the flour and the milk.

"Does your mom give you homework?"

"All the time." Robin made a face.

Stephen threw his arms around Robin and kissed her cheek which was chubby and soft. He loved Robin's blue eyes that twinkled most of the time.

"Want me to take you for a ride after breakfast?" Robin asked Stephen.

"None of that," said Rosemary. "Stephen's much too big now to be sitting on your lap. Besides, I don't want the two of you knocking things over."

"The wheelchair isn't a toy," said Mabel.

"Mom. He's simply too big. Let's leave it at that."

"I'm getting a new wheelchair," Robin shouted at Stephen. "It'll be motorized so I'll be able to speed around and really knock things over."

"Can I try it out?" Stephen bounced up and down in his chair.

"Rosemary, are you listening to this?"

"Hmmm."

"Shouldn't you say something to the boy?"

"It'll be another couple of months before we get the new wheelchair, Stephen. But whenever you come to visit you'll be welcome to take a ride in it."

"Rosemary!" Mabel cut her finger while slicing a strawberry. "You're as bad as the children."

"Worse, Mom. I'm kinda hoping that I'll be able to fit in it too."

"Mom, if you drive the wheelchair like you do the car we should get special insurance for it."

Rosemary and the children laughed. Mabel washed the cut on her finger and shook her head.

☆ ☆ ☆

Late in the evening Robin and Stephen sat together in the boy's room. Rosemary had placed Robin on the bed allowing the children to play a game of checkers.

"Robin?"

"Yeah."

"Did you ever walk?"

"Not really. Mom said I was never able to take more than a few steps as a baby. I spent most of my time falling on my face."

"Do you have bones in your legs?"

Robin looked up from the board with a mixture of surprise and mirth.

"Of course I have bones in my legs." She pulled up the right pant leg of her jeans and invited Stephen to feel her bones.

Cautiously he rested his small hand on her shin and squeezed. Robin didn't react.

"I didn't squeeze too hard?"

"I can't feel much in my legs."

"Your missing the nerves in your legs?"

"I think they're there. It's just that they went to sleep. I can feel it a little when the doctor pricks me with pins."

"Why does he do that? Doesn't it hurt?"

"It would probably hurt you more than me." She reached over quickly and grabbed the bottom portion of his left leg and squeezed. Stephen pulled away giggling.

"You're ticklish."

Stephen saw the bright sparkle in her eyes and immediately jumped off the bed.

"No fair. I still have my nerves," he said. "How come you don't?"

"I told you. They're asleep."

"Will they ever wake up?"

Robin shrugged and turned her face away.

"Do you think a witch stole your nerves?" Stephen spoke in a lowered voice.

Surprised, she turned back to him.

"A witch! What would a witch do with my nerves?"

"Make building putty."

"Yuck, building putty. They use mortar, cement, not people's nerves to build houses. How silly."

"But witches might use nerves when they build their cottages."

"They use candy to build houses so they can attract weird kids like you. Whatever made you think building putty was made from people's nerves?"

"I just heard it someplace. I didn't really believe it. I was just making sure."

"Someone was teasing you. Did Molly tell you that?"

"No."

"Ask Molly when you see her, she'll tell you."

Stephen rubbed his thigh against the bedspread.

"Molly's dead. I'm never going to ask her anything 'cause she might come back to tell me."

"I'm sorry, Stephen. I didn't know. How did it happen?"

Stephen mumbled some words and Robin had to ask him to speak louder.

"I think maybe it was a wolf."

"Do you have wolves around here?"

"At the zoo."

"Did one escape?"

"Maybe."

"Come back up here. I'm not going to tickle you. I promise."

Stephen climbed back up on his bed and pulled the socks off his hot feet. Robin lurched for his feet and he jerked away laughing.

"You look better when you're laughing. When you're serious you get little lines in between your eyebrows." Robin rested an index finger on the exact spot and Stephen tilted his head back to take a bite out of her finger. Both children became uproarious, attracting their grandmother's attention.

"Are you two all right?"

"We were just talking about how a witch stole my nerves," Robin explained.

"A witch what?"

"All this time the doctors thought I had some fancy named disease when really a witch stole my nerves. That's why I can't walk."

"You shouldn't make up stories like that, sweetheart."

"It's true. A witch stole into my nursery one

night and and opened a little hole in each of my legs so she could draw the nerves out."

"Don't be telling your cousin such stories."

"Dad tells me stories like that all the time."

"Really? How fun. Can you remember any? I'd like to hear some of them," said Robin

"Not tonight, dear. You two are going to be going to bed soon." Mabel pulled the wheelchair closer to the bed.

"Dad tells me the stories just before I go to sleep."

"Does he read them out of books?" Robin asked.

"He doesn't have to. He's a. . .schola and knows them by heart. My favorite stories are about Brandy and the witch."

"Did she steal Brandy's nerves?"

"No, she wants his hand for some potion because there's a wart growing on it. And she lives in a house made of people's bones, but not Momma's."

"Rosemary," Mabel yelled. "Isn't it bedtime for the children?"

"Before I go to bed Stephen has to tell me a Brandy and witch story." Robin eagerly sought to make herself comfortable.

"I can't do the witch's voice like Daddy does. He sounds like a little old lady."

"Come into my cottage, little boy." Robin hammed the voice of a witch, delighting Stephen.

"No more about witches," Mabel said. "Here,

I'll help you back into the wheelchair, sweetheart."

"But I don't want to go to bed. I want to hear about what witches do. What if I want to be a witch someday?" Robin teased.

"That's enough! No one in this room is becoming a witch."

The children sat stunned by Mabel's loud voice.

"We were just playing, Grandma. Neither of us are really witches."

Stephen sank back onto his pillows and wondered whether witches were bad people. Often witch stories would make him laugh, and Momma . . . He remembered how different Momma was now that she was dead. Maybe dying made her angry. He could see how that would upset a person.

chapter 49

The nurse took the flowers Rosemary carried into the hospital room.

"I'll find a vase. There's a chair near the bed. He's been popular, and we've had to limit his guests, but since you're family there's no problem."

"Thank you." Rosemary worried her bottom lip. The smell of hospitals always made her nauseous. The silence of the room made her appreciate the noises coming from the hall. She felt awkward in the hospital garb required to visit burn patients.

Slowly she crossed the room, immediately seeing the metal chair by the bed. She glanced over at

Jacob, who appeared to be asleep, and she wondered whether she should stay.

You're here now. May as well sit and wait for him to wake up.

When she sat, the chair scraped the floor, and Jacob's eyes slowly opened.

"Sorry. I didn't wake you?"

"Rosemary." He closed his eyes again.

"I can leave if you want."

"No. Did you fly in just to visit me?"

"I thought I'd be able to help Mother out. I've taken a four-month sabbatical and brought Robin with me. She and Stephen get on well, and I thought it might help him to have her around."

"And I bet you all are staying at my house."

"Do you mind? Stephen doesn't want to leave."

Jacob raised a hand and winced with pain.

"I told Mabel it isn't safe there."

"The firemen . . ."

"What the hell do the firemen know? They think I was drunk."

"They didn't find any alcohol in your blood. What were you doing?"

"The demons were partying."

"What the hell are you talking about?"

"Cathy. You knew she was a witch, didn't you?"

Rosemary remained quiet.

"You know what Cathy was doing down in the

basement, don't you?"

"Stop, Jacob."

"Have you been in the basement? Dare you go into the basement?"

"There's nothing down there that will hurt anyone."

"Look at me, Rosemary. I'm proof of the opposite."

"Cathy wouldn't have caused this to happen to you."

"Why not?"

"She was a good person, Jacob. At times she could be moody, but she meant no harm to anyone. Practicing witchcraft was like a hobby. She had an interest in the supernatural but was always careful not to attract evil spirits."

"Have you been in the basement?"

"Stephen doesn't want anyone going into the basement. You can imagine between seeing his mother dead and seeing you . . ." Rosemary's voice trailed off.

"If you care about your family, Rosemary, you'll move everyone out of that house. I want my son safe. I don't want him under his mother's influence."

"She's dead, Jacob."

"Not in that house."

"Mom said you had been talking nonsense and thought it due to the medications they've been pumping into you."

"I'll get a lawyer, Rosemary, and have my son taken away from Mabel."

"What are you going to tell the lawyer, that there are demons living in the house and one of them is my mother?"

"You and your mother are stupid. Cathy didn't have to conjure you and Mabel up. Mabel was Cathy's own nightmare, not mine. Although I do wonder whether she'll become Stephen's nightmare."

"I'll not let that happen."

"I swear I'll take custody away from Mabel if she doesn't take Stephen out of that house."

"No lawyer is going to pay any attention to your talk about ghosts and demons. If I were you, I'd keep my mouth shut, or Stephen may be taken away from you."

"Is that a threat?"

"Good advice." Rosemary stood. "We'll take good care of Stephen."

"Ask him about how he talks to his mother."

"It gives him comfort."

Jacob slowly shook his head.

"Somehow she's communicating with him. I didn't believe Molly either. She's dead, Rosemary."

"Mother told me."

"I beg you to believe me. Cathy got even for the affair Molly and I had."

"That's your guilt dredging up all kinds of fantasies. Why didn't she kill Molly and injure you while she was alive?"

"Because the depression took over. Her pathetic poor-me act cost her her life."

"Once dead she had a change of mind?"

"She blames us for her suicide."

"If this is true, she's gotten even and can finally rest."

"She wants back."

"To come back from the dead?"

"I'm sure of it. She can never rest where she's destined to go."

"You're saying she's going to hell. I thought you were agnostic, Jacob."

"After what I've seen and been through, I don't know what I am."

"Critical patient who needs his sleep. If you're good I might come back."

Jacob smiled.

"What can I do from this bed other than call a lawyer?"

"Don't. You'll be making trouble for yourself. No one is going to believe little demons did this to you."

"I can't die, Rosemary."

She sighed. The doctors had reminded her of Jacob's critical condition. Death lingered close at hand to burn victims, especially to those with the extensive burns Jacob had.

"You're not going to die."

"No. I refuse to die. I'll come home and take Stephen back."

"My mother and I wouldn't keep you from your son."

"Cathy would."

chapter 50

After dinner Rosemary took cleaning duty. Mom had cooked one of her special meals that no one else found special. However, no one told Mom since she had spent so many hours preparing the bland meal. Rosemary's mother didn't believe in spices, but she did believe the longer food was cooked the healthier it would be. No trichinosis would survive Mom's cooking.

As she squeezed every last dish into the dishwasher she heard the children scream with joy when Mom allowed them to watch television for an hour. After that, Mom would require the children to have some cool-down time before bed. Rosemary remembered how she had dreaded Mom's rules when she herself was a child.

"Can we take some ice cream into the living room while we're watching TV?"

" 'May we,' " Grandmother corrected.

"You may and can," Rosemary yelled to her daughter. She immediately went to the freezer before Grandma could get there. She hated watching her mother scoop ice cream out of the container as if she were weighing the exact amount. Rosemary doubled up on the scoops. Somehow her mother managed to remain silent.

The children rushed off to the living room, carrying their ice cream.

"I'm going up to my room to grade some papers," Mabel said.

"Okay, Mom, but remember you'll have to cool down before bed."

"Don't be sarcastic, Rosemary."

Mabel left the room with head held high.

It only took another fifteen minutes to finish up in the kitchen. Proudly she placed the kitchen towel on its rack and checked on the children, who were mesmerized by a cartoon program.

Now for the basement, she thought.

Halfway down the basement stairs Rosemary shivered. Her mother had lowered the temperature on the thermostat, not because she feared the furnace but because she feared the bills that would come in. Rosemary reminded her Jacob still paid the bills and Robin had to be kept warm, but Rosemary had lost the battle.

At the bottom of the stairs she spied the table covered with wax.

"You must have been really busy, Cathy," she murmured.

The furnace and the back wall had singe marks from when Jacob had caught fire. Otherwise no evidence remained of the tragedy.

She looked for the wooden box she had given her sister for storing some of her utensils, finally finding it beneath a tarp. The wood had lost its sheen but looked the same as when she had given it to Cathy. One of the hinges might be a bit loose, but that could be repaired. She found nothing inside.

"I guess no one would notice if I took this back, Cath. You don't have a need for it anymore."

She thought she heard voices. Scratchy, thin voices that spoke too fast. When she heard hissing sounds, she turned toward the furnace, but it hadn't come on.

A glass jar spilled to the floor and fragmented into pieces.

She realized she should clean it up in case someone else came downstairs, but her gut feel was to run.

"Jacob's just spooking me." Her voice almost

sounded like an echo.

She placed the box on the table and searched for something to clean up the glass. While doing so, another object fell to the floor. This time it was a paint can. She picked it up and noticed the can had to be at least two-thirds full.

How did it fall off the shelf? Must have been put down in a precarious position. Near the edge.

She decided to put the basement off-limits until she had the nerve to stay and clean up the mess.

Picking up the box, she thought she saw movement.

Hell, this house probably has mice like most old homes.

She ran her sleeve across the top of the box, trying to regain some of the original sheen of the wood. Occupied with her task, she almost tripped over the first step. She grabbed hold of the banister, and the voices she heard seemed to get louder, as if little people were shouting at each other. Cautiously she began the climb. Midway she heard a whole shelf of jars crash to the floor. She ran the rest of the way until she found herself in the living room.

"Hi, Mom. They're having a part two; can we watch for another hour?"

Startled by her daughter's voice Rosemary almost dropped the box.

"Are you okay, Mom?"

"Sure. And since I don't see your grandma

anywhere around, go right ahead and watch as much television as you want."

"That doesn't belong to you!" screeched Stephen.

Stephen ran toward his aunt and reached for the box but couldn't quite touch it.

"I gave this box to your mother, and I'd like to have it back now that she doesn't need it anymore."

"The uglies need it," he cried.

"The uglies? What are they?"

Stephen's face looked like he would burst into tears.

"Stephen, who are the uglies?"

"Please, Aunt Rosemary, put the box back down in the cellar. Don't make the uglies come look for it."

"They won't have far to go, since I planned on keeping it in my room."

"The show's starting, Stephen. Come on or you'll miss it," Robin called to him.

"Go ahead, Stephen, get back to your show and let me worry about what to do with the box."

"No! You don't belong in the basement, and the box doesn't belong to you. Give it back!"

Stephen's screaming surprised Rosemary. He did need counseling. She knew her mother had suggested the idea to Jacob.

"You have to calm down or Grandma will be coming down and poof, there will go your television show."

"I don't care. The box belongs in the cellar. Momma kept it there."

Rosemary decided not to debate with the boy. He had been through enough.

"All right. I'll put the box back under the tarp in the basement. But I would like to take it with me when I go. I thought Robin could use it for some of her art supplies."

"She can't have it," Stephen yelled.

"Mom, I don't want the stupid box. I just want to watch the show right now."

"Okay, I'm sorry, Stephen. It was your mother's box, and if you want to keep it, I shouldn't take it. I'll put it downstairs later, or would you like me to leave it in your room?"

"Now. Put it back in the basement now." Stephen's stern voice sounded too adult, which grated on Rosemary.

She had to take several deep breaths before she agreed.

"By the way, where's the broom and a dustpan?"

"The kitchen cupboard," he answered calmly.

"Go back to your show. I'm on my way to the basement."

Rosemary made a detour to the kitchen. On her way out she caught sight of Stephen still standing at the living room threshold, waiting for her to return the box. She waved the broom and dustpan at him and headed back down the stairs.

A stillness settled over the basement. She found it difficult catching her breath, and the ceiling light seemed dimmer.

She could have sworn the bulb grew brighter when she slipped the box back under the tarp. The tarp almost moved of its own accord, carefully assisting Rosemary in covering the box.

"Shit, Cathy, what were you doing down here?"

A peace settled over the entire basement as she swept up the glass and tension flowed out of her body. As the last scoop of glass fell into the garbage bag, Rosemary's arms grew weak. Her head ached and her knees buckled, letting her body fall to the floor.

"Leave it." Stephen's soft voice awakened her failing senses.

"Robin needs to potty," he said from the top of the stairs.

Rosemary stood and nodded.

"Bring up the broom and dustpan," he reminded her as she stood empty handed.

Afraid to bend over because of her dizziness, she asked Stephen to carry them up for her. He obeyed without giving any contradiction.

Standing next to her he asked, "The box is under the tarp?"

She nodded, and they both climbed the stairs.

chapter 51

"Not good," said the old woman.

"What do you mean?" asked the dwarf.

"She'll become suspicious."

"So what! We can handle her."

"We're not strong enough to make ourselves known. We still exist under the mother's thumb."

"Not for long," whispered the dog with the man's head.

The tiny old woman's eyes scanned the basement. Her nose scented the air and her ears listened patiently. Seeing, hearing, smelling no presence of death she turned to the dog with the man's head.

"You are too cocky, Master Dog. You speak before

you know it to be safe. What if she had heard you?"

"She is controlled by death now. She comes only when death wills her back into this world, and for that she must fight."

"Yes, but if she regains a physical presence in this world we will be in great danger of being sent back into limbo."

"I for one would never allow that to happen," stated the dwarf.

"How would you prevent it?" the old woman asked, her chin protruding grandly into the darkness of the basement.

"I have my ax."

"Violence. Ah, you think we are controlled by only physical forces. What of the powers that your ax can't chop into pieces?"

"She is right, dwarf." The snake inched its way closer to the small group. "We weren't only brought to life by blood and flesh. An invisible desire reached out and plucked us from our sleeps. It is her hunger and spiritual strength that keeps us as we are."

"She will rob her son's life and be stronger than before," predicted the old woman.

"Nonsense. The boy—"

"The boy is hers," interrupted the old woman. "She has him firmly gripped inside her fists. He belongs to her more than we do. Look at his eyes. They are hers. Look at his features. They are hers. Soon his soul will

be hers too."

"You live in fear, old woman. Why?" The dwarf approached the old woman and grabbed hold of her staff. "You limp around not as a great spirit of the dark world but as a timid hag who has lost all her powers. Is that true? Have you lost your strength? Were you plucked too soon from your sleep?"

The old woman smelled the dwarf's foul breath and waited for him to rip the staff from her hand.

"You're a coward, Master Dwarf, to pick on an ancient lady. Is robbing canes from the elderly another talent that you displayed in your former life?" the snake taunted from a distance.

"I know you, serpent, from somewhere although I can not immediately place the time or land."

"Perhaps he didn't look like a snake in another life. I certainly wasn't a pig. At least not a barn animal pig. As a seaman I rarely bathed although my girth equaled that of a well fed pig." The pig snorted in delight reminiscing about his pirate days.

"He always was a snake, I'm sure of that." The dwarf let go of the staff to rub his beard. "I never met you on the battle field. No."

"Does it matter, Master Dwarf?" the old woman asked.

"Yes, it does. For I am sure I owe him something and it wouldn't be a pat on the back. More like a dagger between his ribs."

"Not between my ribs, Master Dwarf."

"My ax can cut you into tiny pieces and I can force each slice into your mouth." The dwarf moved closer to the snake.

"You have met me before, Master dwarf. At that time you caused me great pain, not to my body but to my heart and mind. I had a wife, children. Many children. Each a prize for a man growing old too quickly."

"Our former lives mean nothing here," interrupted the gargoyle. "Stop this conversation now."

"An old man." The dwarf reviewed all his ancient battles and the ravaging he had done of villages and castles. Too many to place an old man with a family. "Did I know you, Master Serpent?"

"Of me, yes."

"Daylight is drawing near. Stop this talk. We have the box back. A place to hide while the sun is up." The gargoyle interposed his body between the dwarf and the snake.

"An old man that I had heard of but didn't meet in person. A counselor for a king, no doubt. A bag of bones slinking about a castle, whispering perversions into the ear of some king." The dwarf walked around the gargoyle. "A woman stolen from me."

"Hardly stolen. Whatever would she have wanted with a dwarf?" The snake's voice dripped with derision. It inched its way closer to the dwarf. "Remember Rebecca? The pretty daughter of the-"

"The jester's daughter! The trollop!" The dwarf

laughed so hard he bent over holding his stomach.

"You wanted her. Watched her night after night."

"Yes, counting the number of men she seduced."

"Liar."

The old woman came forward.

"This is tiresome. The woman and her children are dead. You no longer have a wife, Master Serpent. A jester's daughter. Certainly you wouldn't hold a grudge this long for a jester's daughter, Master Dwarf."

"I remember the woman. Her soft flesh, her sweet breath, the long fingers plucking the harp, driving men mad with the music of her voice. Yes, Master Serpent, I recall Rebecca. There's something else though that causes me more fury. At the end the king who you advised had me disemboweled before lowly villagers at your behest."

"A fitting punishment for the death of my family." The snake lifted its head high.

"We are here now, in the present. We have work to do," the gargoyle said. "That work takes precedence over grudges. When we are freed from this woman's control then the two of you can decide this whatever way you please."

"Hatred is impossible to control." The dwarf spoke slowly, articulating each syllable clearly. "We have been drawn back into the world at the same time for a reason. It is to meet and settle our dispute."

"What will the two of you settle?" asked the pig. "You've both been destroyed before and will be again.

Then you will be called back for another round of making these human lives miserable. You really gain nothing by sending each other back to hell. How can you enjoy the turmoil we cause in this world when you're busily worrying about getting the spirit next to you? Master Dwarf, I think both you and the serpent managed in a previous life to bring hell down to earth in each others lives. I call it a draw."

"The first sensible thing to come out of that pig's mouth," said the two-headed bird. One head addressed the other but the words were overheard by the entire collection of demons.

"The pig is right," said the gargoyle. "You both will live on for eternity. Does that mean you will seek each other out in every life you snatch from the world?"

"Rebecca pleaded for her life. The servants heard her cries for our children." The snake drifted closer to the dwarf.

"A human's reaction." The dwarf gloated, reminiscing over the pain he had inflicted over the generations.

"That pain will never end." The serpent's flesh became a paler shade of black. Its tongue flicked the air reaching for dark memories he knew should be forgotten. "Human she was, Master Dwarf, and knew not the evil we shared and brought upon her people. But I think we both will always love her. That is why you had to destroy her."

The dwarf opened his mouth to deny such a feeling

but could not pronounce the word that would reject the woman Rebecca.

Daylight struck the basement like thunder. A frosty wind lifted the demons and distributed them about the rectangular box. The snake and dwarf were separated. The dwarf settled upon the lid of the box, his arm letting the ax droop to his feet. The snake coiled into a ball on one side of the box and didn't lift its head until night.

chapter 52

"Why were you so mean to my mommy?" asked Robin.

"Mean? She doesn't understand what could have happened to her. To you, even, if she had kept the box in the room where you sleep."

"What could have happened?"

"Bad things."

"Like what happened to your mommy and daddy?"

Stephen hung his head in a sulk.

"Tell me," Robin said. "Tell me so that I can understand."

Stephen upended the chessboard, scattering all the pieces onto the floor.

"Why are you so mean?" she asked.

"I'm not." He heard his own voice ring loudly in his ears.

"Yes, you are."

"I'm trying to protect everyone." He looked at a blurred image of Robin.

"Don't cry, Stephen. I don't want to make you cry. I want to help."

"I think my momma is doing bad things." Stephen muttered the words, and Robin had to ask him to repeat.

He looked at her wondering whether she would believe or laugh at him. She had never made fun of him before, and maybe she could understand. At least she might not have the same doubts as the adults.

"My momma is back."

"Back? From the dead?"

Stephen nodded.

"Why would she come back? Does she want to protect you?"

"She says she loves me, but her hugs and kisses are different. I used to feel warm in her arms, but no more. When she hugs me I feel colder. It's like someone threw open the door in the middle of winter during a big snowstorm."

"Maybe that's because she's dead."

He looked at Robin and didn't see her laugh. She intently listened.

"Yeah, maybe. But she's not as nice as before. She's angry."

"At you?"

"No. At Daddy and Molly. And Molly died and Daddy is in the hospital and I don't know when he'll be coming home."

"What if he doesn't come home?" asked Robin.

"He can come home because I can take care of him. I can do everything the hospital is doing."

He saw Robin make a face.

"You don't believe me?"

"It's just that I heard Mom say he isn't in good shape. He doesn't look the same, Stephen."

"Have you seen him?"

"No, but Mom has, and so has Grandma."

"They won't take me to see him."

"Hospitals don't allow little boys."

"I'm not little anymore. I can do things that adults can't."

"You mean the somersaults you do?" Robin smiled.

"Not dumb stuff like that." Robin started to irritate him. He stood to leave the table where they both had been sitting.

"Don't go, Stephen. I'm sorry if I hurt your feelings." She shrugged. "I like it when you do somersaults, and I've never seen anyone who can do as many as you at one time."

"I've increased the number. Dad counted them for me, and I can do at least six more than before."

"Would you show me?" she asked shyly.

Stephen scratched his nose thinking about whether he should or not. He always made her laugh when he did the somersaults, and he liked it when she laughed. Her laughter was catching, like the flu, Dad used to say.

Stephen started to go into his tumbles when a scream sounded from the basement. Instantly Stephen jumped to his feet and beat his aunt down the stairs.

Grandma stood next to the table covered with a rainbow of wax. She held her hand to her heart and took deep breaths.

"Mom, what's wrong?"

Rosemary pushed Stephen out of the way to reach her mother.

At first Grandma didn't speak; she kept huffing for air. Finally she uttered one word. "Mice."

"Oh, Mom, all that noise over a mouse."

"There was more than one."

"I don't see any now."

"They scurried behind the furnace. We have to get traps."

"Not traps," Stephen said. "The traps could

hurt them."

"We'll get little mouse hotels and let them go outside the house," Rosemary suggested.

"Hotels?" Mabel said, shocked at the idea.

"It traps them without killing them, Mom."

"Who cares . . . ?" Mabel stopped when she looked into Stephen's face. "Yes, we'll get nice hotels for them. They'll be very happy there, I'm sure."

"You shouldn't be down here. Why is everybody coming down here? This place belongs to Momma."

"It did belong to your mother, Stephen, but now we have to clean up a bit. This table could be donated to charity once we clean it up. You could help me, Stephen." Mabel attempted to draw him into the activity.

"Everything down here is Momma's." Stephen felt anger building inside him. If everyone left Momma's things alone nothing bad would happen.

Rosemary squatted down in front of Stephen.

"Do you think your mother caused the bad accident that happened to your father?"

"We just want to be alone together," he said, a hint of a quiver in his voice.

Rosemary hugged him and whispered in his ear.

"What did your mother do down here?"

Stephen broke free from her embrace.

"I don't care about any of you. If you want to die, go ahead. Die, and Momma will still take care of me." He ran up the stairs.

chapter 53

"Oh, my God, Rosemary, what did Cathy expose him to?"

"Jacob thinks Cathy caused his accident."

"You think he's influenced the boy?" Mabel moved closer to her daughter, leaning lightly on Rosemary's shoulder.

"Mom, you know Cathy practiced witchcraft."

"Don't tell me you think Cathy is a ghost willing awful things to happen. Next you're going to tell me we should bring in an exorcist."

"No, Mom, but Jacob thinks that somehow Cathy also caused Molly's death, and no one has figured out what happened to her."

"A stray animal. Maybe she took some rabid dog or something into her car. She may have felt sorry for the animal, but it turned on her."

Rosemary took her mother's arm and suggested they go upstairs.

"We have to clean this place up, Rosemary. Once all this stuff is gone Stephen will start healing. He comes down here, and all he sees is his mother's paraphernalia. What the hell is a pentagram doing in a Christian house?" Mabel reached over to the table and picked up an oval inscribed with a pentacle. "This is a sin to have, Rosemary."

"Mom, the pentacle isn't a sin. It's what a person uses the pentacle for that can be evil."

"The damn thing doesn't belong here." Mabel broke the slim plaster cast in half. "Stephen doesn't need to see pentacles sitting around. How could Jacob be so stupid as to leave it here? Perhaps it's just as well the accident happened."

"Mom!"

"He doesn't know how to raise a child." Mabel hesitated. "I'm not sounding very Christian now, am I?"

"You're sounding scared." Rosemary searched her mother's face.

"There's been one tragedy after another in this family. I don't know how much more Stephen can take, but I'm certainly near the breaking point. Thank God you came to help."

The two women embraced. The pentacle slipped from Mabel's hand, hitting the floor and breaking into smaller pieces.

"I'll clean it up, Mom. Go upstairs and lie down."

"There has to be a key to that door," Mabel said, glancing up at the basement door. "If not, we should get a new lock."

"Maybe Stephen is right. We should only come down here when the furnace needs attention or a repair is needed."

"Still, the door should be locked. I don't want Stephen down here."

Rosemary agreed and led her mother to the foot of the stairs.

"I don't like leaving you down here alone, Rosemary."

"I'm fine. It won't take long to clean this up. I'll just use a bit of cardboard, and there are several brushes in the corner. I'll use one of them."

"I could wait."

"Mom, you're sounding more and more like you believe in witchcraft."

"I know it's nonsense," Mabel huffed, taking the first step.

After her mother disappeared, Rosemary took one of the brushes and a stiff piece of cardboard.

As she swept the pieces up, she became more curious about what Cathy had been up to and what she could have possibly left behind. She dropped the pentacle pieces into a trash can. She dropped the brush and cardboard onto the table and looked over at the tarp.

She remembered there had been nothing inside the box and thought it odd. Maybe her sister hadn't liked the box and kept it under the tarp the whole time. She wondered whether she could sneak the box up to her room without Stephen seeing.

She walked over and lifted the tarp. The tarp shadowed the wood box. She reached down and picked the box up, turning it onto its side. A muffled cry escaped her lips and she dropped the box.

The plain wooden box now had carved figures all over it. Perhaps this was a different box. She shook out the tarp in hopes another box would fall out. None did. It had to be the same box. The color, shape, and size were all the same.

"Cathy, what is this?"

She looked around and waited, thinking she would suddenly hear her sister's voice giving an innocent reason for the finding. Realizing how foolish she was, she clasped her hands in prayer.

Finally Rosemary decided Stephen must have played some trick on her. This couldn't be the same box she had given to her sister. He must have exchanged the boxes to scare her away from the basement.

"No, Cathy, you're gone. You don't have anything to do with what's been happening. Stephen needs his hide tanned."

The furnace exploded into action, making Rosemary jump.

"Now Mom decides to turn up the heat." Rosemary shook her head and climbed the stairs, leaving the box on the floor next to the tarp. She wouldn't confront him tonight. She would speak to her daughter's psychiatrist first. He'd be able to tell her how to deal with Stephen.

chapter 54

"I need some sun," declared Brandy.

"Sun? What for? You'll only get burned." The witch had just brought down Brandy's lunch. "You're much too pale for sunbathing. Besides, there is no sun today. It's raining. Has been since early this morning."

"It's not going to rain forever," said Brandy, hesitating in lifting the lid from his plate.

"Could rain for a long time. Eat, eat! Don't be so finicky." The witch whipped the cover off the dish.

Brandy couldn't tell whether the smell of the food or the sight of the food made him sicker.

"Do you eat this stuff?" he asked.

"It's for my guests."

"Why can't I eat what you eat?"

"I have an ulcer. My diet is limited."

"I don't mind a limited diet as long as the food is edible."

The witch looked closer at the plate.

"That's snails smothered in rats' feet. Do you know how many rats I had to kill to get all those feet?"

"Please, ma'am, let the rats live. And the snails too, unless you put them in garlic butter."

"You'll get no dessert if you don't eat what's on your plate."

"Dare I ask what's for dessert?"

"Chilled bees covered in their own honey." The witch smiled proudly. When she noticed he didn't seem impressed, she said, "I pulled off the stingers."

"I'm not hungry," said Brandy, passing the plate back to the witch.

"Not hungry? You complain all the time that I starve you. Yet you hardly ever touch the food I bring.

"Your father never was like that." The witch sashayed her way toward the stairs.

"Madame, I refuse to believe that you ever met my father."

The witch paused, one foot lifted in the air, ready to settle on the bottom step of the stairway. She changed her mind and set her foot back on the cement floor of the basement and turned to face Brandy.

"Why can't you recognize me?"

"Because I never met you before I entered this house."

"Look under my sagging flesh, Brandy. Don't my eyes hold some hint?"

"All I see is a mean old woman."

"Not as old as you think."

"Had a hard life, then?"

"Hard work being a witch. Must dedicate self. No one likes you."

"If you did nice things people would like you."

"But I do nice things." The witch's voice sounded frustrated. "No one appreciates what I do. Look at your plate. Not a crumb eaten."

"Why don't you ask me what I'd like to eat?"

"You don't know what is good for you. You should follow what I say. Your father didn't. See what happened to him?"

"Nothing has happened to him. Certainly you've never caused anything to happen to him."

"Think! Who am I? What do I want?"

"If you don't know, how should I?" Brandy dropped to the floor of his cage.

"You want to practice witchcraft but don't want to learn the rules."

"I just want to get out from under your roof," Brandy said. "Maybe I could disappear with a special magic trick."

"Can't. You will always be mine. You were mine before you even walked into this house. I will tell you what

to do. Give me your hands."

"What are you going to do with my hands? Are you still searching for that stupid wart that will never grow?"

"I need your hands to make things happen."

"Good things or bad things?" Brandy asked.

"You wouldn't understand. I must have the use of your hands." The witch lunged forward and put her arms between the bars in an attempt to grasp Brandy's hands. But she couldn't come near to them.

Brandy sat on his hands.

"First tell me what you will do with my hands."

The witch jumped up and down. Her full skirt ballooned around her. Her worn shoes split apart, leaving her bare-footed.

"Look what you've done, you fool," she screamed.

"I haven't done anything. You're the one having a tantrum, not me. You look worse than me when I throw . . ." Brandy's words slowed down. He didn't throw tantrums, did he? His father would . . . What?

"Your father would tan your hide," the witch said.

"But how do you know what I'm thinking? You've never read my mind before."

"You and I are becoming one, sweety. Someday those hands . . ." the witch pointed to where he had hidden his hands, "will be mine."

"I tell you I have no wart."

"Wart? It's not the wart I want."

"You want the hands."

"I want you," the witch said, her eyes squinting into the darkness of his cage.

chapter 55

Stephen woke in a damp bed. For the first time since he was a baby he wet the bed. Ashamed, he pushed the covers onto the floor and stood. Dawn peeked in at him as he quickly pulled the wet sheet off the bed.

The dream had caused him to wet his bed. The stupid witch dream. He wished he could forget Brandy and the witch. He wished his father had never told him the story.

He pulled down the bottom of his pajamas and stepped out of them. Grandma would be angry if he put them in the laundry and what would she say when she made the bed?

For the first time in his short life he wanted to make his own bed. He'd surprise Grandma when she got up and have the bed all tidied up. But how to dry the sheet? The clean sheets were kept in the hall closet. Would Grandma hear him if he tried to retrieve a new one?

"Daddy," he called inside his lonely room.

He wanted his father home. He didn't care what Daddy looked like. He'd take care of Daddy even better than the hospital could.

Stephen went to his bedroom door and holding his breath slowly opened it. The dimmed hall light showed no one else. He crept forward, hoping he could reach the shelf on which the sheets lay. The closet door stood ajar, and he nudged it gently, opening it just enough so he could slip inside.

A whiny creak sounded in the hall.

"Oh, my Lord, you scared me, Stephen." Grandma stood at her doorway, her right hand clutching her chest the way she had been when she saw the mice in the basement.

"What are you doing up so early?" Her hand went quickly to her mouth. "What are you doing running around half-naked?"

Ooops, in his hurry he had forgotten to pull on a pair of pants.

"I'm going to the bathroom."

THE WITCH

"That's not the bathroom, child."

Stephen peeked in the closet.

"Oh!" He acted surprised.

"Don't tell me you don't know where your own bathroom is."

"I had a dream, Grandma."

"You were sleepwalking?"

Stephen vigorously nodded his head.

Grandma moved forward and opened the bathroom door.

"Hurry, you don't want Robin to see you like that."

Stephen made a run for the bathroom, shutting the door behind him. Suddenly it hit him that Grandma might go into his bedroom to remake the bed. He opened the door and ran into his grandmother's thighs.

"How could you be finished so quickly?"

"I really had to go."

Grandma heaved a sigh.

"Come on, I'll tuck you back in."

"No!" He made a dash for his bedroom and slammed the door behind him.

chapter 56

At breakfast Stephen proudly announced he made his own bed.

"Is this a first?" asked his grandmother.

"Yes." His pride beamed out from his brown eyes.

Robin applauded, and he slyly gave her a small smile.

The doorbell rang, and Stephen quickly ate what was on his plate. Grannie Smith had an early doctor's appointment and had volunteered to take him to school.

Mabel pushed a brown paper bag into his hand as Stephen ran out the door.

"Thank you, Mrs. Rosen."

"No problem. Stephen and I have become great friends."

"Grannie Smith cooks the best food. Can Robin and I come for dinner? I've been telling her about your pies."

"Stephen, that's rude," Mabel said.

"No, no. I'd love to have both children for dinner."

"Not to eat, I hope," said Rosemary, passing by the door.

"I don't want them to be a bother, Mrs. Rosen. Besides . . ." Mabel lowered her voice. "I don't approve of too much in the way of sweets."

Mrs. Rosen lowered her own voice to match Mabel's.

"I'll serve fruit for dessert."

"Apple pie is fruit," said Stephen.

Grannie Smith turned to him and placed an index finger over her lips.

"Mom, let the kids have a night out. Robin enjoys visiting."

Finally, Mabel agreed. It would give her a night off from the cooking, and she and Rosemary could enjoy an evening out.

"I'm going upstairs to check Stephen's bed," Mabel said closing the front door behind her.

"Why? I think he's too young to be hiding Penthouse magazines under the mattress." Rosemary grinned at her mother.

"I hate sarcasm." Mabel began to climb the stairs and Rosemary followed.

"Stephen seems to like Mrs. Rosen, which is good, since poor Molly is gone."

"That was terrible, Rosemary. And the scary part is they've not found the stray that killed her."

"Maybe it wasn't a stray. I read about the pit bull owners who don't secure their dogs. They can do a lot of damage."

Mabel opened the door to Stephen's room and saw the coverlet dangling sideways on the bed.

"That's what Stephen calls a made up bed." Mabel leaned to the side and waved at the disarray inside the room.

"He tried. He's too small to get all the sides even."

"Can you imagine how wrinkled the sheets and blankets are underneath?" Mabel walked into the room and started to reach down for the coverlet.

"Don't, Ma. He thinks he did good. Don't ruin it for him. He'll never make another bed if he thinks you're going to remake what he's done all the time."

"I'm doing him a favor. He can learn by example, and besides, he'll thank me for tidy sheets tonight."

Mabel whipped the coverlet off the bed, dropping it on top of a toy chest.

"I wish you wouldn't do this, Ma."

Ignoring her daughter, Mabel went on to lift the

blanket and top sheet off the bed.

"Oh, my."

"What?"

"He wet the bed."

"Not surprising."

"I caught him trying to make it to the bathroom this morning. Poor thing. Had I known, I would have insisted on changing his sheets."

"And you would have embarrassed the hell out of him."

"I'm changing them now. No sense having him sleep in this mess again tonight."

"I'm going to call Robin's psychiatrist today and make an appointment to discuss Stephen's problems."

"Will he go with you? I've been trying to get Jacob to take Stephen to a doctor."

"No, I'm not going to mention it to Stephen for now. I'll ask the doctor how this should be handled. Obviously the problem is getting worse."

"And if Jacob doesn't make it home the problem will be even worse."

"Jacob will make it home, Mom. He wants to live for Stephen. He's afraid of Cathy taking hold of the boy. All the meds muddle his mind, but I think he means it when he talks about the obsession the boy has with his mother.

"Mom, do you think she was teaching Stephen witchcraft?"

Mabel stopped in the doorway with an armful of laundry.

"Jacob believes that?"

"She had all her utensils in the basement, and Stephen followed her everywhere."

"I assumed she'd have some common sense and not involve her son."

"I tried to bring a box up out of the basement and Stephen wouldn't let me. He said it belonged to his mother, and she wanted it to stay in the basement."

"What kind of a box?"

Rosemary hesitated.

"Initially it was a plain wooden box."

"How did change?"

"I took it back to the basement and the next day I found there were images carved into it. I think somehow Stephen must have exchanged boxes."

"You mean he hid his mother's box." Mabel turned and her eyes searched the room.

"Ah, no, Ma, don't start ripping his bedroom apart."

"He won't know."

"Cathy and I always knew, even though we didn't say anything to you. Give me a few days to speak with the doctor. Please."

"Okay, but I'm still changing these smelly sheets."

"Actually, I could use some fresh sheets too, Ma," Rosemary called out as her mother headed for the laundry.

chapter 57

"There are too many people in the house," said the gargoyle. "They are all too nosey."

"I could smell the sister's scent on the box when we returned to it," said the dog with the man's head. "We must be rid of her."

"But the little one's mother hasn't freed us to act yet," The gargoyle's frown grew darker.

"Damn that woman. She moves too slowly. She wants the boy's body but refuses to snatch it from him."

"She wants him to come to her willingly. The body will be more pliant if he wills her to enter." The old woman, holding the staff, nodded her head as she spoke,

remembering old spells that bound living flesh to the dead.

"The grandmother is next. I feel the tide turning against her. She doesn't have much longer. She will be easy. If a mouse could send her into a fright, think what we can do." The dwarf smirked while leaning on his ax.

All the demons rested against the box. They were a part of the box, and yet separate when the sun lost the battle with the night.

"Shhh! Here comes the sister," whispered the snake.

Rosemary walked over to the table and began scraping the wax off. Layers splintered and gave way as she dug deeply with a spade. Careful that she didn't gouge the table top, she moved slowly, testing the depth of the wax.

"She thinks by banishing the evidence she can make us go away. Stupid woman." The dwarf leaned out as far as he could to watch the sister.

"What if she should take that spade to us?" whispered the snake. "What if she cuts up our bodies before the dark has come?"

All the demons waited in silent fear. Their bodies trembled with each jab she made into the rainbow-colored wax. The gargoyle was near to fainting. The dog with the man's head cowered and its hair stood on end. The bird with two heads settled each head deeply under each wing. The old woman lowered the hood of her cloak over her face, shielding her face from the ravages of daylight. The snake insinuated itself under the witch's cloak.

THE WITCH

Even the pointy tips of the witch's shoes couldn't drive the snake away.

Rosemary spent the hour smoothing the surface of the table. The visible wax was gone, but when she ran the palm of her hand across the surface, she felt an even skin of wax that would be harder to remove without damaging the table.

She decided to come back later with a liquid cleaner. Turning, with the spade still in her hand, Rosemary spied the box. The figures still decorated the sides and top. She thought about how much work the artisan must have put in to do such a work. But the figures looked so ugly it seemed a shame the time had been wasted.

Reaching down, she picked up the box.

"Vulnerable," thought every one of the demons. Their powers were not useful while they were attached to the box. Except one figure knew how he could wield at least some strength. The dwarf turned his ax slightly outward when the sister's fingers came nearer to him.

"Ouch!"

Rosemary looked down at her right index finger and saw a bubble of blood. What the heck could she have caught her finger on? She raised the box closer and let her eyes retrace the path her fingers had taken. She thought she saw something on the tiny ax held by the dwarf. Could the ax have been made so realistic it could cut into flesh? She wasn't about to test it. Instead she placed the box on the table and decided to shower before taking in a movie with her mother. She readjusted the box on the table and started for the staircase.

The dwarf couldn't keep from chuckling out loud. Rosemary stopped, glanced around the room, then resumed her climb to the basement door, all the while hearing tiny, muffled sounds she couldn't place.

"Why did you do that?" asked the pig of the dwarf.

The dwarf continued to chuckle and only took a slight break to say that he couldn't help it.

"What good is drawing blood if we can't drink it?" The old woman placed a hand on her empty stomach. "It's a waste. When it comes time to take her life, Master Dwarf, you may cast the first blow, and I shall be there for the first sip. But to draw blood and let it evaporate into the air is certainly a crime against all of us comrades."

"Comrades? I am forced to tolerate each of you. Comrades are those one chooses to ally oneself with. I fell into this group by chance. None of you have the skill to fight by my side."

"This isn't a war being fought on a field. This is a psychological drama that chills the humans' hearts, sending them to their places of worship for support before collapsing in front of us in defeat." The old woman hated the constant embellishments the dwarf engaged in.

"Pain is what the humans recognize. They know the

burn of a flame, the piercing frigid feel of a dagger, the suffocating tightness of a ligature, the humbling weakness of disease, and the ache of failing organs. Bah, they know only the drive to keep themselves alive even when they should be dead. I've had many humans kneel before me, tears streaming down their cheeks, their bladders unable to control their flow, their bodies shaking from fear, and they begged for a painless death. And a second later they attempted to escape when I agreed to their wishes. Do you know what I did then, old woman?"

"I'm sure you kissed them softly on the cheek and allowed your bad breath to kill them instantly."

The other demons roared with laughter, but not the dwarf.

"I flayed them alive. I took as long as a week to finally let them die. Pain is the humans' greatest misery. We feed on their pain when we imbibe in their blood and taste their flesh. It is the fear and pain we live off. How many of you will deny that?" The dwarf spun in a circle, looking into each of the faces until he reached the black snake. There he stopped to gaze at the recoiled snake wavering in the dimness of the basement. "You speak of love, Master Serpent. We have all heard you say you loved a human. Did that love inspire you to heights, or did it make you a lowly creature creeping around a castle hiding your true nature whenever possible? That was not a complete life and it is why you recall that time with such bitterness."

"I should have killed her like you and I too could be bragging about my accomplishments." The snake twisted his body away from the dwarf.

"You lived to revenge her instead of seeking revenge on her, Master Serpent. She weakened you. The babes she gave you were all human because the seeds you spilt were not your own. They belonged to a man with no supernatural powers and so weak willed that you snatched his soul from him. I watched them die."

The demons drew back, waiting for a battle.

"They died whining and screaming just like every other human. When the guards tore my guts out I did not scream; it was the human I possessed recognizing the end who screamed. We all die multiple times, and some of us die in great pain, but we know some time in the future we will return, and then we will visit all the pain we've ever had on each and every human."

The old woman followed the black snake that glided across the box, its head low, its mouth shut. By the time she reached its side, the snake had found a dark corner.

"Were you always a spirit, or did someone curse you into being a demon?" The witch reached out a hand to the snake but did not intend to touch the scaly skin.

"A curse fell on me the moment I was born, old woman. My life in true human flesh form ended at an early age. I barely remember the sensations of being human. Rebecca reminded me of them. I lost more than a woman I loved. I lost my humanity twice."

chapter 58

Stephen caught his aunt coming up from the cellar. She held one of her index fingers between her lips. She acted startled when she saw him.

"Stephen, I thought you were going over to Mrs. Rosen's."

"It's too early. Besides, Grandma says I have to do my homework first."

"She would, being a teacher and all." She smiled, but Stephen didn't return the smile.

"Why were you in the basement again?" he asked.

"You shouldn't be worried about that, since

you've exchanged boxes. Now there is a delightfully ugly box with gnomes and such all over it."

"Stay away from the uglies."

"I shall from now on. I managed to cut my finger on that box somehow. I'm going upstairs now to wash the wound. Is that okay?"

Stephen nodded, standing out of her path. She thanked him and lightly brushed her fingers through his hair. He watched her mount the stairs and didn't budge until he heard her bedroom door close.

He needed to check on the uglies. Make sure his aunt hadn't moved the box again. As he went down the stairs, Stephen still caught the scent of the fire that had burned his father. The smell would never leave. It would always remain in his memory.

He saw the box on the table. Layers of wax had been removed from the table. No doubt his aunt's work. She wouldn't leave things alone. His trembling hands reached for the box that seemed to jump into his tiny hands.

The uglies were all there. The dwarf even winked at him, the ax still wet from Stephen's aunt's blood.

"What's that?" Robin asked from the top of the stairs, her wheelchair precariously near the edge.

Looking up he admired her wild red hair that sprang into curls in every direction imaginable. The shadows hid the freckles on her cheeks that seemed to increase each time he saw her.

"It's just a box that belonged to my mother."

"Was it important to her?"

"Yes."

"Anything inside?"

"No; the uglies are all clinging to its sides."

"The uglies?"

"You can't see from there, but ugly demons are attached to the box."

"Can you bring the box up here so's I can see?"

The box became heavy in his hands.

"I don't think they want to be stared at."

"Then why are you staring at them?"

"They don't mind me." He heard a creak and immediately checked to make sure Robin remained safely on the staircase landing. "Be careful. You could get hurt."

"But I want to see the box. Why would they be bothered by my looking at them? I promise not to stare. I'll only take a peek."

"They're mean and ugly. You don't want to see them. Suppose they don't like you? Maybe they'll find their way out of the basement and find your bedroom."

Robin chuckled.

"Silly. They can't come off the box. Besides, they're so tiny they couldn't climb the stairs to get out of the basement."

"They can do anything."

"Why don't they slip off the box now and come up and meet me? Aren't they social?" Her voice held a hint of laughter.

"This is serious, Robin. Momma brought them into our world. And now Momma is angry and the uglies do her bidding."

"I'm sorry, Stephen. I didn't mean to laugh at you. But why would your mother be angry now that she's in heaven?"

"Momma's not in heaven. I don't know whether she'll ever go there."

"That's a terrible thing to say about your mother. Of course she's in heaven."

Tears came to Stephen's eyes.

"No, Robin, I was bad and I called Momma back down and now she's angry at so many people."

"Like who?"

"Molly. Dad."

"You don't think your mother caused those accidents, do you?"

Stephen remained silent.

"My mother said Molly was killed by some stray animal."

"Animal?" Stephen looked back up at his cousin. "What kind of animal?"

"A wild dog. A pit bull. There aren't any free wolves or big cats around here."

"A wolf could have killed her?"

"I just finished telling you—"

"I gave Molly back the wolf costume she made for me." Stephen found himself gripping the box tightly.

"So? A costume can't kill anyone."

"My costume came alive. Only for a little bit, but it came alive in my bedroom."

"Don't say stupid things like that. You only imagined it coming to life. Do you hear me, Stephen?"

"I wish Daddy had told me how she died. I asked about the costume, but he said it wasn't right for us to ask for it back. Now I don't know where it is or who it's looking for."

"Maybe we should stop watching television for a while. You're becoming looney."

"Honest, Robin," he pleaded. "I brought Momma back to this house, and now she won't leave. And I don't know if she wants more people hurt. What should I do?"

"Let me see the box, Stephen."

Carrying the box, he climbed the stairs. At the top step he stopped.

"I'll show it to you, but promise not to touch it."

"Cross my heart." Robin leaned closer to Stephen and he presented the box in the palms of his hands.

"Why would your mother bring such ugly creatures into this world?"

"I think they have something to do with vengeance."

"But they're not real, Stephen." She reached out with an index finger and Stephen pulled the box back to his body.

"I told you." His dry mouth made it difficult for him to speak clearly.

"Bring it closer. I want to see the images."

When Stephen hesitated, Robin threatened to call down her mother, and Stephen shoved it forward under her nose.

"Look at the chubby dwarf." Robin giggled.

"Oh!" Robin's body fell back against the chair. "He stuck his tongue out at me. Is this a trick?"

"It's not a trick. It's real magic. My mother's a witch."

"Stephen, the demons are wiggling as if they were caught in sticky mud."

The children watched the demons writhe.

"I think they're getting ready for the nighttime," Stephen said.

"What do they do then?"

"They run free in the basement."

"You mean they jump off the box."

Stephen nodded.

"But what if . . . ?"

Stephen interrupted: "I think they've already hurt my Daddy."

"Destroy them! Chop them up into little pieces

and flush them down the toilet."

"Toilet? I'd never be able to go to the bathroom again."

"Then throw them in the lake, or better, throw them where your mother's ashes are. She brought them here. She should take them away with her."

"She wants me to keep them safe," Stephen said.

"But they set your father on fire."

"I don't know that for sure. Although I saw the dwarf hiding behind the furnace."

"Your mother couldn't want them to cause anymore harm. Throw them into the furnace."

"I can't. Momma wouldn't love me anymore." Stephen broke into soft sobs, and Robin put her hand on his cheek.

"Your mother will always love you. You can never stop your mother from loving you."

chapter 59

"Your mother will always love you," the dog with a man's head said to the bird with the crooked beak.

"Idiot children." The dwarf paced the table, swinging his ax in time with his step. "She'll love her boy for as long as he is useful."

"I love my son," protested a voice that came from every corner of the room.

"I'm sure, mistress." The dwarf bowed, his eyes steadily searching the basement.

"We are one."

"Not yet," hissed the snake.

"He began life inside my womb. He suckled at my

breast. He sat with me when I was quiet and needed someone to hug. He helped me bring each of you into this world. And now he protects what is mine. His father is useless, bedridden. Disfigured."

"But he still lives," said the gargoyle. "And if I look for him I can see the father. I can't see you."

"Stephen sees me in the shadows."

"He imagines you, for you have no body. Hubby made sure of that," the gargoyle argued.

"Why so brave? Do you little ones scheme to be free of me and my son? You'll always be prisoner of the box you now circle. I won't free you of that curse."

"I don't suppose you will, dear." The old woman with the staff came forth to speak to Stephen's mother. "But tell me, has the child offered you his body as yet?"

"Already he dreams of me, even though he doesn't recognize who I am. Soon he will know and will stretch his hands out for me."

"Maybe not. He is a smart boy. What if he should decide to rule us alone without you?"

"He doesn't have the-"

"Exactly," the demon old woman said. "He doesn't have courage. He'll be frightened of your coldness. The chill of death frightens all humans. When he feels his tiny heart slow down he'll pull away from you. The rancid breath of death you'll attempt to breathe into him will make him run from you. His love will vanish along with the ashes of your body."

"No!" cried the mother. "He would not leave me here alone in a vacuum. Stephen will usher me into his soul without a single doubt. My son carries my blood and flesh with him. You see me when you look into his eyes and hear his voice."

"Sounds nothing like you," said the pig, who immediately was shushed by his fellow demons.

"You belong on a spit in hell." The mother's angry voice shattered the pig's eardrums, leaving a high-pitched ring in its ears.

chapter 60

Stephen heard the chatter between Grandma and Aunt Rosemary in the kitchen. He didn't pay attention to what they said. He knew they planned on going out while he and Robin visited with Grannie Smith. But he had to check the basement one last time before he left.

He closed the basement door behind him before he clicked on the light. Night had crept into the basement without his knowing it and he felt uneasy about leaving the house. What if Grandma and Aunt Rosemary decided not to go out? Would they foolishly go down into the basement, churning up the malevolent demons patiently waiting his mother's return?

At the bottom of the staircase he spied the wooden box still on the table. The figures remained glued to the box, barely moving as if waiting. Even when he touched a figure, nothing moved. The dwarf ignored him, and the old woman had her hood pulled down over her face.

"What are you up to?" he asked, knowing they wouldn't answer. Too preoccupied with their own anticipation, they ignored him. They should be free of the box, but chose to cling to its sides. Why?

"Momma, please don't let them do anything bad. Make them behave."

He didn't feel the coldness of his mother's embrace, didn't smell the stink of death, or hear the lilt of his mother's voice. He felt alone with the uglies. He wished for a single mouse to come out and squeak at him. He wouldn't mind. Mice didn't scare him, but the uglies did. He wanted some noise just to know the real world still existed beyond the horror living in his basement.

A loud crash answered his wish. He looked up at the window over the furnace and saw pieces of glass scattered atop the furnace and back down on the floor. Standing at the base of the furnace was a wolf. A tired, ragged wolf with flesh made of rags and face colored the same as his own brown paints. The beast staggered and finally righted itself as its eyes began to focus. It opened its mouth, and its ragged teeth seemed stained with blood.

As night drew on, the beast's flesh and fur firmed, and the face grew harder, sterner. The eyes carried hate, and the ears pricked high to listen while the nose scented for prey.

"Momma." Stephen slowly backed away, and the beast padded toward him. "Momma." Afraid to raise his voice and attract his grandmother and Aunt Rosemary, he kept his voice soft. The dead cannot be called back by a loud scream. He knew that. The dead came when ready, but he didn't mind trying to remind his mother.

The wolf nuzzled its head against Stephen's hand before sidling over to rest under the table. Above, the uglies danced on the table. Their little legs kicked high, and they extended their arms outward in joy. The dwarf had dropped his ax and held hands with the witch, her staff dancing along next to them.

"Stop!" Stephen said, but the uglies ignored him, not a one bothering to look his way.

He couldn't leave the house now. He'd have to fake illness.

"Stephen?"

He looked up to see Robin hovering near the basement door.

"Go away!"

"But we have to leave soon."

"I'm not going. I'm sick."

"It's the uglies again, isn't it?"

"The wolf is back, Robin. The wolf costume that I gave to Molly. Its mouth and fur are bloody. I killed Molly."

"No, Stephen. You didn't know it would come to life."

"But I did. I saw it briefly come to life on my bed."

"It was probably a trick of the lights."

"No. I saw it for a brief moment breathe and its body fill out with bones and muscle."

"Where is it now? I can't see anything."

"Under the table, resting. I don't know where it's been, but it seems very tired."

"Fine, then let it rest, and we will take care of it in the morning when it's just a pile of rags."

"But tonight . . ."

"If you stay home, so will my mother and our grandmother. They'll be in greater danger then. You can't guard the door while you're supposed to be sick."

Robin made sense. And then he remembered his father coming home and going to the basement before picking Stephen up from Grannie Smith.

"What if they get home before us?"

"Make it difficult for them to get into the basement."

"How?"

"I don't know. Don't you have a pile of old toys or something you can pile up on the landing? Block their way. Grandmother probably will yell at you and make you clean up the mess, but she'll be alive to do so."

Stephen followed his cousin's instructions and barely completed the task before Grannie Smith rang the doorbell.

From one of Grannie Smith's windows the children watched Robin's mother get into her rental car and honk her horn. Shortly after, Grandma locked the front door and slid into the passenger seat of the car.

Stephen and Robin looked at each other with great relief.

"My, are you two homesick already, and I haven't even gotten the apple pie out of the oven?"

The children smiled, sniffed the air, and hurried to the kitchen right behind Grannie Smith.

chapter 61

"I'm going to try this cleaner on the table in the basement. See if I can get the excess wax up. Let me know when the kids come back from Mrs. Rosen's"

"Mom, do you have to do that now? The basement gives me the creeps. What about those mice you saw?"

Mabel carried a rag and a household cleaner in one hand and a bat in the other.

"You're not going to beat the poor things to death. Besides, you'll be too scared to go after them."

"I just want to drive them away from me, Rosemary. The loud noise this bat makes should do the trick. I won't be long." Mabel opened the basement door, flipped on the light, and shrieked.

"What was that child thinking?"

Rosemary arrived in time to see her mother tossing toys, old clothes, magazines (some not fit for small children) into a garbage bag.

"Mom, what are you doing?"

"That boy left all this garbage right in front of the basement door. I could have tripped over this stuff and broken my neck falling down the stairs."

"You can't throw that stuff out. It doesn't belong to you."

"It now doesn't belong to Stephen, either. Most of this stuff is for babies."

"Jacob may want to save those toys and clothes to remind him of Stephen as a baby. And the magazines . . ." She picked one up and flipped through the pages. "The magazines can go out."

"Oh, I'm not throwing this into the garbage can. I'm merely getting the junk out of my way. I'll put it all in the pantry room and let Stephen think I threw it all away. Let him worry a bit. What could he have been looking for?"

"Something that belonged to his mother or father?"

"You may be right. I won't chastise him. I want to hear what that psychiatrist you're going to see says. Normally this would have called for a scolding, but with all he's been through I don't want to say or do the wrong thing."

Rosemary hugged her mother and helped clear a path.

"The kids will be home any minute. Forget the basement, Mom, and sit down in the living room with me."

"After cleaning up that mess? I could have left it for the morning if I didn't intend to take care of that table in the basement. Besides, it will give you a chance to spend time alone with the children before I come up and ruin the evening with a reminder of bedtime."

"It's Friday night; go wild, Mom. Join us for some fun. You can fall back in to your job as dungeon master tomorrow night."

"I want that basement cleaned up as soon as possible. Everything down there is a reminder to Stephen of what his mother used to do. I don't want him trying to follow in her footsteps."

Mabel grabbed her cleaning equipment and descended the stairs. The basement had an odd odor.

At the bottom she skidded on glass.

"Oh, Stephen, what have you been up to?"

She resigned herself to staying in the basement for at least an hour to cool her temper down. She had to keep reminding herself that Stephen, like the rest of them, was going through a very traumatic period. A little boy can't cope and would certainly act out under the current circumstances.

She looked at the table.

"Hmf. I wonder what that box is for?" She placed the cleaner and rag on the table and picked up a plain, brown wooden box. She left the bat leaning against one of the table's legs. "Could be handy for recipes, or maybe Rosemary could find a use for it." She placed it on the floor near her feet, planning to take it upstairs when she finished with the table.

She poured out a small amount of the cleanser and used the rag to scrub hard. The wax dissolved slowly.

"This could take all night." She shrugged her shoulders, thinking at least she could make a start.

The door to the basement crashed shut and Mabel jumped. She cursed, realizing how stupid she had been in not propping the door open. Shaking her head, she continued with her task.

The door to the furnace flew open, and she felt a hot draft almost scald her back.

She turned to the furnace and remembered what the fireman had said. "*Make sure the lock catches.*"

Mabel shut the furnace door but had to work the lock for several seconds before it felt secured.

She thought she heard some vague chatter. Even thought she heard her own name used.

Those damn mice, she thought, checking for the baseball bat. The bat no longer leaned against a leg of the table. She circled the table, but no bat.

She caught a flash of movement near the tarp. The baseball bat floated away from her and seemed to scurry under the tarp.

Mice can't do that. But she wasn't about to shake out the tarp to make sure.

Something brushed across her slippered foot and Mabel held her breath but refused to look down at the floor.

The place is infested. Okay, I'll just calmly head for the staircase and leave.

A twittery chuckle filled the basement.

"Rosemary," Mabel called out in a low voice. Her throat felt raspy, dry, tight. "Rosemary," she tried again, forcing more lung power into the name.

Mabel moved toward the staircase but stopped abruptly when the furnace door again opened. Positive she had secured the lock, she broke out in a cold sweat.

A long growl caught her attention, and she saw a wolf standing midway up the staircase. Her eyes shifted to the broken window over the furnace.

"Rosemary," she called. The damn girl must have hunkered down in front of the television.

Cold dampness moved up her ankle, and a sharp pain splintered her flesh on the other ankle. She looked down to see a tiny snake-like blackness slipping up her calf. She tried to brush it off, but the thing clung.

Leeches, she thought. *How the hell could there be leeches?*

Another sharp pain stunned her into checking her other ankle. Blood dripped from a wound in her flesh, and a little man ran around her foot waving a tiny ax. She went to kick him, but lost her balance when something else appeared to bite the back of the bloodied flesh. She lay on her back looking at the table, where a small old woman waved a staff and shouted out a curse she could barely hear.

"Let her blood move swiftly through her veins and let the pressure build inside her skull. Feel it, dearie." The old woman tilted her head toward Mabel. "The heart speeds to move the blood through the veins that snake and coil through your brain. Feel the pressure build each second as the veins' walls come near to bursting."

Mabel felt out of breath. Panic rose quickly, and her head seemed filled with a battering pain. She tried to rise but found she could no longer see.

"Rosemary, help me." Mabel's garbled words sounded choppy, indecipherable even to her own ears. Her chest ached and her head pounded. Still she tried to stand, yet her limbs no longer belonged to her. Her vision cleared, but she wished it hadn't when she saw little bodies swarming over her. Most seemed eager to taste her flesh and drink her blood. Inside her head she heard the echo of soft chomping and slurping. She wanted to call out, but couldn't think of the words.

Who was she trying to call? The name eluded her. Where was she? Her home or someone else's? She had known. Why didn't she know now?

Her flesh seemed pricked by dozens of needles, yet gradually the pain faded and a blessed numbness enveloped her flesh.

chapter 62

"I'm sorry, but Jacob's having his dressings changed. It takes at least an hour to complete. Perhaps you could grab some lunch."

Rosemary breathed in the stench of antiseptics, blood, urine, feces, and disease. She hated hospitals. Hated those who peopled hospitals. Especially the doctors who wore colorful hats into surgery. Who did they think they cheered? And what of the nurses who spent more time gossiping than taking care of patients? Laughing in the middle of the night. Covering their hands with latex to add another layer separating them from the patients.

The woman across the desk from her touched her arm and Rosemary took a step back.

"Can I get you some water?"

Rosemary shook her head and turned away.

The glass doors to the hospital kept opening and closing with the rush to and from lunch. Rosemary couldn't find her way out amidst the crowd. Always someone coming toward her or knocking into her on their way out.

She had been here all night, lying in bed in a small room just off the Intensive Care Unit. The sheets had been stiff, the pillows had the consistency of mud, and the crinkle of the mattress protector echoed with her every toss and turn.

"Excuse me. Oh, I'm so sorry."

Rosemary looked down at the arm of her sweater. Someone had splashed the wool with coffee.

"Let me get some napkins. I'll certainly pay for the dry cleaning."

Rosemary ignored the intruder. She walked into the parking lot and didn't know why. She hadn't come by car. The ambulance had taken her and her mother directly to the emergency room.

She didn't know what direction to take. The freeway noise hummed in the background. A young man sat in his car, running his engine while his exhaust polluted the air. The hospital gardener lined up clay pots of unknown flowers that must have been hardy enough for the cooler fall weather. An ambulance sped out of the driveway. A block away she heard the siren start, and she shuddered, remembering last night.

A cab, she thought. Reception could call a cab for her, and she would be able to spend an hour or two with the children before returning to the hospital. An hour or two consoling the innocent victims. But she wondered how innocent Stephen was. How much had he learned from his mother? She wondered whether she should talk to him about his grandmother. And what about his father's injuries? He missed his father. Wanted him back home. But . . .

She couldn't do anything more at the hospital but sit and twiddle her thumbs. Not very productive.

Both children stayed the night with Mrs. Rosen and were still presumably at her house. Guilt swept through Rosemary. She hadn't bothered to call Mrs. Rosen about the children since she had left with her mother for the hospital last night. How safe was Robin with Stephen? He adored his cousin, but what did he think his mother wanted him to do?

Jacob had been sure Cathy's influence on Stephen was negative. He actually believed Cathy's spirit remained at the house. And maybe he was right.

Rosemary hurried back to the reception desk of the hospital. She had already given her cell number to her mother's doctor, and it would be a while before Jacob could be seen.

"I need a cab," she hurriedly said, interrupting another visitor's request.

"Give me five minutes and I'll get you one," the receptionist said.

The man in front of Rosemary gave her a dirty look, but it didn't really register with her. The five-minute wait did.

"But I need the cab now. Give me the number and I'll call myself."

"You'll have to wait," said the receptionist. "Right now I'm helping this gentleman."

Rosemary looked at the man as if she noticed him for the first time. His sour expression forced her to back off. Antsy, she twisted around to look out the main door. A cab had pulled up, and two nurses were assisting an elderly man out of the back seat and into a wheelchair.

She ran out the door and to the cab, seating herself in the back seat before the elderly man had completely cleared the vehicle.

She rattled off the address and the cab driver shook his head.

"I ain't been paid yet, lady."

The elderly man fumbled through his pockets.

"Hell! I'll pay his fare. Go! Go!"

chapter 63

"What do you think happened last night?" asked Robin.

Stephen sat on the window ledge, waiting. He didn't know what he waited for, but knew that he couldn't do anything else. He had begged Mrs. Rosen to take him back to the house, but she had refused. His aunt's rental car sat in the driveway, but all the house lights were out.

"Who do you think the ambulance was for?"

Robin kept asking questions, and this was the only one he had an answer for.

"Your mother is fine. She was at the door last

night talking to Mrs. Rosen. I couldn't hear what they said, but your mother looked fine."

"You think Grandma is hurt? Do you think she tripped and fell down the basement stairs? Maybe you shouldn't have piled all that stuff at the top of the basement stairs."

"You told me to do that." His angry face turned to look at her. "You said she wouldn't try to go down in the basement if there was a mess."

"Could she have not seen it? Maybe she didn't have any lights on."

"I told you the uglies were getting ready for something and the wolf had come back."

"You think Grandma is . . ." Robin hesitated. "Is sick like your father?"

"I didn't see any firemen."

"That's good at least, isn't it?"

"She could have been eaten by the wolf."

"That only happens in fairy tales, Stephen. That's silly."

"I saw the wolf, Robin. My wolf. The one Molly and I made."

"And your mother brought to life."

"With my help." His voice quivered.

"Don't cry. You didn't want anyone hurt. You thought you were obeying your mother."

Stephen turned and looked at Robin.

"I have to stop Momma."

"Look, there's a cab pulling up." Robin leaned forward in her wheelchair, anticipating her mother's arrival. She smiled broadly when her mother exited the cab.

The two children watched Rosemary pause and consider whether she should go into Stephen's house first.

"No!" Stephen cried out.

And although she couldn't have heard him, Rosemary changed directions and headed for Mrs. Rosen's house.

Robin swiftly moved to the front door while Stephen lagged behind.

"Where's Stephen?" he heard his aunt quickly ask. No one replied, but soon she appeared in the living room, where Stephen stood with his hands in his pockets.

"What have you been up to?" asked Rosemary.

Misunderstanding the question, Mrs. Rosen listed the tasks and games they had been doing all morning.

"May I speak to Stephen alone?"

Mrs. Rosen politely left the room, leaving Robin behind.

"You too. Go help Mrs. Rosen in the kitchen."

"No. Stephen never wanted to do anything wrong, Mom. You shouldn't blame him. I told him to put all that stuff in front of the basement door."

"What?" Rosemary faced her daughter.

"It seemed like a good idea. We thought Grandma wouldn't go into the basement if she had to clear away all that stuff first."

"What do you know about that basement? You haven't been down there, have you?"

"No. I've only been at the top of the stairs."

Rosemary whirled about to face Stephen.

"Why did you bring Robin to the basement?"

"I told you, I haven't been down in the basement, and Stephen didn't invite me. I caught him down there one day on my own. He didn't want me there." Robin placed her wheelchair in front of her mother. "Don't blame him. He's confused."

"Confused?"

"His mother is angry, and he doesn't know why."

"What about your mother, Stephen?"

"She's come back to him," said Robin.

"She's dead, Robin. Don't talk nonsense."

"I believe Stephen, Mom. I think he . . ." Robin stopped and looked over her shoulder at her cousin. "He has been talking to someone. She may not be your mother, Stephen."

"Momma is back." Stephen's voice cracked.

"What does she want you to do?" asked Rosemary.

He shrugged because this was where he was confused. He had wanted his mother back, but didn't realize the cost he and others would pay.

"Is Grandma all right?" asked Robin.

"She's in the hospital."

"The same one they took my daddy to?" Stephen asked.

"Yes. Convenient. I can run back and forth between the two wards while I worry about you kids."

"I can stay with Daddy," Stephen offered.

"This has already been explained to you, Stephen; I'm not going to waste my time telling you again."

"But Momma and Daddy once sneaked me into the hospital when Grandma was sick."

"I'm beginning to think you're best locked in a cage."

"Momma!" Robin wheeled herself over to Stephen. "She doesn't mean that. Only Grandma's sick, and Momma wants her to get better."

Rosemary walked out of the room. Robin reached out and touched Stephen's shirt sleeve. Both children sunk into their own private thoughts.

Ten minutes later, Rosemary returned carrying several of Robin's schoolbooks, which had been left over from the day before.

"I called a cab. It should be here in five minutes. What did you do with your jacket, Robin?"

"Why?" The girl sat tall in her chair.

"I've got it," called Mrs. Rosen entering the room.

"Thanks. Let me help you put it on."

Robin backed away, the wheelchair hitting a table and knocking over a small statuette.

"That's okay. It didn't break. Just an accident. Don't worry about it." Mrs. Rosen lifted the statuette off the carpet and placed it on a table farther away.

"Is Stephen coming?" Robin asked.

"Don't give me a hard time. Not now."

"Stephen's staying to help me make some pies for this evening. Isn't that right, sweetheart?" Mrs. Rosen placed a hand on Stephen's right shoulder. He didn't budge.

"Mom, you're acting as if you think Stephen would hurt me."

Rosemary forced her daughter into the jacket.

"Go with your mother, Robin. Maybe you'll get to see my Daddy. Tell him I miss him. I want him home."

"This is a mistake. Maybe that woman who visits you isn't your mother. Make her go away. If she loves you she will. She won't want to hurt you or get you in trouble." Robin's voice filled his head with a cloud of nonsense words.

Rosemary began to wheel her daughter out of the room.

"Mom, you can't leave him here alone. What if he gets hurt?"

"Mrs. Rosen is here, and she won't be letting

him back into his house," Rosemary said, staring into Stephen's eyes just before she turned the wheelchair into the hall.

Within ten minutes the cab arrived and took both his cousin and aunt away. He watched from the window and Robin waved to him. His aunt never turned to acknowledge him.

"What's all this talk about a woman who visits you, Stephen?" asked Grannie Smith.

Stephen left the window and walked over to the couch, where he buried his face in the pillows with his rear-end pointing skyward.

Grannie Smith lifted him up and carried him up the stairs to the guest bedroom, which faced his own bedroom next door. She tucked him into the bed and left him sucking on his thumb. She had never seen him suck his thumb before. She swept back the hair falling onto his forehead, but never dared to remove his thumb from between his lips. On her way out of the bedroom she closed the door quietly.

chapter 64

"The troll doesn't like you anymore. He'll never visit you again. He told me so." The witch stood in front of Brandy's cage, her hands settled upon her ample hips.

"It's your fault. You told him bad things about me."

"Me?" the witch screeched. "I hardly think it worth while talking about you. No, no. He came to this decision on his own. He tired of hearing you complain, and of those silly stories you told him about me."

"I merely answered his questions. I volunteered nothing."

The witch scrunched her face into an ugly prune shape.

"Don't make faces at me. You're ugly enough."

"Ugly? Sweets, you don't really think me ugly, do you?"

"I certainly do. You do ugly things so you'll always look ugly to me." Brandy turned away from the witch and marched the short distance across his cage.

"You've hurt my feelings."

"I don't care," he murmured.

"Yes, you do. You don't really want to hurt me. We are too much alike."

"I'm nothing like you, madame."

"You have my eyes."

"I have my mother's eyes."

"Exactly." The witch reached out her hands and took hold of the bars on the cage. "Come, turn around. Look at me, sweets."

"I'm not your sweets." Brandy stamped his foot.

"No tantrums here, sweets."

"I told you . . ." Brandy swung around. "I am not your sweets."

The witch's brown eyes softened. Her eyelids flickered in innocence. She attempted to wipe a tear from her eye, except Brandy couldn't see the slightest sign of dampness.

"You're trying to trick me. You have no remorse or love for anyone. Your heart is an iceberg."

The witch grasped at her chest.

"And I thought it was indigestion."

"You would have me believe you knew my father. He

would never associate with a woman like you."

"Yes, he would."

"I'll never believe that. My father is good."

"That is highly questionable, but I'm not here to argue over your father. Continue to love him if you wish. My vengeance is complete."

"You can't hurt my father."

"I don't want to anymore. Keep him in your heart, sweets. It won't bother me."

"I'm very tired, madame. Please go away and let me rest."

"Tsk, tsk. You've hardly slept lately. What's been preventing the sandman from visiting you?"

"I cried last night."

"The whole night?"

"Most of the night. I don't want to play with you."

"Play. Child, I don't play." The witch's face grew broader and sterner. "This has never been a game. I want what you have, sweets. Give it to me."

"I have nothing but the rags on my back. You've taken everything else. My favorite pen that I kept in my inside pocket. My notebook with pages and pages of my memories. My hankie with the initials embroidered in red. My favorite monster cards given to me by my daddy. Even the pennies I saved for Christmas."

The witch leaned an elbow on a cross bar and settled her chin in the palm of her hand.

"Minor. All minor in comparison to your greatest gift."

"I will gift you with nothing else, madame. Go away."

Brandy and the witch stared at each other. The witch calm, relaxed, patient. Brandy sullen, cross, agitated.

"Can you not guess what I want?" The witch stood to full height.

"My life?"

"I only want to share it," the witch whispered. "I want to be very close to you. I want to be one with you. Our souls can mesh. Your heart will beat for two." The witch reached out her hands toward Brandy.

"If our souls mesh, mine will fade and yours will grow. My heart will do your bidding, and I'll be left to watch."

"Give me your hands, Brandy."

"Your hands are scratchy, with big brown spots."

"For you they will always be soft. Try them," she said, raising her hands up so she could fit them through the bars.

Brandy looked at the hands, raised his own to compare them to hers. Her hands were old but strong. Her hands could take care of both of them. His hands were young and weak. He wondered how they would fit together.

Their fingertips barely met.

"I need your young flesh, and you need my old wisdom," the witch said.

chapter 65

Stephen woke up lying on his back, propped up by several pillows. He faced the window that peered over at his own home. His mother sat at his bedroom window, her hands resting flat against the pane.

"No one likes me, Momma. Aunt Rosemary is afraid of me."

His mother's brown eyes crinkled into a smile, and he watched her lips mouth *I love you*.

He sat up, drawing his knees to his chest. His arms circled his legs.

"Can I trust you, Momma? Will you make me hurt others?"

A soft knock came on the door. Just as softly Stephen answered before the door opened.

"Are you feeling better?" asked Grannie Smith. "Well enough for a cup of hot chocolate? I can bring it up if you'd like."

"Grannie Smith, do you still like me?"

"Of course. And so does your aunt. She's under a lot of pressure now between visiting your father and her mother. She doesn't know what to make of all the troubles the family has been experiencing."

"She thinks I caused it all."

"No. You weren't even at the house when those accidents happened." She sat down on the bed.

"Do you think Aunt Rosemary will come back?"

"Why not? She loves you."

"Will she let Robin and me play again?"

"Certainly. How could she keep the two of you apart?"

"Robin can't run away from home because a witch stole her nerves."

"I don't think anyone will be running away from home, do you?"

Stephen thought about it.

"I don't know where I'd go."

Grannie Smith cupped his cheek in the palm of her hand.

"Stay with family, Stephen. Family will always take care of you."

"Even when they're scared of me?"

"How could someone be scared of you? Would I be sitting here if I were afraid?"

"Maybe you shouldn't sit with me," he said, glancing out the window, still seeing his mother staring back. "But then the uglies don't know how to get over here. They're locked in the basement of our house."

"Your daddy had a terrible accident. He didn't mean to hurt himself, and no one else wanted him hurt."

Stephen's mother beckoned to him. She wanted him to come back to the house. She stretched her arms out as if to hug him.

"Momma still loves me."

"Love doesn't end when a person has to go away. My husband, Lord rest his soul, still loves me, I'm sure. And I love him, but in a different way than before. We can't hug or kiss. Still, I talk to him in quiet moments, and I knew him so well that I can hear the replies he'd make."

With astonishment in his eyes, Stephen looked up into Grannie Smith's face.

"Your husband talks to you?"

"I imagine him talking to me. Advising me what to do, offering support when I need it. Everything he did when he lived with me."

But Stephen didn't imagine his mother's voice or

her touch. She wanted back into his life, and he had welcomed her without thought of what it could mean.

chapter 66

"Mother, where is your little boy? Why doesn't he come to release all of us from this stifling, filthy basement?" asked the gargoyle

"Do not rush him, or he will balk," replied Cathy.

"Aye, he's been balking ever since we came here. No stomach for this evil business." The dwarf paced back and forth on the table until he skidded on a slippery spot. "Batty old woman. Cleaning wax off the table. What did she think? We'd disappear along with the wax that brought us here?"

"She's no longer a problem," Cathy reminded him.

The wolf attempted to leap up to the broken window

but couldn't make it.

"He's getting restless. If the boy doesn't come soon we may lose control of the wolf." The dwarf never trusted animals, which meant he trusted hardly anyone in the room.

"He watched us feast on blood and flesh last night without participating." The gargoyle shook his head.

"He couldn't be trusted," said the dwarf. "He would have eaten her up in two gulps. There would have been none for us."

"I ordered him not to kill my mother," said Cathy. "I want her to suffer. He wouldn't have been able to control his appetite."

"He's starting to look at us too much. Sometimes he lays his head down but doesn't sleep. His eyes watch us." The dwarf shivered with the thought.

"Oh, don't worry so much, Master Dwarf, you taste much too sour, I'm sure, to interest the wolf." The black snake slid across the dwarf's path, who barely had time to stop.

The wolf padded over to the table and set its front paws on the surface.

"Aye, his breath. Truly putrid." The dwarf danced back away from the wolf. "What does he want? Make him go away. Don't allow him to have complete freedom. He's much too dangerous."

The wolf shivered and its ears settled back on its head.

"Down," Cathy commanded.

The wolf's paws slipped off the surface of the table

and landed on the cement floor with a loud tap.

"When will you take your son's body?" demanded the dwarf. "We've been waiting a long time. The brat has nothing to offer us except little baby flesh and blood. He has no powers."

"Yes, he does." Cathy's voice rang out like a bell. "He isn't aware of what he can do yet."

"Excuse me, mistress." The old woman with the staff came forward. "Pardon my opinion, but he has the power, yet lacks the evil intent. I've seen this before. Many children lose their way. He was born to serve the devil, but his heart isn't in it. Too much goodness spoils his abilities. His powers are rancid with self-doubt. He loves you, mistress, yes. However, don't trust him, for he will fall in line with the good, even against his own mother."

"He is troubled by what he has seen, old woman, but eventually he'll do what is best for me. I trust him and only him."

"What of us?" demanded the dwarf. "We follow your instructions. Never ask questions. And most of all, wait."

"You enjoy the revenge you take. And especially you *ask too many questions. The wait has been short in comparison to the length of time you've existed. My son does far more thinking than you'll ever be able to do. He sees beyond his own needs. He'll understand what is necessary to keep me with him and why I must come back."*

"You want back because you are just as selfish as us," the dwarf said.

"I left too soon. I thought I had finished with the earth, but I hadn't."

"You mean you don't want to go to hell," the dwarf niggled.

"My life had always been limited. First by my mother and then by Jacob. My rebellions were ignored. My love rejected. Now I intend to own my life."

"And what of your son?" The dwarf cocked his head and the snake looped up his body to knock the dwarf's hat off.

"We will share the same life as we did before he was born. He lived inside me. Now I will live inside him."

chapter 67

Rosemary woke up in a semi-private room at the hospital. Her daughter slept in the next bed. The hospital staff had been kind in allowing her and her daughter to stay the night. Rosemary's mother still remained in a very critical state, and Jacob had a relapse. Currently antibiotics flowed through his IV line, fighting the bronchitis he had come down with. Pneumonia could bring death to Jacob, given how serious his burns were. His lungs would be unable to clear themselves, and he could easily drown in his own fluids.

"Mom?"

"Hi, Robin. Did you sleep okay?"

"I kept thinking about Stephen. Maybe we shouldn't have left him alone."

"Mrs. Rosen is taking good care of him. She is very fond of him. Makes up for the fact that she doesn't have her own grandchildren to pester her."

"Neither will you, Mom."

"Don't talk like that, Robin." Rosemary immediately got out of bed. "Do you need to use the bathroom?"

Rosemary helped her daughter get ready, and the nurses generously provided breakfast in the room. All of the staff enjoyed Robin's company. Robin had no fear of hospitals because she had spent so much time in them, as much time as she had spent at home.

Leaving Robin doing her homework in the waiting room, Rosemary visited with her mother. Her mother never opened her eyes, and one side of her face sagged. The doctors couldn't be sure Mabel would ever regain consciousness.

Rosemary wheeled her daughter out of the waiting room to the burn unit. Instead of using the mask and aprons required while visiting burn patients, Rosemary rushed into Jacob's room.

His labored breathing made her pause for only a moment.

"Jacob, can you hear me?"

He opened his eyes, the blue irises tinged with red.

"Rosemary," he hissed.

"Momma." Robin panicked. She knew about the equipment the hospital used, but the sight of her uncle wrapped in gauze sickened her.

Rosemary knelt down beside her daughter.

"Be strong, Robin. Please, I want you to tell your uncle what you told me last night."

"About the uglies?"

"Yes."

"Don't put her through this, Rosemary." Jacob's breathing became more difficult. One of the machines began to beep.

A nurse entered the room almost immediately.

"What are you doing? Are you trying to kill him? Get out of here now, or I'll call security."

Rosemary wheeled her daughter out of the room at the same time Jacob's doctor entered. He grabbed her arm.

"What is the meaning of this?"

Rosemary had no answer. She had acted out of selfishness and disbelief. She wanted Jacob to explain to her what her daughter had told her about the demons living on the wooden box.

"Momma, is Uncle Jacob going to die?"

Rosemary pushed past the doctor and returned her daughter to the waiting room.

"Momma, he can't die, because then Stephen

won't have a mommy or daddy."

"He'll have us, Robin."

"But you hate him."

"No. I don't understand him."

"He's haunted, Momma, by some evil spirit. We have to help him."

"Rosemary."

She looked up at Jacob's main doctor.

"I'm sorry. I went crazy. I won't do it again."

He stood, saying nothing.

"My God, he isn't dead?"

"No, but we'll have to watch him carefully over the next few days. I don't think you should visit him for a while."

"I'm taking care of his son. He'll want to know how the boy's doing."

"Too risky," the doctor said. "We're trying to fight pneumonia, and his flesh is open to all kinds of bacteria. No, we'll tell you when you can see him again."

The doctor turned from her and walked down the hall back toward the burn unit.

"What did we do, Momma?"

Rosemary closed her eyes and brought her fingertips to her lips.

"Did we do something wrong?"

"Not you, Robin. Me." Turning back to her daughter, she opened her eyes to see the fear in Robin's eyes.

"We won't do that again, will we?"

"You must be hungry. Why don't we grab a cab and ride down to the—"

"I'm not hungry. I'm scared. What if Uncle Jacob dies? Stephen won't be able to take that. What if his father haunts him too?"

"Stop, Robin. His father will be coming home to him. In the meantime we'll help Stephen get through this."

"We can't do that if we stay hiding at the hospital."

She had isolated her nephew. Turned her back on him in self-defense.

"We can't live in that house, Robin."

"Mrs. Rosen has an extra bedroom."

"There's three of us."

"You don't want to go back to Stephen, do you?"

No, Rosemary didn't. The innocent little boy had turned into the demon child.

chapter 68

All night Stephen sat at the window and watched his mother fade in and out of the moonlight. She rarely moved except to occasionally mouth *I love you* or to place her palms against the window pane of Stephen's own room across from where he sat.

"Momma, can't you come here?" he asked, desperately needing her frigid embrace. The tinkle of her voice could soothe him into sleep. But did he want sleep?

His dreams were of Brandy and the witch. The witch who wanted to steal Brandy's flesh and soul.

"Momma, I'm so scared. What happens if Daddy

doesn't come home? Will you stay with me forever?"

His mother must have been able to read his lips, for she nodded her head in assent. Tears filled his brown eyes, and he briskly wiped them away, not wanting to lose the image of his mother.

However, as daylight overcame night, she began to fade. No amount of pleading from Stephen prevented it. Slowly, she dissolved along with the darkness of the night.

He leaned against the arch of the window, feeling the sun soak into his body. Warmth filled his thoughts with peace, and he gradually fell asleep.

He woke hours later realizing that he hadn't dreamt. Brandy and the witch, like the uglies, were nightmares of the dark night. He guessed that today the sun refused to welcome leftovers from the darkness of night. Daylight brought different dreams or none at all. He preferred the empty sleep he just had.

Stretching his limbs, he stood, arching his back cat-like after the uncomfortable position he had been in. The lights remained out in his own house, and the window pane of his own room stood vacant, darkened. No one stood at the window. He couldn't even see into the room.

He heard a telephone ring downstairs and crept to the door to open it a crack.

"Rosemary, how are you and Robin doing?" A few seconds of silence followed. "Oh, he's still asleep, I guess. I haven't looked in because I didn't want to wake him. I don't think he's been sleeping well. The poor boy has little dark circles under his eyes." A few more seconds of silence. "Shall I have him ring your cell phone when he gets up?" Silence. "I see. Shall I at least tell him that you called?" Silence. "When can I say anything about his father? The boy is worrying so much he's quickly growing into a little old man." Silence. "Pneumonia?"

Stephen opened the door wider and stuck his head into the hallway.

"They're giving him antibiotics, I'm sure."

Stephen stepped into the hallway and leaned against the banister, thinking that seeing Grannie Smith would also make it easier for him to hear his aunt.

"I'll say a prayer for Jacob and for your mother. Don't worry about Stephen. I love having him here."

He might be there forever, he thought. Would Grannie Smith love having him then?

Grannie Smith hung up and immediately looked up at Stephen.

"You're up. That was your aunt. Everyone's doing fine at the hospital."

"When is Daddy coming home?"

"He'll need to stay for some time."

"Is he going to die?"

"Lord, your father's a tank. How could you say

that? I used to watch him go out running every morning."

"He ran four times a week," Stephen corrected.

"To me it seemed like every morning. I certainly don't have that kind of energy."

"He has new mona?"

"'New mona?. Oh, you mean pneumonia. A bad cold. The hospital is giving him the best of medicines. Come on down and I'll give you some breakfast."

"Why won't Aunt Rosemary talk to me?" He poked his little face between the slats of the banister.

"I told her you were asleep."

"But she doesn't want me to call her."

"Your aunt is very busy at the hospital. She might be in with your grandmother or father when you call, and that might disturb their sleep. You don't want to do that, do you?"

Stephen withdrew his face from between the slats and sat down on the hall rug. If Daddy didn't come home, who would take care of him?

Grannie Smith climbed the stairs to squat down beside Stephen.

"You can stay with me for as long as you want. Matter of fact, it would be fun helping you pick a college the why I did for my son."

"It'll be a long time before I'm a scholar."

"I think you're a little bit of a scholar now."

"I'm not as smart as Robin."

THE WITCH

"Maybe you're smarter, but in a different way. I think in your heart you're a scholar." She touched his chest where his heart was.

"Mean I know how to love?"

A surprised look came to Grannie Smith's face.

"Exactly. That makes you easy *to love*."

chapter 69

"Doctor, how is Jacob doing?" Rosemary had waited by the nurses' station for most of the morning to ask this question.

The doctor looked surprised to see her.

"He's doing better."

"May I see him?"

"He's groggy most of the time."

"But can I try to speak to him?"

"What were you thinking yesterday when you charged into his room?"

"My mother is in the hospital. She suffered a stroke. With all this on my mind I was confused.

I'm calmer today. I even took a Xanax this morning to quiet my nerves." She held out her hands in front of her. "First time in days they're not shaking."

"Don't stay long. I want Jacob to get as much rest as possible." He began to walk away then stopped. "And no children."

"Sorry."

A nurse assisted Rosemary in putting on a mask, head covering, and a gown.

When she entered the room, her knees almost gave way. She rounded the drape-covered bed and saw Jacob with his eyes shut, breathing with the assistance of oxygen.

"I apologize, Jacob."

His eyes opened. She moved closer, enabling him to see her better without having to adjust his own position.

"Mother's hospitalized. She suffered a stroke in the basement."

His eyes looked weary.

"She had small bites on her body. They can't understand what they were from, but they healed within twenty-four hours."

She lifted a hand as if to take his in comfort but realized she might hurt him.

"Mom's not able to talk. She . . ." Rosemary felt her throat close off. "The doctors say the stroke did a lot of damage. Asked whether I want to take extraordinary . . ." She began to cry. "Mom won't make it."

Jacob slowly raised a bandaged hand.

"I'm not allowed to touch you. I don't have gloves on."

He kept his hand in the air, and she gently covered his bandaged hand with her naked one. Almost immediately she pulled away.

"If the doctor catches me, he'll throw me out for good. Besides, you have to come home, Jacob. Stephen needs you. I don't think Cathy will give him up. That's what I really wanted to tell you. I believe you. Cathy is very angry, and she wants to keep her little boy all to herself."

Jacob tried to speak.

"Stephen is out of the house. He's staying with Mrs. Rosen. I've been staying at the hospital. I want to be there when Mother's end comes. She looks so much older than before the stroke. Her skin has wrinkled. Half her face is slack. I just wish she would open her eyes once before she . . . leaves us."

Both Jacob and Rosemary were silent for a while, but the room hummed with the sound of the equipment that kept Jacob alive.

"Stephen really likes Mrs. Rosen. You might have a hard time talking him into leaving.

"What am I saying? He asks for you all the time. He wants to take care of you himself. A few days ago he tried to sneak in to see you, but he didn't get very far. Mrs. Rosen kept vigil in front of the men's room, not giving him a chance to roam off on his own."

Jacob's eyes remained open and fixed on her.

"By the way, you'll need a place to stay when you get out. I know you don't want to move back into that house. When you're better, we can see about selling the place. But in the meantime when you first get out, I think you and Stephen should live with Robin and me. I know what you're thinking. *Rosemary hates my guts.* Not true. I think I understand you more. Had I known how far Cathy had gone, I would have tried to stop her, or at least warn you to watch over Stephen.

"Get better, and you and Stephen will never have to go into that house again."

chapter 70

Stephen threw his ball at the fence separating his house from Grannie Smith's. He paused to look up at the sun that had started to set. Grannie Smith warned him to come in before dark, but if she couldn't find him she couldn't make him.

At this time of day she usually laid down for a half-hour. If he were inside the house she would sweep him off to the guest bedroom for a nap. He hated naps. Today she'd let him play outdoors until she awoke.

Stephen walked along the side of Grannie Smith's house, opened the gate, and rounded the bend to his house. The house looked sad, deserted. He knew how that felt. He walked up the steps to the front porch and tried the door. Locked. Aunt Rosemary hadn't forgotten in all the haste she had been in. He jumped down to the ground. The wolf had broken the basement window. Had Aunt Rosemary taken the time to have it fixed?

He gave a last look at Grannie Smith's bedroom window before heading straight for the broken basement window. Some glass lay on the ground, but most had fallen into the basement, and no one had repaired it.

Crouching down, he peeked into the basement and saw shards of glass and heard the furnace kick in. Soon it would be dark, but if he entered the basement now, he'd be able to find the flashlight under the stairs.

Stephen carefully pulled some of the broken glass from the frame of the window before sliding his legs through. If he could set a foot on the furnace, he could let himself down slowly. He extended his right leg as far as it would go and found nothing to rest his foot upon.

What a long way down.

And he'd have to make sure he didn't cut himself on the loose glass lying on the cement floor.

He wiggled farther inside the window, his belly pressed against the ledge. His arms became tired, his fingers slipped on the smoothness of the inside ledge, and he dropped to the floor with a loud thump.

Small pieces of glass bit into his palms, and his left knee ached. He took a moment to catch his breath before rising to his feet. Limping away from the broken glass, he checked his hands. Small cuts cris-crossed his palms. When he leaned over he saw his jeans had ripped at the knees and the skin on his left knee had broken open and was bleeding.

Looking up, he faced the wooden box on the table. The dwarf stared at him while the others turned their faces away. Stephen rushed under the staircase but almost fell from the sharp pain in his knee. He found the flashlight and tested it. Good battery power. He sighed with relief.

A low growl caught his attention. The wolf peered up from its bed of old clothes. Its flesh and fur had just begun to take on life. Giggles coming from behind Stephen's back reminded him that darkness had almost arrived.

"Momma, I want to talk to you. Please show yourself."

"The child wants his momma. How cute."

Stephen ignored the scratchy whisper.

"Momma, Grandma is sick. Did you let the uglies hurt her?"

"Uglies? Find this boy a mirror."

Chuckles filled the room.

Stephen spun around and shouted, "I'm not talking to you. Keep quiet!"

To his amazement, the room went silent.

"Momma, where are you?"

"She must wait for death to free her from its fist." The old woman had stepped away from the others. *"Death is very selfish. It doesn't care to give up its own easily."*

"Can you ask her to come for me?"

"Child, the only one who may call her is you. She will come. You have something she wants."

"What is that?" he asked.

"Life. She wants life back again. Your mother carelessly tossed it away, and now she would steal someone else's life."

"Momma wouldn't hurt people. It's you uglies who make people sick."

"We fulfill your mother's fondest wishes, child."

"Momma," he cried out, spinning in a circle, hoping to catch a glimpse of his mother's specter.

"Are you so willing to lose your own life?" The old woman walked to the edge of the table to be closer to Stephen.

"What do you mean?"

"Look at you, so innocent, so trusting."

"Momma loves me."

"Yes, yes, she does. She loves every inch of you." Chuckles backgrounded the witch's voice. *"What,*

child, you have no daddy, no grandma? I am saddened for you. Ah, but you do have a dead mommy who intends to resurrect herself in the guise of a small child."

"Don't try to scare me. This is the way you hurt people."

"We hurt people with fire and chants. You've seen our work. Ooops, perhaps you didn't get to see your grandma."

"They took her to the hospital to make her better."

"I think she will die. She's not strong enough to survive."

"My daddy will."

"Daddy, your one hope in the world now."

"Stephen, come away from that old woman."

"Momma, you're back." He saw a shimmer of light in the darkness under the stairs. Gradually the shape of a hand rested upon the head of the fully animated wolf. His mother's body and face wavered in the darkness before showing as a thin cloud of smoke. He started toward her, but the wolf snarled.

"It's merely rags and paper, Stephen. Don't be afraid of him."

"It killed Molly."

"No, no, Stephen. Our wishes killed her."

"I never wished her dead. I only wanted her to go away because you didn't like her."

"We did it together. Don't you remember placing the costume on the bed and imagining a real wolf that could

come alive inside the suit? Touch it, Stephen."

Carefully Stephen reached out a hand and placed it on one of the wolf's ears.

"It feels like paper."

"*Our desires keep it alive. It exists only to do our bidding. Otherwise its face could blow away in a breeze.*"

He ran his hand down onto the body. Cloth. Nothing but fuzzy cloth. The wolf flexed, its breath shallow, almost non-existent. Stephen dug into the cloth and felt the zipper that Molly had shown him.

"*He can't hurt you, Stephen, because you can banish him with your mind.*"

"Or with my hands?" he asked, gripping the catch on the zipper and pulling it down quickly. The wolf convulsed before Stephen grabbed its face and ripped it to shreds.

"*You will be a powerful warlock, Stephen.*" His mother held out her arms to him.

He walked toward the shade that appeared to be his mother. She caught him in her arms, freezing his flesh until his fine hairs stood on end and goose bumps spread on the surface of his skin. She kissed him on the mouth, and he tasted the bitter flavor of death and smelled the putrid rot that clung firmly to her lips.

"*Take him! Take him!*" cried the dwarf.

"*He is becoming too wise to our ways,*" warned the the old woman.

"Momma?"

"Yes, my baby." His mother freed him.

"Are you happy being dead?"

"No."

"Then why don't you go to heaven?"

The uglies chuckled and cooed to each other.

"Because I don't want to stay away from you for good."

"I'll let you go to heaven. You don't have to stay here if you're not happy."

"But I am happy when I'm with you."

"We can't always be together."

"Why not?"

"Because you disappear when death calls to you."

"I don't have to if you take me within your heart and soul. I need a place to live."

"I think of you all the time but I can't see you all the time."

"Give me your hands, Stephen." She extended her hands palms upward.

The stillness caused Stephen to whirl around to check on the uglies. They all stood on the table staring at him. Not a single one moved. The dwarf's ax had fallen from his hand, but he hadn't bothered to pick it up. Stephen turned back to his mother.

"I pray for you every night 'cause I want your soul to go to heaven."

"You don't want me so far away, Stephen. That's much too far for me to go."

"But that's where you belong now. I would be selfish to hold you here."

"Give me life, Stephen. Don't deny me your flesh."

He turned from his mother and walked toward the uglies.

"They exist because we called them up. But we can send them back to hell, can't we?" He looked back over his shoulder. "Like I destroyed the wolf."

"Come back to me, Stephen. I have shared my knowledge with you. Share your body with me, and we can live together forever."

Stephen looked at the puny uglies. He had helped give them the power to destroy, to terrorize, but they couldn't disobey him. They existed on his flesh and blood.

"You each came from tiny blocks of clay. You I molded with my own hands," said Stephen, pointing at the black snake. He scooped up the snake and rolled it into a ball. His palms turned scales back into clay, which he threw back inside the wooden box.

The dwarf raised its ax.

"You are especially mean," Stephen said.

The dwarf swung his ax wildly, trying to fend off Stephen's small fingers. Once he managed to slice open Stephen's flesh, but he lost the battle when the boy pronounced the dwarf "Nothing but clay."

Stephen picked up several of the figures and crushed them together until there were no more uglies. He carried the box across the room to the furnace. With difficulty he managed to swing open the door and toss the box into the flames. The same flames the uglies had used to burn his father.

"I taught you so much. I had faith you would follow me in the magic."

"Black magic," Stephen dully said. "You can't go to heaven if you practice black magic. You taught me that also."

"We use what we can when desperate. As you grow old you will understand."

"No, Momma, you tricked me. You promised me love, but at a price that's too high. I kneeled next you and said my prayers. I prayed to God. You prayed to the devil."

The front door of the house slammed. Feet could be heard running down the entrance hall.

"Stephen, where are you?" The door to the basement flew open.

"Aunt Rosemary? You came back for me?"

"I told him to come in before dark. I fell asleep, and the alarm clock never went off." Grannie Smith peeked from behind Aunt Rosemary's shoulder.

"Momma's here," he said.

He watched his aunt's eyes search the basement.

"Stephen, come up here to me."

"Can I say good-bye to Momma first?"

"Make it quick." Aunt Rosemary's voice was

sharp, demanding.

"I'll keep praying that you go to heaven, Momma, but I have to go now. Good-bye." He walked several paces before a chill erupted inside his body. He found it hard catching his breath. He reached out for the banister, but his hands were too numb to grasp the wooden rail. A rancid odor made his stomach roil, and food flew from his mouth.

An arm gripped him tightly around his middle and he floated up the stairs, blood pouring from his nose. His eyes saw nothing but a whirl of colors fly by.

The wet earth penetrated his clothes, blades of grass pricked the wounds in his hands.

"Stephen, can you hear me? Stephen?"

He opened his eyes and saw Aunt Rosemary bending over him. The night sky haloed her head.

"Will he be all right?"

He recognized the voice of Grannie Smith and sensed the pastry smell of her hands and clothes.

"Momma didn't want to let me go," he said.

"I know, but you're out of the house now, and you're safe."

He rolled his head to the side and smiled when he saw Robin in her wheelchair waiting on the sidewalk.

"The uglies can't hurt anyone now. And Momma . . . Momma knows that I want her to go to heaven. She shouldn't try to stay here on earth with me. She's not meant to be here anymore." He spoke to Robin but his Aunt Rosemary crushed him to her breast.

"I can drive you all to the hospital," said Mrs. Rosen.

"Am I going to visit with Daddy?" Stephen felt strong enough to pull away from his aunt and ask the all-important question.

"I think you need to see a doctor yourself," Aunt Rosemary said, wiping blood from Stephen's face.

"It's just a nose bleed. I'm not sick. I can't give Daddy any bad germs."

"How about I let you talk to your daddy's doctor?"

"That's a start, I guess."

Mrs. Rosen's car pulled up to the curb. Both children were loaded into the back seat of the car, the wheelchair slipped easily into the trunk.

Robin slid her hand across the back seat, finding Stephen's cold hand. She squeezed as hard as she could but couldn't get the boy to turn away from his house until they rounded a corner.

☆ ☆ ☆

Cathy reached out with her tongue to lick at the spot of blood her son had left on the banister. Another few spots lay splattered against the wall. But none of them retained the sweetness of her son. All she tasted was a sticky bland goo.

She looked back at the destroyed wolf.

"Stephen, you lost our vision. We designed the little people to keep us together. Why didn't you stay? Death wants to pull me under and I fight so hard to remain here that I almost think death has given up on me."

The lock on the furnace door clicked and slowly the door opened. She looked inside to see ashes where the box should be and in the center of the flames an irregularly shaped mound of clay lay lifeless. Hell had managed to retrieve some of its inhabitants.

chapter 71

Robin laughed the loudest when Stephen broke his record for somersaults on the day his father came home from the convalescent home. After months of surgery and physical therapy, Jacob walked into Rosemary's house with the aid of a single cane. He had shaved his head, since his hair grew now in patches. He wore a Jobst plastic mask to keep his facial skin from scarring too badly. Mrs. Rosen declared that he needed to eat a whole pie by himself if he was to gain back the weight he had lost.

"You never were fat, Jacob. Sturdy, but never fat. Now you're skin and bones."

"And happy to still have some skin and bones."

Aunt Rosemary rolled her eyes, but Stephen gave his father a hug. He had been allowed to visit his father at the convalescent home and learned how much pressure he could use without causing his father to flinch.

Five months ago, when Grandma was buried, Stephen wasn't sure if he would ever see this day. The house was sold, and strangers had packed up all his belongings and delivered them in big boxes. In the very last box he found the fat goddess, her hands still shaped in an oval over her head. He sometimes wore the goddess at night when he went to bed right after he said his prayers, always remembering to pray for his mother's passage to heaven.

He liked holding the goddess in the palm of his hand. She wasn't ugly, and she never twitched, but she did have a power he still didn't understand. Someday maybe she'd reveal herself to him. He didn't think she'd ever be mean. Molly had said the goddess helped to bring babies into the world. That was certainly good.

"I'm so glad I could be here for your homecoming," Mrs. Rosen said. "This was my first trip on an airplane, and I rather liked it."

"You'll have to come back more often," said Rosemary, assisting Jacob into a chair.

"I'll definitely be back. How could I stay away

from the children? I've already promised to help Stephen in selecting a college."

Jacob moaned.

"Are you all right?" Rosemary immediately asked.

"Fine. I just can't envision Stephen leaving for college. Hell, that's over ten years away. Besides, how am I going to pay for it? With all the medical bills I'm totally in hock."

"Some money has been put into an account for Stephen. Besides, we'll be putting him out to work as soon as we can."

"What can I do?" Stephen asked.

"Somersaults, of course," cried Robin, gayly laughing as her cousin resumed his favorite acrobatics.

"What about your mother's house, Rosemary? Have you had a chance to clean it out yet?"

"No, Jacob. I wanted to wait until you were released from the convalescent home. Since the kids are free for the summer I thought I'd take them back with me. We could fly back with Mrs. Rosen. A nurse will be starting tomorrow to care for you."

"A nurse! You think I'm an invalid?"

"Yes, I do. She won't be full-time. Half the day you'll have to manage on your own, but you'll need assistance with bathing and the like. This was not my idea, though. The doctor wouldn't release you until I found a nurse to come in."

Jacob sighed and looked over at his son.

"What would have happened had Cathy won?"

"Well, I can tell you that the new owners of the house seem happy there." Mrs. Rosen placed her coffee cup on the table. "I haven't seen any sign of ghosts. The new people did some renovation work. New kitchen, redid the bathrooms, that sort of thing. I understand they replaced the furnace with a new one and whitewashed the basement walls to get rid of the . . ."

"Singed walls," Jacob finished.

"Yeah. The people are quiet. Don't really talk much to the rest of us, but they wave when they see me. Not like having you and Stephen living next door."

"I know my son could cause quite a racket sometimes."

"Having a child around made me feel a little bit young again. You know I actually spied a gray hair on my son's head. If he's getting old and gray, what am I?"

"I'm sure it's premature," Rosemary consoled. "Your son still looks like a kid. Does he actually shave?"

chapter 72

"Will I have to go back to the house?" asked Stephen.

"No way," his aunt answered. "We'll be staying at Grandma's house."

"But she's dead."

"Stephen, she's not going to come back and haunt us."

"How do you know?"

"She loves all of us."

"I thought Momma loved me."

"She did love you, Stephen, but she . . ." Rosemary hesitated.

"She was afraid of going to hell."

"No, Stephen. Your mother did not go to hell.

Maybe she had to spend some time in purgatory."

"Is that where she is now?"

"I am sure of it."

The plane descended for its landing and Stephen's stomach balked at the change in altitude.

"You think she left earth when I stopped calling to her?"

"None of this is your fault. Your mother didn't know what she was doing."

"Yes, she did. She planned it all before she even died. That's why she wanted me with her when she made the uglies."

"Look, look. I bet that's our little town over there," Mrs. Rosen shouted out. "It was fun visiting Austin, but I'm so happy to be going home."

"Do you ever see Momma?" Stephen asked.

"No. The house has new owners, and they're taking good care of the place."

"Maybe I should have left you with your father."

"No, Aunt Rosemary. I want to see my friends again. Besides, I can help you with Robin."

"More like I'll be helping Mom take care of you, Stephen." Robin made a face at her cousin and stuck out her tongue.

"Instead I think I'm going to be breaking up all sorts of rumbles between you two."

The plane dropped through an air pocket and Rosemary had to grab the air sickness bag for Stephen.

chapter 73

Aunt Rosemary took a wrong turn one day in the car and drove by Stephen's old house. He got to see the new owners with their twin Labrador retrievers running around the front lawn, chasing a sprinkler that went round in a circle.

The house was painted, but otherwise it looked the same. He stretched to see the side basement window that had been broken, but it was impossible to see it from the road. He imagined it had been repaired probably before the house was sold.

Twilight hovered over the house, and he thought he saw a familiar sad face weeping in a window. He hoped he had imagined it.

☆ ☆ ☆

Cathy roamed from room to room in the house. She couldn't quiet herself. The old people who had bought the home had few visitors. No children ever crossed the threshold.

The man's sallow face was engraved by years working under the sun. His wife dyed her hair a bright orange she called red. Once in a while the grown children visited. Cathy paid no attention to them, couldn't even recall what they looked like until . . .

A baby came into the house, wrapped in a pink blanket in her mother's arms. A grandchild.

"Very young," the old woman said, grasping her staff tightly.

Ah, yes, Stephen had missed one of the uglies, and she kept Cathy company each night in the basement.

The baby's eyes were blue; or had they not changed color yet? wondered Cathy, hovering above the carriage.

"Charming," the old woman declared.

"And so vulnerable." Cathy smiled down at the babe.

"Can she see you?" the old woman asked.

"I'm sure she can. She hasn't forgotten where she came from yet. She still remembers the prior world."

"To which you belong," reminded the old woman.

"I'll never meet God again. I now belong to hell like you."

Cathy touched the blanket and gently let her icy fingers travel over the baby's fisted hand.

But always the baby left. Her parents visited but once a week and never did they stay overnight.

"How will you win the young thing over?" the old woman asked.

"Slowly. Patiently," answered Cathy.

chapter 74

"Grannie Smith's here with her apple pies."

"Good Lord, Mrs. Rosen, we're going to look like blimps if you keep this up."

"Rosemary, if someone invites me to dinner then they have to suffer through my desserts."

"I like your desserts, Grannie Smith. Who suffers?" Stephen looked around the hallway and saw no hands being raised. "Besides, we need something home-cooked, 'cause Aunt Rosemary had the dinner delivered."

"I just didn't want to poison anyone."

The small group gathered in the dining room

with the table already set for four. As the man of the house, Stephen sat at the head of the table. Robin sat to his right, and the two women fought over who should be closer to the kitchen.

"Robin, why do adults want to be able to run to the kitchen during the meal?"

"I think it has something to do with politeness, Stephen."

The children gobbled down their food quickly in order to rush on to the dessert, but the adults languidly finished their meal, taking long pauses to exchange conversation and laugh.

"You should see the grandchild the neighbors have. She is beautiful. A tiny bit of fuzzy hair and the itsy-bitsy fingers. I forgot how miraculous small babies look."

"What baby?" asked Stephen.

"Oh, the people who bought your house have just become grandparents for the first time. Suddenly they're talking to everyone. I think it's because they want to show off their granddaughter."

"The baby doesn't live there?"

"No, Stephen, although I think the grandparents would like to kidnap her."

"That's not nice."

"Stephen, Mrs. Rosen didn't mean they would really kidnap her. They would like to see more of her, but they aren't going to rob their own children of the joy of having a child." Rosemary reached over and took hold of Stephen's hand. It was cold. "Hey, it's pie time."

The adults removed the dinner plates and promised to return with apple pie and vanilla ice cream.

"What if Momma's still in the house?"

Robin turned to Stephen and held her breath for several moments before speaking.

"She went to heaven."

"You don't know that. I thought I saw her face when your mom drove by my old house. I didn't say anything 'cause I thought I imagined it."

"Probably you did. She can't hurt the new owners."

"What about the baby?"

"The baby isn't you. She wanted to be one with you."

"She wanted to live again, Robin. She didn't want to go to hell forever."

"Stop, Stephen. You're out of the house and as long as you don't go back you're safe."

"But I brought her back and now she has a baby to attack. The baby won't know what's happening to it. I gotta go back and make sure Momma's gone."

"No one will take you back to that place."

"What if I visit Grannie Smith?"

"The last time Grannie Smith trusted you, you almost lost your soul."

"But Momma can't rob a baby of its life."

"How do you know she will?"

"I remember her holding on to me. My insides felt all mushy and I started to black out. You saw me when your mom took me out of the basement."

"And I never want to see you like that again."

"Why are you kids looking so grim?" asked Rosemary.

The children didn't answer.

"Don't tell me you two had some sort of fight."

"We never fight, Momma. Only . . ." Robin kept from looking at Stephen but sensed his eyes glaring at her.

"Only, Stephen's scared for the baby," Robin blurted out before Stephen could cover her mouth with his hand.

"Sit down, Stephen." Rosemary passed out the apple pie with Mrs. Rosen's help. "What baby are we talking about?" Rosemary grabbed hold of her fork and made a deep stab into the pie.

"The grandbaby Grannie Smith was talking about. Stephen's afraid his mother still haunts his old house." Robin looked over at Stephen with downcast eyes.

"The house doesn't belong to you anymore, Stephen, so what goes on inside the house is none of your business," said Rosemary.

"But I brought Momma back. I never got to banish her."

"Banish? Such a fancy word for a little boy," Grannie Smith said. "Where did you learn the word? Do you know what it means?"

"It means sending a spirit away from earth so's it can't hurt anyone. Momma taught me a little about it."

"She did?"

"Stephen, your ice cream is melting. We can talk about this later on. Mrs. Rosen wouldn't be interested."

"I am. What I didn't know is that Cathy actually was teaching witchcraft to Stephen."

"He watched her a lot, that's all."

"No. She had me help her," Stephen clarified. "And I helped make the stupid uglies who hurt so many people. I'll never forget that."

"Dr. Fisk told you it wasn't your fault because you had no idea what your mother's plan was."

"But, Aunt Rosemary, I'm the only one who can make Momma go away."

"How?"

Stephen shrugged.

"Since I brought Momma back I should be able to send her away."

Mrs. Rosen looked at Rosemary.

"Do you think that poor, dear baby is at risk?"

"You said they only visit, never stay. Besides, I'm sure they don't go down in the basement."

"Momma isn't limited to the basement."

"But you destroyed the demons. She has no one to help her."

"She doesn't need help to take over the baby's body. She only needed the uglies for her revenge."

"He says he thought he saw someone crying in the window when we went past the other day," said Robin.

"That could have been a real person."

"No. The people were outside with the dogs."

"They could have had a visitor. I'm sorry, Mrs. Rosen. I didn't mean for this evening to be so grim."

"I brought the topic up, Rosemary, and to tell you the truth, I might keep a watch on the place."

"I can help, Grannie Smith. We can take turns watching."

"Stephen, Mrs. Rosen can take care of her end."

"No, she can't 'cause she can't see Momma. I can. You have to let me stay with Grannie Smith to watch the house." Stephen felt a slap on his right knee. Robin reminded him that he might be going too far. He leaned back in his chair and watched the ice cream melt while the others ate.

chapter 75

"Why did you tell your mother what I said?"

Robin flipped through the television channels. Nothing appealed to her.

"Why?" Stephen repeated.

"Because I didn't want you to get yourself in trouble."

"So you did it for me?"

"No, Stephen." She dropped the remote control to the floor. "You wanted to go to the house. No one will take you there. And how do you know the people who live in your old house want you around? Are you going to sneak in like a burglar?"

"I'll tell them I used to live there and I want to look around."

"Why should they let you?"

"Grannie Smith could get me in."

"She didn't jump at the chance to invite you over."

"That's okay. I can talk her into letting me stay. She likes me."

"Yes, and she doesn't want anything to happen to you."

"They won't know whether Momma is going after the baby's body."

"How will you know?"

"It feels awful. The baby would be miserable. Probably cry a lot and not be able to sleep."

"You can't do this by yourself, Stephen. If my momma hadn't shown up you wouldn't be you. You'd be your mother."

Stephen's face turned perplexed.

"Where would I be right now, Robin?"

"You're the witch. Where do people go when their bodies are stolen?"

Stephen had no answer but he worried about the excited feel he got hearing Robin say that he was a witch. Could his mother have passed on her powers to him? He had enjoyed participating in the basement rituals with his mother. He felt guilty.

"What's the matter?" Robin asked.

"Do you believe that I'm a witch?"

"Maybe you have no magic power. Maybe your mother's magic brought the uglies to life. If they depended on you they may have remained lumps of clay."

"But I brought the wolf to life."

"Your mother was present for that also."

"But she couldn't touch this world. That's why she needed the uglies and she needed me. But I do know she can invade a body."

"Maybe because you're her son you're more susceptible. She might not be able to take over the baby's body, since they're not related."

Stephen thought about this while Robin went back to watching the television.

chapter 76

Since the box had been destroyed the little old woman with the staff had nowhere safe to go during the day. She hid herself behind cardboard boxes infested with bugs and under the dirty laundry that seemed to sit in the basement for weeks.

When Stephen began destroying the other demons she had wisely slipped off the table and onto the hard, cement floor. The landing had been painful, and she had flattened both her feet but had escaped the harsh lick of the fire.

At first she thought about escaping into the outside world. The pane of glass was still missing from the win-

dow over the furnace. The wall leading up to the window had tiny grooves and with the aid of her staff she might have been able to climb the wall. Instead she had decided to wait. When the meddling sister rushed the boy out of the house the mother had gone mad. So mad that the little old woman thought she might be able to rule her creator.

The old woman waited many days before revealing herself to the witch, and she only did when she felt the spirit of the witch fading.

"Mother, why do you mourn?" the old woman asked.

The witch immediately spotted the old woman.

"You exist. And the others?"

"Into the fire."

"Stephen missed seeing you?"

"He was much too busy in his righteous snit to count heads. But, again I ask, why do you mourn?"

"My son is gone."

"There are many other children in the world."

"Children?"

"Yes. If you were . . ." The witch hesitated. She wanted to say "more accomplished," but thought she should choose her words more wisely than that. "If you were weak and had no power then I could understand. But why fade away when you can renew your quest with another child?"

"Can I?"

"Of course. The younger the child the easier it is. The fewer the memories, the easier to squelch the resident

personality."

"But the house is empty."

"Not forever. There is room in this house for many children. Do you think some old maid is going to want the task of caring for a house this size?"

"Will you help me?"

"That is why you called me into this world." The old woman staggered out from behind the furnace and didn't stop until she stood on the center of the basement floor. "I've been waiting here for you to notice me, and while waiting I've met numerous cohorts who knew me in another existence." The witch tapped the floor three times with her staff. A second later a crow flew in through the broken window.

"This is Asmodeus. An old lover. He appears here not in his usual form, but with his three heads, feet of a cock and wings it would be difficult for him not to attract attention. He has volunteered to watch over us. To be our spy."

"We don't need a spy. We need to bring my son back."

"That may be impossible, my dear. We must not obsess over the past. Asmodeus and I can certainly vouch for that. If we wallowed in our histories, we'd never accomplish anything with our futures. However, if the boy should still be near, Asmodeus will find him."

"Will he recognize my son?"

"Yes, by the scent of his flesh and by the pain in the boy's heart. I'm sure he cries nights over losing you,

Mother. That pain will give him away."

"But how will Asmodeus bring Stephen back to this house?"

"First let Asmodeus look for him. But always remember there are others who can take your son's place."

"I want my boy with me forever."

Time, however, changed the mother's longing, and the infant girl soon became the prime target.

chapter 77

Mrs. Rosen peeked out her living room window when she heard a truck stop in front of her door. The driver had a delivery for the neighbors, but he couldn't park any nearer their door because of an overhanging tree. The side panel advertised BABY WORLD in big letters. Curious, she decided to just happen to step outside to check for her mail.

At her mailbox Mrs. Rosen saw the neighbors signing a sheet of paper on a clipboard. She waved when they noticed her. Waving back, the couple glowed.

"Beautiful day, isn't it?" said Mrs. Rosen.

The delivery men returned to the truck and pulled out a big box.

"A gift for your granddaughter?" asked Mrs. Rosen.

"Much more exciting than that," said Mrs. Crowther, the neighbor. "We'll be having our granddaughter staying with us for several months. The kids have to go off to South Africa for their jobs and didn't want to chance taking the baby along. They themselves have to get all sorts of shots."

"How delightful for you."

The delivery men passed by, carrying a box that obviously contained a crib.

"When does the baby move in?" Mrs. Rosen asked.

"Soon. We're getting ready in advance. The small room on the way to the kitchen has been done up as a nursery."

"You mean the one near the basement?"

"Near the basement door. Yes." Mrs. Crowther let her husband guide the delivery into the house and she approached Mrs. Rosen. "The kids think we're overdoing it, but I haven't had a baby in the house since . . . Never mind, I don't think I want to admit to how long it's been."

"Are you enjoying the house?"

"Yes, very much. We have lots of room for my husband's library, and we can keep the dogs downstairs away from our bedroom. Although once in a while Ginger whines in front of the gate we have barring the stairs. We figure she misses being pampered. She used to sleep every night at the foot of our bed. Spike doesn't seem to care."

"Any problem with the heating?"

"We got a brand new furnace. Why would we have problems with the heat?"

"Just wanted to make sure you weren't too warm."

"Too warm?" Mrs. Crowther waited for an answer.

"The former occupants had some trouble with the heat, but as you say, you did install a new furnace."

Mrs. Crowther nodded and excused herself. "My husband is probably wondering what happened to me."

"Yes. Well, I look forward to seeing more of your granddaughter."

Mrs. Crowther gave her neighbor a broad grin and hurried back to the house.

"Oh, Stephen, I hope your mother has moved on," Mrs. Rosen muttered to herself.

A horn broke Mrs. Rosen's reverie.

"Rosemary. Stephen."

Both got out of Rosemary's Jaguar.

"He's been dying to pay a visit." Rosemary made direct eye contact with Mrs. Rosen, sending a signal that Stephen still worried about what he had let loose.

"You needn't have come over here. I would have

dropped by before the end of the week."

The deliverymen returned to their truck and almost immediately pulled away from the curb.

"A gift?" Rosemary asked.

"Sort of." Mrs. Rosen nodded and led her guests to the house when a crow swooped low, barely missing the top of Rosemary's head.

"What was that?" Rosemary asked.

"I've never seen anything like that before. I don't know how to explain it."

"I don't like that bird," Stephen said.

"I think the feelings are mutual." Rosemary ran her fingers through her hair.

"Come inside before we get dive bombed again."

Stephen trailed along behind the two women, searching the sky for the crow.

"Pay attention or you'll trip."

Stephen heeded his aunt's advice and stepped over the garden hose.

chapter 78

As night filled the sky with darkness, the old woman came out from her hiding place behind the piled-up cardboard boxes.

"Old woman, there is a delightful treat on the first floor. A nursery is being prepared. It's bright pink with various-sized stuffed animals and a rocking chair containing a musical box."

"Mistress, has the house once again changed hands?"

"No. But I believe a baby will be staying here."

"Perhaps it is there to enable the baby to nap more comfortably. It doesn't necessarily mean the baby will stay."

"Cursed old woman, why do you destroy my dreams?"

"Mistress." The old woman bowed low. "I merely—"

"First you deride me because I dream of my son. Now you want to steal the baby from me."

"Hardly, mistress. I speculated. That is all."

They both heard a tap on one of the basement windows. The crow stood so still he almost blended into the night.

"What does he want?" Cathy asked.

"He has found someone."

"Stephen?"

"Yes." The old woman walked nearer to the window and raised her staff to be rid of the crow.

"Why did you send him away?"

"We wouldn't want someone to notice him."

"You're annoyed that he's found Stephen," Cathy said.

"Your son, the baby girl. It makes for more complications. The baby is pure, new, untouched by this world as yet. Your son suffers prejudices fed to him by the authorities he must obey."

"You're saying it would be easier to take possession of the baby."

"Yes. More than that, we must make sure your son does not interfere."

"He fears me now and probably won't come into this house."

"Maybe we should reinforce that fear."

chapter 79

"Are you satisfied now, Stephen? I took you over to Mrs. Rosen's and you saw how quiet your old house looks."

He wiggled his nose.

"What's that supposed to mean?"

"Aunt Rosemary, that bird wasn't really a bird."

"What?"

"It was a spirit. I could feel the evil in him."

Rosemary rested her hands on his shoulders.

"I was wrong to bring you back. Your dad could use some cheering up."

"Is he sick?" Stephen turned around to face his aunt.

"No. He's not sick, but he is finding the physical therapy very taxing."

"I think the bird is spying for Momma," Stephen said, ignoring his aunt's comments about his father.

Rosemary sighed.

"I find this hard to comprehend. I'm afraid you've become obsessed with witchcraft. On the other hand, I didn't believe you the first time."

"And two people died and Dad got hurt."

"Momma?"

"Yes, Robin?" Rosemary turned to see her daughter in the doorway of the living room.

"Maybe we should pay attention to what Stephen says. If we stay close to Stephen, then his mother won't be able to attack him."

"Neither of you can stop her," Stephen said. "But I can talk to her. I can ask her not to hurt anyone."

"What if your mother won't listen?" Robin guided herself into the room. "What if your mother has become evil, or what if she isn't your mother at all? Maybe it's some demon imitating your mother. Could you tell the difference, Stephen?"

"She's my mother."

"But you don't know that for sure. Maybe a demon has possessed her dead soul."

"Robin, I don't think we should encourage Stephen in these fantasies."

"I'm not. I'm trying to make him see the dangers he faces if he goes back to the house."

"No one has invited us to the house. The people deserve their privacy," said Aunt Rosemary.

A crow crashed into the window, its wings spread wide and its head tucked low, close to its body.

Rosemary screamed as the bird seemingly fell to the ground.

Robin started for the front door.

"Where are you going?" her mother called out to her.

"The bird could be hurt. We should do something."

"No. Stay in the house."

"But, Mom . . ."

"He's here for me. It's the same bird we saw at Grannie Smith's," said Stephen.

"Both of you stay in the house and I'll check on the crow." Rosemary threw on a cotton sweater on her way out the front door. Once outside she wondered why she had bothered with the sweater. Her body instantly broke out in a sweat. She rounded the corner of the house, hoping there would be no bird prostrate on the ground, but there it was. Its head bent in an awkward position, the wings spread wide, allowing the shine of the black feathers to glow under the sun. As she drew nearer the bird shuddered. She looked toward the window and saw that both children watched her.

I'll get a bath towel, she thought, looking back down at the crow. Wrap the poor thing in a towel and take it down to the veterinary hospital. Had the children not been watching she probably wouldn't have bothered to touch the crow.

"Here's a blanket."

Rosemary jumped at the sound of Stephen's voice behind her.

"I told both of you to stay in the house. Besides, that blanket's decorative. Mom uses it to cover . . ." Mom didn't use it anymore, she reminded herself.

"Come on, let's go back into the house and find a towel."

"Which towel? I can get it."

"Fine, Stephen, get one of the bath towels. Get two," she corrected herself.

A minute later Stephen stood behind her again, this time with the guest towels. Again she had to remind herself that it didn't matter. Mom wasn't going to be using them for guests ever again.

She took the towels from the boy's outstretched arms.

"Want me to do it, Aunt Rosemary? The bird won't hurt me."

"How do you know that?"

"Because Momma sent him."

"If she sent the bird, what kind of message did

he bring? And couldn't she find a bird that was less of a klutz?"

"He wanted to get our attention."

"And kill himself?"

"Maybe he's not really hurt." Stephen moved in closer to the crow, and when he did the bird suddenly became very still. There didn't appear to be any sign of life.

Rosemary quickly threw one of the bath towels over the crow. Still no movement.

"What are you going to do with him, Aunt Rosemary?"

"I don't know whether to throw it in the trash or take it to the hospital."

"The same place where they took Daddy?"

"No. That hospital is only for humans. There's another hospital not far from here that's for animals."

"I think maybe we should leave him there under the towel."

"Don't you want to help it if it's hurt?"

Stephen shook his head. "It's not hurt. It's faking."

The boy had been right before.

Robin knocked on the windowpane. She waited for them to pick up the bird. *Is it hurt? she mouthed.*

"I'll tell her it's dead; then no one has to pick it up," Stephen said.

"She'll want to bury it. She always does."

"We can have a private ceremony and tell her

she wasn't invited."

"Robin will believe that one, all right. Step aside and give me some room."

Rosemary held up the second bath towel, a bright periwinkle with tiny daisies decorating one end. She sighed, took a deep breath, and bent over to wrap up the bird. Surprised by the weight, she almost dropped it.

"Now what?" Stephen asked.

"Exactly. That's my question. I guess I could put it into the car and drive it over to the hospital."

The bird didn't move. She thought about digging a hole and simply dropping the crow in and covering it with as much dirt as she could shovel. Holding the bird at arm's length, she turned to the window and smiled at her daughter, whose green eyes couldn't have been any larger. Robin was such a sucker for animals.

A flurry of activity inside the towels made her let go of the bundle. The crow screeched out from under the cover and attacked her face, clawing at her cheeks and pecking around her eyes, until finally its beak did a dead aim into her right eye. Her screams matched the deadly caws of the crow as it swept out of Stephen's reach and up into the sky.

"Momma," yelled Robin, gliding down the path on which her mother stood, the towels wrapped now around her mother's legs. She could feel the blood covering her hands but couldn't see. Stephen had obviously gone for the neighbors. She heard his voice calling out for help. She fell to her knees and wept as Robin wrapped her arms around her mother.

chapter 80

"You do have to do something about your mother," Robin said, sitting across from Stephen on Grannie Smith's porch. "You can't let her continue hurting people. Even if it isn't your mother but a demon you have to stop it. And I'll help you."

Stephen stared over at his former house. Most of the lights were on, and the dogs lay in front of the house enjoying the light breeze that rustled their fur. He stood and walked to the very edge of the porch for a better view. One of the dogs flexed its legs as if dreaming about chasing a rabbit. The other dog stared back at Stephen.

"Hello," Stephen said.

The dog ears perked up, and when Stephen repeated his greeting the dog stood.

"Come here, boy."

The dog came immediately, giving a brief glance at Robin before setting its jaw on the boy's thigh. Slowly, Stephen petted the dog.

"I wish you could talk. I have so many questions to ask."

"He's just a dog, Stephen. He can't tell you who's haunting the house."

"He could if he could speak. He knows me because of my mother."

"Are you telling me she sent him over to you?"

"No. But he can sense who I am."

"And what are you?" Robin asked, a chill touching her voice.

"Are you afraid of me?" he asked Robin.

So much time passed that Stephen had given up on an answer until she moved her wheelchair closer to him.

"I'm afraid of what's haunting you. You don't mean any harm, but horrible things happen to people around you."

"Maybe you should stay away from me."

"No. Instead I'm going to pay attention to everything you say. I'll not doubt you the way the grown-ups did."

As he petted the dog it began to whimper.

"Is he hurt?" Robin asked.

"He's trying to talk to me." He looked over at Robin.

"Don't look at me. Momma started teaching me French, not dog talk."

"Let's bring the dog home."

"What? He lives right next door."

"But Robin, we can say he joined us on the porch and we wanted to be sure he belonged to someone."

"Why not?" Robin carefully maneuvered her wheelchair down the ramp, leading the way.

Stephen rang his old doorbell while holding onto the dog's collar. The other dog merely looked at them quizzically and went back to sleep.

"Oh, hello. I almost missed you down there."

"Hi. Robin and I are staying with Grannie Smith." He pointed toward the house next door. "And we were sitting on the porch. And this dog came up on the porch to sit with us. But we're not sure whether he has a home. Is he your dog?"

"Yes. He's usually very good, never wanders off the property. He must be getting a bit jealous of our granddaughter. He's used to being fussed over. I hope he didn't bother either of you."

"No. I used to live here."

"In this house?"

Stephen nodded.

"We moved to Austin to live with Robin's mother."

"You must be the Zaira child. Your father had some sort of accident. Listen, do you both want to come in and have some soda or ice cream?"

"Ice cream would be great," Robin shouted out.

"I'll get my husband to help you up the steps."

Inside the children couldn't recognize the place. The pale walls were now painted in deep hues, and instead of shades the windows now had velvet curtains.

A piercing shriek came from down the hall.

Startled, the woman excused herself and went to check on the baby.

"I think she misses her parents. She's only a few months old. A terrible time to leave a child." The lady's husband shook his head and invited the children into the living room.

"My wife said you both used to live here."

"Only me," answered Stephen. "Robin lived in Austin and she still does, but now Dad and I live there too."

"I guess you miss your friends."

"Sometimes, but I got Robin." He listened as the woman helplessly tried to quiet the baby.

"We thought this would be a joy having our granddaughter around, but it's not such an easy job."

"Can I see the baby?"

The man led the children to the back room, which had become a nursery. The woman sat in a pale pink rocking chair holding the baby close to her breast while singing an old lullaby Stephen recognized.

"My momma sang that to me," Stephen said. "Is it a favorite song of yours too?"

"Actually, I hardly ever sang to my own children. I don't know how this tune popped into my head, but it seems to soothe her down after a while."

The baby held her hands in tight little fists, her beet-red face soaked in tears.

"Stephen, you're back."

He looked to see whether anyone else had heard his mother's voice, but the adults and Robin kept cooing over the baby.

"Will you stay with me this time and not run away? That was very bad of you."

Embraced by his mother's coldness he shivered.

"Take me out of this house, Stephen. There's nothing left of our former lives here. Take me to your new home."

"No!"

Everyone turned to look at him.

"Are you all right?" Robin asked. "We should really head back to Grannie Smith's before she notices we're missing."

"Of course. I'll walk the children back to their house, dear. Will only be a few minutes."

The husband helped Robin back down the front steps and stayed with them until they climbed the porch stairs.

"Thank you, we're okay here. Grannie Smith said we could sit on the porch until bedtime."

The husband nodded and headed back to his own home.

"What happened, Stephen? Why did you yell out like that?"

"She's still there, Robin. She spoke to me. She wants me to take her back to your house."

"What are we going to do? That poor baby screamed so loud. Your mother must be hurting her. We can't let that happen, but you certainly can't take her back to Austin."

Stephen's shoulders drooped. It would be so much easier if he didn't believe the woman really was his mother. He didn't want to cause her to suffer, and she sounded so sad.

He walked to the edge of the porch and looked up at his old bedroom window. Momma stood there, her hands pressed against the windowpane, her hair a riot of smoky white; her flesh shone with the paleness of death, and her frightened features pleaded for his help.

chapter 81

In Grannie Smith's guest room Stephen kept his curtains open and the window ajar. Momma stood across from him in his old bedroom window, staring. Not saying a word and not trying to communicate with her hands, she simply stared at her son.

"Momma, you hurt me so badly. Daddy has trouble moving around. He can't play rough with me anymore. I have to be careful when I touch him. Grandma's gone. Molly's dead. Aunt Rosemary's in the hospital, and Robin was so scared that she'd loose her momma. Why do so many people have to suffer?"

He reached under his pillow and pulled out the

wooden goddess.

"I still have the fat lady. You said she's very important. She's not mean like the uglies, but she hasn't told me what to do about you." He fingered the figure, rubbing the swollen belly gently as if he had an Aladdin's Lamp. The belly shined under the dim nightlight. He looked closely at the face of the goddess but it seemed amorphous, the features blurred purposefully by the hand that created the figure. The longer he looked at the face, the more different forms it took. Was she young? Yes, she had smooth skin. Was she old? Yes, her pinprick eyes held wisdom. Was she gentle? The softness of her brow revealed her love and patience. Was she strong? Yes, her firm jaw jutted out in defiance.

"Please, naked lady, tell me what to do. Don't let me make a mistake and cause others to be hurt." He rested his head on the pillow and lay the naked lady next to him. She'd watch over him and keep his momma away.

☆ ☆ ☆

Brandy stood outside the witch's house. He couldn't remember how he had gotten there. How had he escaped the cage? Had the lady come back? Did the troll change his mind and save Brandy? Brandy wished he could remember, for he didn't like empty space inside his brain.

The cottage looked the same. Snakes still wiggled and sunned themselves on the path leading to the front door. The knocker in the shape of garlic on the door tempted him to knock. But why would he? He was free. This is what he wanted. He looked down at his clothes and saw that every stitch he had arrived in was back on his body. His shoes looked polished. His shirt pressed. His pants were even clean.

He should run away, he thought. Far away and never have to see that old witch ever again.

The door to the cottage swung open, but no one stood in the doorway. He moved forward to peek inside.

The cottage was still. No ticking clocks, no clanking pipes, no patter of the witch's big feet.

He realized he didn't know her name and doubted he really wanted to.

"She's found herself another."

Brandy spun around to stare at the troll.

"She mourned a little bit for you but then moved on, as you should do."

"Who has taken my place?"

"It doesn't matter," replied the troll. "Go home, Brandy."

"If I go home, will she follow me?"

"She never travels far from this cottage."

"Then she won't look for me?"

The troll shook his shaggy head.

"What will happen to the person in the cage?"

"She'll probably boil her and serve her for dinner."

Shocked, Brandy didn't know which way to turn.

"I wouldn't go back into the cottage if I were you. I'd go far, far away."

"But I can't abandon the person in the cage."

"Why not?" The troll looked very perplexed.

"Because I should be in the cage instead. It isn't fair for someone else to suffer."

"Do you think it fair that you should suffer?"

Brandy could see the logic to running far from the cottage. He liked standing outside under the sun, smelling the flowers, hearing birds chirp.

"I can make a passage for you among the snakes," the troll offered. "I'll make sure you come to no harm. Down the road there's a bus stop. It's due in twenty minutes."

"Twenty minutes? Then I must have at least a few minutes to say goodbye to the witch."

"She'll not let you go. If she finds you, it will be the end. There'll be no second chance." The troll spoke in a stern voice.

"Why is she so mean? She wasn't always mean, was she?" Brandy asked.

"Disappointments. She's had many disappointments. They've hardened her heart."

"That's sad. We should feel sorry for her."

"Why?" The troll scratched his head with his huge six-fingered hand. Lice alighted from his mane.

"Maybe if she hadn't had so many problems she'd

be nice."

"Not her. Too selfish."

"What should I do, Mr. Troll? I feel I owe her something."

"Not at all. She birthed you and abandoned you."

"My mother. She wouldn't harm me."

The troll looked skeptical.

chapter 82

"Wake up, Stephen." Robin pushed against his shoulder. "What's that thing sticking in your cheek?"

Alarmed, Stephen immediately felt the cheek that lay on the pillow. He had rolled over onto the goddess during the night, and now his cheek felt semi-numb.

"What's that?"

"A goddess. I keep her close at night so Momma won't visit me in my dreams."

"Does it work?"

"It did last night. I only talked to the troll."

Robin sat back in her wheelchair and covered

her face with both her hands.

"Robin?"

She dropped her hands into her lap.

"I hardly ever know what you're talking about. We certainly don't need to add trolls to the problems we have."

"He's a friendly troll. Although he did kidnap Brandy."

"This is making less sense as you explain it. Grannie Smith has breakfast on the table. And your dad called."

"I missed his telephone call? Didn't he ask for me?"

Robin shrugged.

"Grannie Smith didn't give me any details. I think he called because my mother's in the hospital. I get the feeling he wants to come and take us all back to Austin."

"He can't come here. Momma will hurt him again. She watched me all night."

"Why didn't you close the window?"

" 'Cause I feel sorry for Momma."

"Sorry? She tried to steal your body. She killed Grandma and Molly. She hurt my mother and your father badly. How could you feel sorry for someone so cruel?"

"You're sounding like the troll," Stephen said, thinking that maybe both might be right.

"I don't care about your stupid troll. And you may not be able to save the baby."

"I won't be able to forget the baby. Her shrieks sounded so painful. Momma's trying to push the baby's soul out to make way for her own spirit." He looked down at the goddess in the palm of his hand. "I feel stronger when the naked lady is near me. I'll know what to do if I keep her close to me."

"The people who bought your house aren't going to believe you if you tell them your mother is haunting the house. They'll think you're making up stories."

"Wouldn't you like to see the baby again, Robin?"

"If you insist."

chapter 83

The old woman grunted as she tucked herself farther behind the water-stained cardboard boxes. Not only did she have to stay out of the sun, she also had to worry about the horrid dogs that followed their master every place he went, including the basement.

"Where is the boy?" she muttered to herself. By now Asomodeus should have caused some sort of chaos at the child's house. She expected such an incident would prick the child's guilt and send him searching for his mother. The witch didn't know how to do a true possession. All she did wss terrorize the infant without sending its spirit fleeing. The witch's son seemed far more able, although he

still didn't know the breadth of his skills.

The old woman heard the dogs bark and drew deeper into her filthy crevice. She became caught in a giant spiderweb; the sticky threads clung to her cloak, whitening the dark material. She pulled forward but the web dragged her back. In her fury she flailed about, managing only to coat her fingers in a slimy glue. For a second she stopped to rest and felt the tango of the large, black spider coming to greet her. Lifting her head she saw the slender legs scurry down the web. Unfortunately her hair became entangled in the carefully patterned threads.

The staff remained gripped in her right hand. Sending all her power into that hand, she set the staff on fire, burning the web but not the staff itself. As if made of straw, the web flared and the unwary spider didn't have time to withdraw. The old woman pulled away quickly as the web's fibers dissolved. The spider instantly became ash.

The basement door opened.

"I think I have some down in the basement. It'll just take a second."

"Now what?" the old woman wondered out loud. She peeked carefully around one of the boxes and saw the man had not come down but had left the door ajar. She heard an annoying whine, and then one of the dogs slipped his snout into the crack and opened the door wide enough to give him space to enter. Down the steps clicked the dreaded paws. She hated dogs. They didn't mind their own business.

"I'll get him for you," cried Stephen's voice.

"The boy is here," the witch whispered to herself, almost forgetting the Labrador retriever that skittered directly toward the box she hid behind.

Again she withdrew to the narrow crevice where the spider ash dirtied the hem of her cloak.

"Where are you, Spike?" called Stephen, coming down the familiar staircase. "Have you found something?"

The dog whimpered and stood in front of an old, stained cardboard box.

"Is there something in there?" Stephen touched the box haphazardly.

"Momma, are you down here?" he asked.

"No, foolish child, death is keeping company with her today."

Stephen pulled back the dog, holding it by its collar.

"Sit," he demanded, and to his surprise the dog did.

The old woman sniffed the air and relaxed when she couldn't smell the dog's bad breath. Slowly she moved forward, leaving a trail of ash behind her. Once near the edge of the box she peeked around.

"My goodness, Stephen, you look bigger and healthier. You were awful pale the last time I saw you. Except of course for that red flush your mother put in your chubby cheeks."

"I thought I destroyed the uglies."

"You did. Almost. I may have an old body, but I can

get it to move pretty quick when I have good reason to."

"How are you surviving without the box?"

"In dark corners, beneath dirty laundry."

"You sent the crow."

"The crow?"

"The one that hurt my aunt."

"Your aunt! How is she? Brilliant of her to come when she did last time."

"You hate her."

"Your mother has reason to hate her more than I."

"But you sent the crow. Don't lie."

"Why would I bother?"

" 'Cause you want to get even for her taking me away."

"Who had more to lose when you vanished?"

Stephen sulked for a few seconds before answering.

"Momma."

"Am I your momma?"

"I wouldn't want you to be my momma."

"You hurt my feelings, boy. I've been sitting with your mother for months now. Making the long nights bearable. She was very upset when you rejected her."

"She wanted to steal my life."

"Your body. She's willing to take you along with her as a silent partner. Worse than sending you from your body, since you'd have to partake in her scheming. And that would be such a shame because of the potential bubbling inside you. I feel it. You have abilities you can't imagine. You could call to the great ones and have them

bow before you."

"Like the uglies." Stephen's derisive voice made the witch clench her hands.

"Not those fools. Greater spirits who can bring their own disguises to life in this world. The charm you wear can release the energy you possess."

Stephen reached up and felt the naked lady beneath his shirt.

"You wear her because you must."

"I wear it in memory of Momma."

"Liar. She keeps you safe in bed, protecting you from your momma. *Why else would you be wearing it now?"*

"The naked lady belonged to Momma."

"But it rarely worked for your mother. She needed you and the wooden goddess to spark her magic."

"You owe your existence to Momma."

"I owe an act of revenge to her. I have completed my contract. I want now to work with a great conjuror." The witch bowed to Stephen.

"You're a traitor," spat out Stephen. "My mother may not be powerful, but you are weaker. You need to latch on to someone of this world to survive. Alone you will be destroyed. The sun could drive your spirit back into the hell from which you came. A curse laid upon you would subdue you into slavery. Just as my mother did."

"An irritating child," the witch muttered.

"You speak of her being a weak witch; what are you that she could bind you to a stupid wooden box? And

when it is no more you are left cowering in the basement."

"I offer you lessons. Perhaps you may surpass my skills, but first you must learn how to use the magic that travels with you."

"My Mother could give me that information."

"But at a price. The price is your soul. She has lost hers to the devil and will take you with her if willingly you combine with her. The blackness of her sins will rot your guts, child. The pungent smell of death will always be within your nostrils, and the coldness that makes you shiver will freeze your blood until your heart and mind are ice."

"Momma doesn't have to go to hell."

"She'll certainly not be invited to the Lord's banquet." The witch chuckled and leaned heavily on her staff.

"It's you that can't change the future. You were born of evil. Momma said so. You neither love nor hate. That clay is the best you can do for a body."

"This clay? It is the worst vehicle I have ever had to use. You and your mother aren't even skillful in the art of sculpturing." Abruptly the old woman stopped speaking. A frown darkened her brow, and her lips moved in a nervous quiver before she could speak again. "We argue. We fight. Yet we forget how much we can give to each other. Work together and we drive our powers forward into this world's mass confusion. No one will suspect the sway we would have over all that rules. Nothing could be changed or continued without our express wishes."

"You and I? Where does that leave Momma?"

The old woman gave Stephen a weary smile.

"Your mother's existence is in your hands."

"I think it's time she went to heaven."

"Heaven? Can you define that word for me?"

"It's where the dead can rest without being bothered by evil things like you."

"Your mother isn't ready for a rest. She wants life back."

"Daddy says I'm responsible for the consequences of my own actions. Momma took a bad action, and now she—"

"Must pay," the old woman interrupted. "What did she do that was so bad? Abandon you? Tie a noose around her neck and hang herself in this very room?"

Stephen squeezed his eyes shut.

"Yes, you remember, boy, the doll-like limpness of her body dangling in mid-air just about where you are standing."

Stephen's eyes flew open.

"No, she was across the room!" he shouted.

"Yes, you remember and always will. 'Momma needs help,' weren't those your words? 'Help Momma,' you pleaded, tears streaming down your cheeks because Momma didn't answer your call, and in your heart you knew she never would again."

"Her hair covered her face and her feet were bare."

"The clothes she wore were dirty and stained. She

hadn't washed in days. She hadn't spoken in days." The old woman moved closer to Stephen.

"Momma touched my cheek and kissed me goodnight. When she saw me she would give me a faint smile."

"Still, she didn't take you to the basement with her the very last time. Her last act she needed to do alone. She never stopped to think how you would feel. It didn't matter to her."

"She hurt really bad."

"How did you feel her last days? Did she hurt you, Stephen?"

"She didn't mean to."

"The truth is she didn't think of you at all. You would serve as her way back. She would rob you without a pang of regret."

"Momma loved me. Momma loved me." His voice quivered within his throat. "Only she's not Momma anymore. She's been soiled by you uglies."

The witch attempted to reach out to the boy, but the dog growled from behind Stephen's legs.

"Don't be a fool for your mother. I will show you how to use the goddess. Her secrets will spill out onto your hands and seep into your flesh. Love your Mother but also beware of her."

Stephen grabbed Spike's collar and walked toward the staircase. He stopped at the first step to look down at the dog.

"Wait!" the old woman screeched as she moved onto

the center of the basement floor. "Pay attention to what I say." Her age turned her voice to gravel. She breathed in his innocence and she wanted to puke. "Come back here," she demanded, her voice filled with disgust.

Stephen let his hand slip from the dog's collar. Spike instantly sprang on the old woman. The staff flashed a few sparks before being broken into bits by the chomp of the dog's powerful jaws.

Stephen didn't look back. He climbed the stairs hearing first the laughter coming from the living room and then the squawk of a baby in pain.

chapter 84

After leaving the basement Stephen walked to the nursery. Mrs. Crowther sat in the rocking chair singing Momma's lullaby.

"Don't sing that to the baby."

"Pardon me, Stephen?"

"The baby doesn't like the song. That's why she's crying."

"Do you have any suggestions?"

"Rock-A-Bye Baby. Anything, but not that lullaby."

"But it was your favorite, Stephen."

His mother wrapped him in her cold arms and

the baby quieted.

"Perhaps you're right. She's seems to be settling down. Do you think it was the lullaby or my singing?" Mrs. Crowther smiled at him.

"I'm ashamed to say I didn't sense you were in the house."

His mother's voice sounded apologetic. The baby had captured all her senses. The baby with the chubby body and the dimpled cheeks. The baby that could give Momma life again.

"Since she's being so good, why don't we take her into the living room where my granddaughter can be the center of attention." Mrs. Crowther stood and walked toward him. She touched his arm and immediately pulled away. "You're so cold. Are you feeling all right?" The woman called her husband who came in a hurry followed by Robin in her wheelchair. "He doesn't look well. I'm afraid he may have something that the baby can catch," Mrs. Crowther said to her husband.

"You look a bit pale. Would you like to sit down?"

"Maybe we should go back to Grannie Smith's. We just wanted to visit the baby for a short while," Robin said.

"Sorry she wasn't more amenable to company."

"More what?" asked Stephen.

"She was cranky, Stephen," Robin clarified. "She's better now, but it's time for us to go back for lunch."

"We can set some food on the table for you kids," said the husband.

"Let them go home, dear," Mrs. Crowther said, glancing down at her granddaughter and back to her husband.

"Don't go, Stephen. I've missed you. I want you to stay with me forever. Let us be one, please."

The soft, pleasing voice of his mother made Stephen sleepy. He almost lost his balance except that Mr. Crowther supported his small body.

"I'd better carry him over."

"No, he can walk, can't you, Stephen?"

Robin's voice came from so far away, and yet she appeared to be right in front of him. He reached for her and she grabbed his hand.

"Just help me down the steps, Mr. Crowther, and we'll be fine. My cousin needs some fresh air."

Once outside and on the front lawn Stephen withdrew from the cavernous tunnel in which his mind had gotten lost. Robin held his hand and Mr. Crowther stared down at him.

"I'm okay," Stephen said, letting go of Robin's hand.

"He had an allergic reaction. He's allergic to dogs," Robin explained.

"I must say you and Spike were down in that basement for quite a while. Robin and I got so wrapped up in discussing Three Stooges' films that we forgot about you. Did you ever get him to come up?"

"No. He's probably still down there."

As Stephen spoke, Spike came out of the house and dropped a smoking object under the direct rays of the sun.

"What the heck have you got there?" Mr. Crowther walked over to pick up the ball of clay. "Can't imagine where you found this, Spike." He turned to Stephen. "Is this some leftover play clay you left behind when you moved?"

"I don't want it."

The dog barked several times.

"Guess if you want to roll it around in the grass a bit, it can't hurt." Mr. Crowther threw the lump of clay into the grass and the two dogs nudged it about, occasionally biting into the sun-softened clay.

chapter 85

"I'd take the bus if I were you," said the troll.

Brandy couldn't decide. Should he run away or face the witch one more time?

"She can't be trusted. I remember once when she kidnapped a husband. Brought him to the house by advertising for a tutor. Of course she had no intention of advancing her education. Instead she turned him into a zombie and led him around with a collar round his neck."

"What happened to him?"

"I believe he's the third window frame from the left, top floor."

They both stared upward until they heard a cry come

from deep within the cottage.

"Don't have much more time to catch the bus," the troll said, looking at the sundial he wore on his wrist.

"Won't there be another bus tomorrow?"

"Sure, but you might not be able to be on it." The troll tapped his large, ugly, naked foot on the cement pathway.

"Can I at least go in and check on her prisoner?"

"Why? The prisoner doesn't mean anything to you."

"But she's taken my place."

"So? Be glad she did."

"She didn't do it voluntarily, did she?"

"None of them do. You've seen what that basement looks like. Who'd want to spend time down there?"

"Then I must save her."

"Who?"

"The prisoner."

"What if you miss the bus?"

"You told me there'll be another."

The troll put an arm around Brandy's shoulders. His body odor caused Brandy to almost faint.

"Listen, if you go back into that cottage she'll never let you go again. She may not even free the young lady who has taken your place. Why should she?"

"But she doesn't need both of us."

"The witch will feed off her soul."

"But if you help . . ."

The troll dropped his arm from Brandy's shoulders

and took several steps back.

"I can't help. I'm just as dependent on her as she is on you."

"But you're a troll. You're strong and scary."

"I wouldn't double-cross the witch. She'd cast a spell on me. Make me small and frightened like a mouse."

Brandy turned away from the troll and walked into the cottage.

"Oh, you're back," the witch twitted from the end of the hall. "I did miss you. I checked everywhere for you. Under the beds. Under the pillows. Even under the stove. But I couldn't find you. Bad boy." Even as she said "bad boy" she smiled.

"Free the woman you have captive in the basement and I will come back."

"What woman?"

"The troll told me that you—"

"He *did?*"

Stephen woke in the middle of the night, his sheets wrapped around his legs and his pillow tossed to the side along with the naked lady. Hurriedly he freed himself from the bed linen and jumped out of the bed. He ran to the window and looked across at his mother, who sat with her palms against the windowpane. He swept the curtains across the window, erasing her image.

He opened the drawer in the night table and pulled out a burgundy velvet cloth and laid it on the bed. The smooth material eased the tension in his body. For a few minutes he simply ran his palms across the fabric. Finally he pulled apart the corners and revealed the items that had belonged to his mother: a pair of pearl earrings, a tortoiseshell comb with a tooth missing, a locket containing the missing tooth, a missal from his mother's first Holy Communion, and a holy picture depicting the Assumption of the Virgin Mother. He reached across the bed for the naked goddess. He placed the goddess inside the fabric with the other utensils he had used to bring his mother back and rolled the entire package into a tight bundle. He no longer wanted to know the magic hidden inside the naked goddess. He decided magic couldn't be trusted. But he might have to use what power he had one more time.

chapter 86

In the morning Stephen bravely opened the curtains and peered across at the room that used to be his. His mother stood wild-eyed and angry. *She's missing the old woman*, he instantly realized. *She senses that I have something to do with the old woman being gone.*

A soft knock on his door pulled him away from the window.

When he opened the door Robin immediately rolled into the room.

"Your father is coming."

"He can't travel. He isn't that well yet."

"He knows all about what happened to my

mother. Mrs. Rosen explained every detail to him. Mom told her all about the crow, and they both agreed it was the same crow that attacked Mom a few days earlier."

"Dad can't come 'cause he'd be in too much danger."

"So are you. I saw you yesterday in that house. You can't fight her."

"The old woman is dead. The dog carried her out into the sun and destroyed her. She has no ally."

"The crow?"

"I can't explain that. She never made contact with live animals when I worked with her. I think it may have been the old woman who worked some magic on the bird. Mom couldn't reach into this world like that."

"She's able to reach inside you and the baby."

"Only because we're especially vulnerable. The baby is very young and I brought Mom back into the world. Otherwise she would have taken either Mr. or Mrs. Crowther."

"Then your father will be safe. She has no allies."

"I don't think she does, but I'm not sure."

"What are you children doing up here?" Grannie Smith peeked into the bedroom. "I have a hot breakfast downstairs waiting."

"Grannie Smith, is my father really planning on coming back here?"

"Come on down to the breakfast table and we'll talk about it."

At the table the children hardly touched their food. Grannie Smith tried to explain what Stephen's father had said.

"His doctor doesn't want him to travel. He's afraid too many days away from physical therapy and your father will lose too much flexibility and not be ready for the next scheduled surgery."

"In two months," Stephen said. He posted the dates on a calender in his room. "The doctor hasn't told him when he'll stop operating."

"Your father has a lot of damage."

Robin reached across and grabbed Stephen's hand.

"And your mother, Robin," continued Grannie Smith, " is scheduled to come out of the hospital in two days. She wants both of you ready to travel. I think she hopes to cut Stephen's father off at the pass, so to speak."

"Grannie Smith, have you visited the baby next door?" Stephen asked.

"I've been over there when the baby screams, tormented by some hell."

"By my mother."

"Mr. and Mrs. Crowther would never believe that. I suggested they go away on a vacation or perhaps take the baby to her parents. I suggested maybe the baby missed its mother, but they wouldn't listen.

They simply believe the baby is colicky. Thinks that since the baby is eating and otherwise seems healthy it's just a stage."

"Momma will wear the baby out."

"You think the baby will die?" asked Grannie Smith.

"No. At least not in the physical sense. Momma wants the body alive, not dead. I need to talk to Momma."

"You can't talk her out of what she's doing." Robin squeezed his hand tighter. "I'm already packed. When Momma comes out of the hospital I'm ready to go home."

"I can't talk to Momma while other people are in the house. They'll think I'm bonkers. Grannie Smith, can't you get the Crowthers and the baby out of the house?"

"And send you in to confront your mother? Stephen, your father would never forgive me."

"The Crowthers won't be happy either if they have my mother as their grandchild. Grandma had to scold her a lot. And where will the baby go?"

"Don't they take the baby to the doctor?" Robin asked.

"Lord, what are you asking me to do?"

"You've got an extra key to their house, don't you? You always kept a key to Stephen's house and *vice versa* in case of an emergency."

"Yes, Robin, I have a key. But what if Stephen doesn't come out of the house?"

"I'll stay with him."

"And what will you do?"

"Drag him out if it gets too dangerous."

"You're not strong enough or agile enough to do that, dear." Grannie Smith stood up and paced the kitchen for several minutes. "The Crowthers take the baby to the doctor on Thursday."

"That's tomorrow," shouted Robin in Stephen's ear.

"I will take Stephen into the house and, Robin, you'll stay here."

"No. I have to go with Stephen. I'll know what to look for in his eyes. I'll know when he's in trouble. We should all go."

"Your parents would kill me if they knew what we planned. But I must admit allowing that baby to be possessed is something I can't do. I wish I was able to confront your mother."

"She'll ignore you 'cause she can't reach inside your heart and soul."

"Let's pray we still have tomorrow to save that child," Grannie Smith said.

Later that afternoon Mr. Crowther picked up something from his front lawn when Stephen wandered over to say hello.

"Hi, Stephen. I guess the dogs are tired of

playing with this lump of clay. They seem to have abandoned it." He threw the clay into the trash bin at the side of the house.

"How's your granddaughter?"

"Still colicky. But sometimes she'll sleep fitfully for hours at a time. I think she tires herself out with all her crankiness."

"Maybe she should be sleeping in the bedroom with you and Mrs. Crowther."

"The kids said she slept alone at their house. Never heard any complaints from them about all her crying. Mrs. Crowther and I can't take much more. We're too old to be minding a colicky baby."

"Maybe she doesn't like the house."

"Or the house doesn't like her."

"What do you mean?"

"Oh, it's silly."

"No, tell me what you mean."

Mr. Crowther placed a hand on Stephen's head. "Did you have any ghosts when you lived in the house?"

Stephen bit his lip. Dare he share the truth?

"We did."

There was a split second of silence before Mr. Crowther laughed.

"Yeah, I suppose I had my own bogeyman under the bed when I was a kid. Now I'm feeling kinda stupid because I know there isn't any bogeyman under the bed."

"The bogeyman isn't real; ghosts are," Stephen said.

"I shouldn't be talking to you about this. I'll be giving you nightmares."

"You feel someone else in the house, don't you, Mr. Crowther? Someone you can't see."

"And I'm a foolish old man for letting it get to me."

"No, you're sensitive. Momma said some people are."

"Was your mother a gypsy or something?"

"A witch."

"Ah, new age stuff." Mr. Crowther nodded his head. "I've got to get into the house and do my chores. You should be running around having fun instead of speaking to an old superstitious man." He waved goodbye and went into the house.

Once Stephen felt sure he couldn't be seen he took the lid off the trash bin and fished out the lump of clay.

chapter 87

The troll stood in the doorway of the witch's cottage. His massive body filled up the space and blocked the sunlight.

"I'm sorry," the troll meekly said. "I couldn't help myself. But it is the truth about the bus."

"It's too late for that damn bus," the witch said.

"Lies. There have been so many lies. Neither of you wanted to be my friend. You both wanted to use me."

"Friend? What's a friend?" the witch asked of Brandy.

"Someone a person can trust."

"I told you not to trust trolls," the witch said.

"She's right. We male trolls can't be trusted."

"Neither could your father," the witch said to Brandy.

"My father never hurt me. He didn't want to steal my hand. He didn't lock me up in a cage."

"I offer you far more than your father ever could. Powers he will never comprehend."

"He loves me and wants me to be me." Brandy looked the witch in the eyes. "You selfishly want to bind me to you. You want to live through me."

"Nonsense. We will share life together. I'll put my arm inside yours and we'll be linked forever. Not my fault that those idiots will see only one when there are two of us. The troll will see two."

Brandy and the witch looked at the troll.

"I'm so sorry," the troll said.

Brandy walked toward the doorway, but the troll didn't move.

"I'm not that sorry. I gave you the chance to run."

"Why would he want to run away from me?" the witch asked. "He and I are very close. Mother and son, I'd say."

"You're not my mother. You are a shade. My mother is dead."

"Dead? How can I be dead when I stand before you? Dead is when a spirit gives up. I never give up." The witch giggled. "And you can never leave me. Always you will be drawn back to me. You'll wonder what I'm doing. Who I'm touching." She reached out and touched

his cheek. "And you'll be jealous. You came back because you thought I had someone to take your place. Admit it. Admit it and join with me forever."

"That's not true," Brandy said defiantly.

"Not true? You chose me over your father."

"I didn't know. I tried to protect him."

"You've protected no one but me and what is mine. Put your hand inside your pocket."

Brandy did. He felt something hard and slippery.

"Take it out," the witch said.

His hand came out of his pocket holding a tiny goddess covered with blood. He tried to throw it away, but it stuck to his flesh.

"I lent her to you. She carried you through the hardest days, didn't she?"

The troll shook his head, stepped outside and closed the door behind him.

From a distance the troll could be heard saying, "Too much blood, way too much to forget."

"I don't want to forget. I want to remember, for then I'll never do any of these deeds again," said Brandy.

The witch laughed.

"Talk. Nonsensical words fly out of your mouth and float high up into the sky and out to the universe."

The witch toddled over to the basement door and opened it.

"The bigger cage is empty now. The circus picked up their cats. I've cleaned it for you. Even put in some

straw for a bed and a lamp for when you want to read."

"I thought you weren't going to give me any of your magic books."

"I will share everything with you, Brandy. All you have to do is take my hand and walk down these stairs with me."

"And lock myself inside a cage." Brandy fisted his hands and screamed at the top of his lungs. "No! No! No!"

"Wake up, Stephen." Grannie Smith sat on his bed and held him in her arms. "She can't have you, Stephen. We'll keep you safe from her."

"I've been afraid of hurting Momma, that's why she's been able to rule me. I was afraid she wouldn't love me. But her shade isn't Momma. Her shade doesn't love me. It only loves itself."

chapter 88

The morning sun sprayed Stephen's room with its light. Everything in the room had a happy shine. No one stood at his old bedroom window, and several birds chose to sing among the branches of the tree flowering outside the house.

Stephen had fallen back to sleep in Grannie Smith's arms. He didn't know whether she had stayed the night with him and left early to prepare breakfast or whether she had tucked him in and returned to her own bed after he dozed off. He had slept that soundly and dreamlessly.

He got up and used the bathroom, dressed, and

checked for his velvet bundle hidden under the mattress. He stared at the bundle, remembering how he had managed to save these few items. His father had sent all of Mom's things to charity. Everything. He never asked whether Stephen wanted something. Dad seemed ready to be rid of Momma. Grandma had been annoyed there had been no wake. Momma went away, and two days later her ashes were tossed into the ocean. No grave to visit. No headstone marking where she lay. Gone.

Yes, they visited the ocean and threw flowers into the water, hoping Momma would find them, but he never got to kiss her goodbye.

He had brought back an evil-stained shade to substitute for Momma. With a few cheap utensils he had brought a bad momma back. He gave her existence and power over him. He gave this to her. She had no way back without him.

Stephen put the velvet bundle back where it belonged and went downstairs for breakfast.

In the kitchen Robin and Grannie Smith sat quietly at the table, their toast cold, their eggs hardening, their bacon shriveling, and their fruit turning brown.

"What time do they take the baby to the doctor?" Stephen asked.

"You don't have to go back to your old house, Stephen. We'll understand if you can't." Robin's green eyes looked too serious for a child her age.

He looked at Grannie Smith.

"They'll leave at ten. Should be back by noon for lunch."

Stephen pulled out a chair to sit at the table, and to the others' amazement he managed to eat a big breakfast.

"Is this your last meal?" asked Robin.

"Child, don't say that," Grannie Smith reprimanded.

"Finally I know what to do. That's all," Stephen said as he reached for another slice of toast.

chapter 89

Cathy watched as the Crowthers dressed the baby. The tiny hands kept trying to grab onto the grandparents.

The baby always sensed when Cathy entered the room. The grandmother lived totally oblivious to her surroundings. But the old man suspected. He hovered over the baby too much. He broke the spell too often that Cathy had tried to weave. His hands were warm, bringing the baby back to be with him. Over and over the baby rejected the cold touch of death.

Cathy missed the old woman. The crow no longer visited. He vanished at the same time as the old woman. Such true love, thought Cathy. She wished she had experienced something at least similar, if not of the same strength. She still had her little boy. He idolized her. He would come round. He would bring her back into the world.

The baby kicked off its blankets, its legs and arms a whirl of movements.

"Dare I touch you one more time? Your innocence weakens me."

Hearing the words, the baby's eyes filled with tears.

"Oh, no. I think she's going to start up again before we even get into the car."

"She'll be all right," said Mr. Crowther, lifting the baby into his arms. "She just wants some cuddling. Right?"

The baby cooed and rested its head against the grandfather's strong shoulder.

"I've turned up the heat in this room, but it hardly ever feels warm in here," Mrs. Crowther said, putting the last of the baby supplies into a canvas grip.

"Don't worry about it now or else we'll be late for the doctor's appointment." The grandfather headed out into the hall. "Have everything?"

"What don't I have in here?"

Cathy watched the family leave and hurried to the window to see the car pull out of the driveway. But someone waited on the porch next door. Stephen with his too-long hair and sad eyes, holding a burgundy velvet bundle in his hands. He held the bundle tightly and close to his body. He didn't glance at the house; he watched the neighbors' car pull away. She looked for tear stains on his cheeks, for worry lines furrowing his young brow, for tense lips drawn into a straight line, for a nose red from rubbing, but none were present, only his sad eyes. Had he resigned himself to joining with her? He certainly didn't look conflicted anymore.

"What are your thoughts, my little one?" Her whisper emptied into the silence of the house. None would hear her words but her little boy. Appropriately he looked toward the window, his brown eyes weighted with whatever decision he had made. He untucked the bundle from his chest and offered it to her. The bundle quivered in his hands, not a trick of the light but a nod to his strengthening determination.

The bundle contained the utensils he had used to bring her back. She could see the outline of the goddess, the trinkets that kept the wooden image company, and something else. The remnants of the old woman. What had Stephen done to her? The piece of clay sat in the bundle unanimated.

Fear passed through Cathy. Why the old woman? How had he managed to reach her?

Her sister's handicapped child appeared behind Stephen, the wheelchair an eternal extension of the child's inabilities. The biddy who lived next door came out to take the handles of the wheelchair and guide it carefully down the ramp that had recently been installed.

Stephen didn't immediately follow. Mesmerized by his

mother's face, he stared until the biddy called his name.

"Leave him be. Let him stay," Cathy spoke to the air. Her words didn't cause the slightest ripple.

He hesitated for a second, tucking the bundle again close to his body, and slowly descended the porch stairs.

chapter 90

"Are you sure you want to do this, Stephen?"

The boy nodded. The bundle became heavier the longer he carried it.

"I have to go to the backyard first," he said.

"What for?" Grannie Smith held her neighbors' front door key in her hand.

"I gotta bury this," he said, showing the bundle to Grannie Smith.

"Why?"

"Because none of this stuff is mine. It all belonged to Momma and she should have it back."

"I don't think she can take it from you."

"I can bury it behind the house and she'll know it's there."

The three of them walked around to the back of Stephen's old house. Upon opening the gate the Labrador retrievers ran over to them with tails wagging.

"I can't pet you now," Stephen said, carrying his package to a flower bed situated against the house.

He knelt and started scooping up the loose soil. The flowers had recently been planted, and he had no trouble burying the bundle among the plants.

"Momma can take them with her," he said, looking up at his two companions. "We can go in now."

The trio retraced their steps to the front door. Grannie Smith fitted the key in the lock and threw open the door. Stephen entered first, with Grannie Smith assisting in bringing the wheelchair over the few steps.

"Is your mother present?" Robin asked, her eyes checking the hall carefully.

He didn't answer; he continued down the hall to the nursery. The too-still room worried the boy. Would his mother hide from him? Perhaps she had given up on taking his body captive. But the familiar cold gradually enveloped him.

"Welcome back," his mother said, her voice charming and close to being human, the floral odor covering the scent of baby powder.

"I came to say goodbye."

Quickly the room filled with the stink of decayed garbage.

"You can't leave me, Stephen. You will *take me with you. Is it to Austin we'll be traveling to live with the cripple and my sister?"*

He looked at Robin in the doorway and realized she couldn't hear his mother's words.

"That's cruel, Momma. You used to speak kindly of her."

"I'm sorry. I don't know why I said that."

"Because you're not really my mommy. You're a shade of her that was left behind. The bad part that was barred from heaven."

"You've a wonderful imagination. Or maybe you attributed kindly wishes to one who didn't live by her words."

"I can't say what exactly you are, but you're not my mommy. You're hurtful and selfish."

The smell in the room grew worse. Grannie Smith pulled Robin's wheelchair back into the hall and Robin protested.

"You have to go to wherever you belong."

"I belong on this earth with you."

"No, Momma gave up on the earth. She didn't want to be here, and you have to go with her. You and Mommy are one."

"This foolish nonsense about there being two mommies isn't going to stop me from returning. If you refuse to

open your heart and soul, then I'll seek another."

"I am the one keeping your shade here. I banish you to . . ." He couldn't and wouldn't say hell. "I banish you to serve the penalty for your crimes. I know then you will be able to rest."

"Stupid, moralistic child. Do you believe you have such a power?"

Stephen swallowed hard.

"Yes, because I received it by birth. You passed it on to me. I keep nothing that belonged to you. The utensils I used are buried in the backyard. I release you from the spell that bound you to me."

He heard his mother laugh but never wavered in his confidence. Not a complete shade, she played on the insecurities of humans. On his fear of being alone, his fear of losing his mother's love, his fear of having to make a choice between parents. His momma had made the choice for him when she killed herself. For a long time he couldn't say those words. She killed herself.

"Leave the house with me."

"Of course I will." His Mother's voice brightened. The stink of death dwindled.

He felt her make a rush for his body, but he expected it and stood firm. He caught his breath after the first attack and waited for her to niggle her way inside his flesh.

"You've turned to stone. There's no love left in your

heart for me."

"Wrong. I love Momma, but I don't like the part of her that was left behind. And . . ." He took a few moments to choose his words. Smiling he said, "I've become a scholar. I can live without you and make friends and love other people too."

He saw her shade form within a white puff of smoke. While trying to hold the image her face look pained. Her form faded, coming back diminished each time she tried.

"Don't fade away here alone," Stephen said. "I'll walk with you into the sun."

"*I need your body for that, fool.*"

"No, you need to be willing to give up the earth for some rest."

Smoke circled his body, and Grannie Smith almost made a grab for him, but he raised a hand to stop her.

"Momma can't get inside me."

He heard curses, pleas; a mad cacophony of words poured forth from his mother's shade. He walked out of the room, the white halo still surrounding him.

Grannie Smith pushed Robin to the front door she had left ajar. Slowly she lowered the wheelchair back onto the cement path before turning toward the boy. As he reached the warmth of the sun the halo withdrew, fading back into the hallway.

Stephen stepped outside and Grannie Smith

locked the door.

"Will she go away?" asked Robin.

"There's no one to keep her here," he said.

The threesome strode to the house, each looking over his or her shoulder, checking for a sign, but the house looked normal and quiet.

chapter 91

"I'm your mother," screamed Cathy. "I birthed you. I am as whole as when I walked this earth." Except for a physical body, a self-doubt reminded her. "I don't need a boy to bring me back. I am here of my own accord. Nothing, no one gives me permission to be here." Her words echoed around her, yet she knew no one heard her.

In the backyard one of the dogs barked, incessantly, demandingly, loudly. She went to the kitchen window and saw the male dog looking up at her, its coat full and clean. Its face never turned away from her. Beyond him, centered in the yard, lay the burgundy velvet fabric, and trailing it lay the items Stephen had used to bring her back. The mound of clay looked singed by the sun, and the other items seemed cheap and used up. The dogs had mauled the goddess. Teeth marks bruised every inch of the wood. Chips missing had either been eaten or spat out onto the grass. But the figure no longer retained any specific shape; it was merely a discarded twig of a tree or broken-off bit of furniture.

For a time the sharp backyard image stayed tattooed upon her vision, but soon it blurred as the surroundings faded. The sight and sound of earth lost the reality she so longed to keep.

Her tired spirit wanted sleep. Death claimed her back into its bounty and cradled her in its arms.

SIREN'S CALL

MARY ANN MITCHELL

Sirena is a beautiful young woman. By night she strips at Silky Femmes, enticing large tips from conventioneers and salesmen passing through the small Florida city where she lives.

Sirena is also a loyal and compassionate friend to the denizens of Silky Femmes. There's Chrissie, who is a fellow dancer as well as the boss's abused and beleaguered girlfriend. And Ross, the bartender, who spends a lot of time worrying about the petite, delicate, and lovely Sirena. Maybe too much time.

There's also Detective Williams. He's looking for a missing man and his investigation takes him to Silky's. Like so many others, he finds Sirena irresistible. But again, like so many others, he's underestimated Sirena.

Because Sirena has a hobby. Not just any hobby. From the stage she searches out men with the solid bone structure she requires. The ones she picks get to go home with her where she will perform one last private strip for them. They can't believe their luck. They simply don't realize it's just run out.

ISBN#1932815163
ISBN#9781932815160
Gold Imprint
US $6.99 / CDN $9.99
Available Now
www.maryann-mitchell.com

TOLTECA

K. MICHAEL WRIGHT

His name is Topiltzin. He is the son of the Dragon, a blue-eyed Mesoamerican hero. He is also a godless ballplayer, a wanderer, a rogue warrior. He will become known as the Plumed Serpent, the man who became a god, who transcended death to become the Morning Star.

In the world of the Fourth Sun, Topiltzin is the unconquered hero of the rubberball game. When he comes with his companions to a city to play, children flock to meet him, maidens cover the roadway with flowers for him to tread on, and people gather to watch the mighty Turquoise Lords of Tollan. They are the undefeated champions of the ancient game of ritual, a game so fanatically revered that spectators would often wager their own children on its outcome. To lose meant decapitation. The Turquoise Lords of Tollan never lost. At least until now.

The Smoking Lord, descended from Highland Mountain kings, has come with vast armies. He has learned of the splendid Tolteca from a priest who tried to teach him the true way of the one god. After offering the old man up as a sacrifice to the midnight sun, Smoking Mirror has now come north to see if the legends are true.

An army has come, and a new age. Topiltzin witnesses its horrors. He finds cities destroyed, villagers raped and ritualistically slaughtered by sorcerer priests sent as heralds to offer up human sacrifice. Unable to stop the blood slaughter of innocents, realizing the vast armies of the Shadow Lords will annihilate even the mighty Tolteca, Topiltzin becomes obsessed with one final objective, one last move in the rubberball game: the death of the Smoking Mirror.

ISBN#1932815465 / ISBN#9781932815467

Platinum Imprint — US $26.95 / CDN $35.95

JOSEPH LAUDATI

IN DARKNESS IT DWELLS

Teen-aged filmmaker Tom DeFrank, through his hobby of stop-motion photography, conceives a monster: he builds and animates a demon puppet. Unbeknownst to Tom, however, the "toy" creates a subliminal bond with a dark entity. As he labors with the miniature beast, making his movie, the boy unwittingly summons a force that wreaks the terrible vengeance of Tom's repressed rage.

Only reclusive psychic Stephen Parrish and his daughter Julie know of the ancient evil awakened in their little town. As romance blooms between the teens, Parrish senses the strange presence within the troubled young filmmaker and seeks to unravel the mystery of the demon.

But people are dying as bitter grudges come to the fore. Rumors abound of a strange creature loose in the countryside, and a fearful public turns suspicious on Parrish. Will he be able to leash the monster and the will of its creator — a boy little conscious of his power to create ... or destroy?

g.a.r.y f.r.a.n.k

FOREVER
will you SUFFER

Unsuspecting Rick Summers had simply gone to the cemetery to visit the graves of his mother and sister, killed in a car accident years earlier. He had the cabbie wait for him. But when he got back into the taxi, he didn't have the same driver. His new chauffeur was a re-animated corpse. And he was about to take a drive into hell.

The doors to hell open in the house of his ex-lover, Katarina, where he is delivered by his not-so-sweet smelling driver. Rick learns that Katarina is missing and has been recently plagued by a stalker. That's just the beginning of the bad news. When the house changes right before their unbelieving eyes, taking them somewhen and somewhere else, a horrifying mystery begins to unfold. At its heart is unrequited love. And Rick Summers.

It seems that several lifetimes ago, Rick, then Thomas, spurned a woman named Abigail. Not a good idea. Because Abigail's great at holding a grudge, some of her best friends are demons, and she's dedicated to keeping a promise she made to Rick long, long ago. "Forever will I remember; forever will you suffer . . ."

ISBN#1932815694
ISBN#9781932815696
Gold Imprint
US $6.99 / CDN $9.99
Available Now
www.authorgaryfrank.com

THE LUCIFER MESSIAH

FRANK CAVALLO

Sean Mulcahy answered Uncle Sam's call. In the autumn of 1917, he left his home, his friends, and the girl he loved. On the killing fields of the Western Front, he vanished without a trace.

Thirty years later his best friend Vince Sicario is a broken man. Split from his wife, run off the NYPD, his world swirls in the bottom of a bottle. Until Sean comes clawing at his door. Bleeding. Delirious. And looking not a single day older.

Vince turns to the only person he trusts, his wife Maggie — the woman Sean left behind three decades earlier. Together they hit the streets of Hell's Kitchen, seeking answers to Sean's disappearance . . . and mysterious return.

But others are on the same trail, and something terrible is lurking in the dark alleys and dirty corners of the West Side. Wise guys are disappearing. Mutilated corpses are turning up. The cops are baffled and gangsters are running scared. Rumors abound of strange gatherings in the shadows, of ancient horrors reborn, of blood feasts and pagan rites rekindled. Some say the savior of the damned has come.

Sean may be in terrible danger. Or the greatest danger of all.

The Lucifer Messiah.

THE DREAM THIEF

HELEN A. ROSBURG

Someone is murdering young, beautiful women in mid-sixteenth century Venice. Even the most formidable walls of the grandest villas cannot keep him out, for he steals into his victims' dreams. Holding his chosen prey captive in the night, he seduces them . . . to death.

Now Pina's cousin, Valeria, is found dead, her lovely body ravished. It is the final straw for Pina's overbearing fiance', Antonio, and he orders her confined within the walls of her mother's opulent villa on Venice's Grand Canal. It is a blow not only to Pina, but to the poor and downtrodden in the city's ghettos, to whom Pina has been an angel of charity and mercy. But Pina does not chafe long in her lavish prison, for soon she too begins to show symptoms of the midnight visitations; a waxen pallor and overwhelming lethargy.

Fearing for her daughter's life, Pina's mother removes her from the city to their estate in the country. Still, Pina is not safe. For Antonio's wealth and his family's power enable him to hide a deadly secret. And the murderer manages to find his intended victim. Not to steal into her dreams and steal away her life, however, but to save her. And to find his own salvation in the arms of the only woman who has ever shown him love.

erin samiloglu

DISCONNECTION

There is a serial killer on the loose in New Orleans. Someone is branding, stabbing and strangling young girls. Their mutilated bodies are being found in the depths of the Mississippi River.

Beleaguered Detective Lewis Kline and his colleagues believe the occult may be involved, but they have no leads. And the killer shows no sign of slowing down.

Then Sela, a troubled young woman, finds a stranger's cell phone in a dark Bourbon Street bar. When it rings, she answers it. On the other end is Chloe Applegate. The serial killer's most recent victim.

So begins Sela's journey into a nightmare from which she cannot awaken, a descent into madness out of which she cannot climb . . . as she finds herself the target of an almost incomprehensible evil.

ISBN#1932815244
ISBN#9781932815245
Gold Imprint
US $6.99 / CDN $9.99
Available Now
www.erinsamiloglu.com

DANIEL'S VEIL

R.H. STAVIS

Daniel O'Brady is a burned out cop. When he sees a child blown away by her own father, he's seen one murder too many. Grief stricken and questioning the validity and purpose of his life, he takes off for a drive in the countryside. Daniel's bad day is only beginning.

Regaining consciousness after the single car accident, an injured Daniel sets out to find help. What he finds is a quaint little village full of people who are more than happy to help him. He's given medical aid, food, clothing and shelter . . . and no one will take a dime from him. If that's not strange enough, after a few days in the tranquil town he discovers an odd house surrounded by streaks of an odd blue light. He decides to investigate.

Dr. Michael Hudson is a scientist bent on proving the existence of supernatural phenomena. His life is consumed with passion to prove his theory, to the exclusion of all else. When his research leads him to a house outside a small village in Northern California, he packs up his team and his equipment and sets out to document and prove his long-held belief in another dimension.

What both men discover will change their lives, and alter their souls, forever.

ISBN#0974363960
ISBN#9780974363967
Gold Imprint
US $6.99 / CDN $9.99
Available Now
www.rhstavis.com